Heart Lamp

Heart Lamp
Selected Stories

Banu Mushtaq

Translated by
Deepa Bhasthi

SHEFFIELD – LONDON – NEW YORK

First published in English in 2025 by And Other Stories
Sheffield – London – New York
www.andotherstories.org

'Stone Slabs for Shaista Mahal', 'Fire Rain', 'Black Cobras', 'A Decision of the
Heart', 'Red Lungi', 'Heart Lamp', 'High-Heeled Shoe', 'Be a Woman Once, Oh
Lord!', 'Soft Whispers' and 'A Taste of Heaven' first published in book form in
Kannada in *Haseena Mathu Ithara Kathegalu* (Abhiruchi Prakashana, 2013)

'The Shroud' and 'The Arabic Teacher and Gobi Manchuri' first published in book
form in Kannada in *Hennu Haddina Swayamvara* (Abhiruchi Prakashana, 2023)

3 5 7 9 8 6 4

ISBN: 9781916751163
eBook ISBN: 9781916751170

Editor: Tara Tobler; Copy-editor: Robina Pelham Burn; Proofreader: Sarah
Terry; Typesetter: Tetragon, London; Typefaces: Albertan Pro and Linotype
Syntax (interior) and Stellage (cover); Series Cover Design: Elisa von Randow,
Alles Blau Studio, Brazil, after a concept by And Other Stories

And Other Stories books are printed and bound by CPI in the UK on FSC-certified paper.

A catalogue record for this book is available from the British Library.

The authorised agent in the EU is LOGOS EUROPE, 9 rue
Nicolas Poussin, 17000 La Rochelle, France

And Other Stories gratefully acknowledge that our work is
supported using public funding by Arts Council England.

This book has been selected to receive financial assistance from English PEN's PEN
Translates programme, supported by British Council. English PEN exists to promote
literature and our understanding of it, to uphold writers' freedoms around the world, to
campaign against the persecution and imprisonment of writers for stating their views, and to
promote the friendly co-operation of writers and the free exchange of ideas. This book has
been recognised through both PEN Presents and PEN Translates, as part of a partnership
with British Council to support diverse voices and underrepresented literatures from
India to reach wider readership as part of the India–UK Season of Culture in 2022–23.

Supported using public funding by

Supported by

| MIX |
| Paper \| Supporting responsible forestry |
| FSC® C013604 |

CONTENTS

STONE SLABS FOR
SHAISTA MAHAL

From the concrete jungle, from the flamboyant apartment buildings stacked like matchboxes to the sky, from the smoke-spewing, horn-blaring vehicles that were always moving, day and night, as if constant movement was the only goal in life, then from people, people, people – people with no love for one another, no mutual trust, no harmony, no smiles of recognition even – I had desperately wanted to be free from such a suffocating environment. So, when Mujahid came with news of his transfer, I was very happy, truly.

Arey, I forgot. I should tell you all about Mujahid, no? Mujahid is my home person. Oh. That sounds odd. A wife is usually the one who stays at home, so that makes her the home person. Perhaps then Mujahid is my office person. Che! I have made a mistake again. The office is not mine, after all. How else can I say this? If I use the term yajamana and call him owner, then I will have to be a servant, as if I am an animal or a dog. I am a little educated. I have earned a degree. I do not like establishing these owner and servant roles. So then shall I say 'ganda' for husband? That also is too heavy a word, as if a gandantara, a big disaster, awaits me. But why go into all this trouble? You could suggest that I use the nice word 'pati' for husband – then again, no woman who comes to your house introduces her husband saying 'This is my pati' – right? This word is not very popular colloquially. It is a very bookish word. If one uses the word pati, there comes an urge to add devaru to it, a common practice, equating one's husband with God. I am not willing to give Mujahid such elevated status.

Come to think of it, for us, that is, for us Muslims, it is said that, other than Allah above, our pati is God on earth. Suppose there comes a situation where the husband's body is full of sores, with pus and blood oozing out from them, it is said that even if the wife uses her tongue to lick these wounds clean, she will still not be able to completely repay the debt she owes him. If he is a drunkard, or a womaniser, or if he harasses her for dowry every day – even if all these 'ifs' are true, he is still the husband. No matter which religion one belongs to, it is accepted that the wife is the husband's most obedient servant, his bonded labourer.

By now you must have understood what my relationship with Mujahid is. At the same time, you must have understood what I think about all this. It is not my mistake; when Mujahid, that is, my life companion, got transferred, we moved into beautiful quarters at the Krishnaraja Sagara dam project. He then left me with the jackfruit and lemon trees, the dahlia, jasmine, chrysanthemum and rose plants in the front yard, and the curry leaves, bean plants and bitter gourd creepers growing in the back. He, on the other hand, was occupied for twenty-eight out of twenty-four hours every day, either working at the office or doing research at the Karnataka Engineering Research Station.

It is the same now too. A cool breeze is tickling my body and mind. Since I don't have anyone to talk to, I am sitting here in the middle of the garden and ranting about this so-called husband to you all. But . . . arey! What is this? Mujahid's scooter, that too at this time of the day! I looked at the clock. It was only five o'clock. I raised my eyebrows; I did not move from my seat. Mujahid flashed his teeth. I imprisoned mine tightly behind my lips. He bowed down, placed the helmet on my head, pulled me up by the hand and said, 'Hmm, quickly! I will give you eight minutes. You have to get ready by then and come out. If you don't . . . '

Hold on a minute. Let me tell you the whole story. We are newlyweds. If I have to be specific, we have been married for ten months and thirteen days. Mujahid has tried a few gimmicks before this. One day, he tried very hard and braided my hair, sticking a hundred and eighteen pins into my head to hold it up. Satisfied that it looked very good, he even took a photo. I looked like a monkey. Another day, he tried to get me to wear trousers, but even his loosest pair burst out of their seams and he had to give up trying. Then he tried to encourage me to smoke so that people would think of him as a very social, liberal person. I get very irritated when other people smoke, so instead of blowing out the smoke, I held it in and acted like I couldn't stop coughing and that I was finding it hard to breathe. Poor thing. He was so upset. But all these disasters passed within three months of our wedding, and we are a very 'normal' couple now.

'Can I ask where we are going?'

'Yes, you can ask. There is a man called Iftikhar Ahmed at the Belagola factory. I met him only eight days ago. He has invited us to his house today, to Belagola,' Mujahid replied.

It did not take me even eight minutes to come out. Cheluva rushed behind me and stood near the gate. He was happy when I told him, 'Don't cook anything for dinner. I will come back and cook myself.'

It seemed like Mujahid was also in a good mood that day. He rode the scooter very slowly. Listening to him whistle a Hindi song, I wondered if I should tickle him. But by then we had reached the Belagola circle.

When our scooter approached a house, the man standing outside smiled and opened the gate wide for us. I got down and walked up the path. The compound alone was bigger than our quarters. When I saw all the amenities there, I wondered whether we were in a garden or a park. On each side of the footpath stood a guava tree with iron ropes tying a swing to its thick branches. Jasmine creepers and varieties of rose plants bloomed around them. I was dumbstruck.

I guessed that the man standing outside must be Iftikhar. Just then, the lady of the house came out, greeted us with a polite salaam and welcomed us to her home. Within just half an hour, Iftikhar Bhai and Shaista Bhabhi were getting along with us so well – I was so surprised! Seeing Mujahid mostly talking to Shaista Bhabhi, I thought I would tease him about it when we were alone. But when I realised that she was not only much older than Mujahid, but also seemed pure-hearted and without any ulterior motives, I did not feel like making jokes about her. She was a very simple and open-hearted soul, and paraded all six of their children before us within a few moments. Three daughters, three sons. Apart from the eldest, Asifa, the rest were all like monkeys without tails. As if she had read my mind, Shaista said, 'What to do, Zeenat, I did not do any planning. Before I even turned round to see what happened, I had had six children. And your Bhai Saheb came in the way,' she said, cocking her head at Iftikhar, 'when I thought of getting an operation done. Now I will certainly get it done after number seven.'

'There is no need, Shaista. I am the one raising them. Why are you worried? Thanks to God's grace, I earn enough to look after all of them well,' Iftikhar interjected.

'Oh! Is it enough to have sufficient earnings? My sweet Asifa has had to say goodbye to her studies because of me. Do you know how much that pains me?'

'It is not like that. I made her stop studying because girls do not need much education. A high school certificate is enough. There is no need for her to roam around in Mysuru for college. We can get her married off next year,' replied Iftikhar.

'Absolutely not. I got married when I was twenty years old. I have become a mother of six children over the last seventeen years. If you get my daughter married off this early . . . ' Shaista trailed off.

Mujahid and I listened to all this quietly. Asifa, the topic of this discussion, was standing by the window, holding her brother. It agitated me to look at her youthful beauty and listen to decisions being made about her future. Come to think of it, Shaista was more attractive than me. Iftikhar got up as if he had just thought of something and said 'Oh, Shaista, you and Zeenat Bhabhi come out and sit here. I will pluck some flowers . . . '

Shaista and I went out. Asifa had given her brother a bottle of milk and was patting him gently. Shaista sat on one swing, while I sat on the other. I liked the swing very much and began to push it higher and faster. The joy of going up, and kicking the ground again while coming down! Just then I saw Iftikhar Bhai begin to pluck tiny jasmine buds with a plastic basket tied around his waist. Mujahid was playing with the kids in the front yard. A short while later, Iftikhar came and placed that plastic basket in his wife's hands and climbed up the guava tree. Shaista sat on the swing and began to string the flowers together.

Iftikhar brought guavas for me and Shaista, nudged his wife along so he might sit next to her on the swing, and called out, 'Asifa, bring us some tea, dear.' Asifa had just then put her brother to sleep and come out, standing by, quiet and hesitant since Mujahid was there too. She went in to make tea the moment she heard her father call. It was Iftikhar's tenth cup of tea in the hour we had been there.

Shaista divided the jasmine buds she had strung into two equal pieces and gave me one. She left the other hanging down from the crown of her head like a rope. It suited her thick, long braid. Asifa came and handed Iftikhar the cup of tea. It did not seem right to me that Shaista was ignoring her grown-up daughter and adorning herself with so many flowers.

'Come here, Asifa.' I called her and tried to give her my share of the flowers. She did not accept them, but I forced her to sit next to me and tied them in her hair. The girl's eyes filled with tears, and she disappeared inside the house, Iftikhar's empty teacup and saucer in hand.

It was getting dark. Just as I was thinking of leaving, Iftikhar said, 'Zeenat Bhabhi, look here, I planted this guava tree for Shaista. Every plant and flower here is a favourite of hers. I grew this Anab-e-Shahi grapes creeper for her. These swings . . . she likes them very much.'

'Iftikhar Bhai, I feel very happy to see you both together. You seem to pay a lot of attention to Bhabhi's likes and dislikes.'

'Not just this. If I were an emperor, I would have built a palace to put even the Taj Mahal to shame, and call it Shaista Mahal—'

Mujahid had by then stopped playing with the children. He came near us and halted him mid-sentence. 'Oh ho ho! Stop, Iftikhar, you don't know what blunder you are committing. The emperor built the Taj Mahal as a grave for his dead wife. May Allah give Bhabhi a long life. She is sitting right in front of you, and you are talking about constructing a Shaista Mahal!'

It seemed like Iftikhar faltered for a minute. 'But no one thinks of the Taj Mahal as a grave. They consider it a mohabbat ki nishani, a symbol of love. I said it in that sense.'

Mujahid did not let the matter go and retorted: 'Yes, yes, a symbol of dead love.'

'But love does not die, Mujahid.'

'Hmm . . . it doesn't. But this is all very filmy, Bhai. If your mother dies, it is the death of your mother's love too. You will not get that kind of love from anyone else. Huh. But if the wife dies, it is a different matter, because one can get another wife.'

I was shocked at what Mujahid was saying.

A tiny smile flashed across Shaista's face. She sprang up and said 'Yes, my grandmother used to say that when a wife dies, it's like an elbow injury for the husband. Do you know, Zeenat, if the elbow gets injured, the pain is extreme for one instant – it is intolerable. But it lasts only a few seconds, and after that one does not feel anything. There is no wound, no blood, no scar, no pain . . . '

I did not like where this conversation was going. But all of a sudden, Iftikhar got up, greatly agitated. He held Shaista's hands and said, 'Shaista, what are you saying? Every cell in my body is alive because of the strength of your name. Every heartbeat of mine is because of your energy and vigour. You – what you said – did those words come from your heart? Is that what you believe?'

I controlled my laughter with great difficulty. I remembered Shaista mentioning that Iftikhar was ten years older than her. This sight of a man near fifty trying to declare the immortality of his love like a teenager, and her, sitting like a queen and looking at him benevolently, as if she would forgive every transgression, was not one I was likely to see again. Mujahid finally broke into a wide smile. Shaista giggled, overcome by shyness.

We soon left.

Since we had eaten a lot at Shaista's house, Mujahid said that he did not want dinner and just had a glass of milk. I felt the same and there was no need to think about cooking. He sat down with a book to read, and although I was also flipping through an issue of *Femina* magazine, my thoughts were all about Shaista's family.

'I know . . . you're only pretending to read that magazine . . . '

'Then tell me, what am I thinking about?'

'Shall I tell you? You are thinking about Shaista's youngest child, the one with black eyes and plump cheeks,' replied Mujahid.

'Maybe. But more than that, I am thinking about what you said back there.'

'I knew it. I knew you would worry too much about that. To be frank with you, Zeenat, you must understand: the emperor who built the world-famous memorial for love did not die with his wife. There were innumerable women in his zenana.'

'It is not about the emperor.'

'OK. I will let the subject of Shah Jahan go. Shall I talk about our modern badshah of love? Fundamentally, Iftikhar needs the company of women. He has a special place for Shaista because they have been getting along very well for many years. Whether it is Shaista or Nargis or Mehrun.'

'Enough. Stop it. Even in ten lifetimes you will not be able to love me as much as Iftikhar loves Shaista.'

'First of all, there is no concept of reincarnation for us; I don't believe in these things. Secondly, I am ready to show you a hundred times the love Iftikhar showers on Shaista, this very instant . . . no matter how much you protest . . . '

Before I had a chance to appreciate how cleverly he had changed the topic, Mujahid hugged me tightly and showered me with crazy love – the animal!

It was nine in the morning that Sunday, and Mujahid was still in bed when Iftikhar came to our house with Shaista. I told them that Mujahid was still sleeping, and they sat down, chatting with me. I brought hot-hot samosas for them, but Iftikhar did not eat even one. He piled his share on Shaista's plate, drank only a cup of tea, and went to the market to buy vegetables.

Shaista, wearing a peacock-coloured sari and few pieces of jewellery, was looking especially beautiful. I placed our wedding album in her hands and went indoors. When I returned, she was looking at one of the photos pensively. It was my graduation photo where I was wearing a gown. When I sat beside her she said, 'Zeenat, it is my wish to see Asifa also wear such a gown and get a photo taken like this. She passed her tenth exams in the first attempt. We did not allow her to study further because there was no one else to look after the house and the children.'

'Hire someone to help, Bhabhi.'

'There was someone. She left saying she was going to visit her hometown, and then never came back. Some agent sent her off to Dammam, it seems. I have not found anyone else.'

'Asifa cannot continue her studies this year anyway. At least let her join college from next year.'

'I will do that. What is the use of torturing that poor young girl just for our convenience? Aiyo, Zeenat, I had forgotten to ask. Is it dangerous to get an operation done to avoid having children?'

'What is the danger in that, Bhabhi? On my mother's side of the family three of my sisters-in-law and two elder sisters have got themselves operated on after having two or three children each. They are all well and healthy.'

'Is that so? In that case, I will get an operation done this time. If you can come with me, even the little fear I have will go away.'

'Bhabhi, you are looking so beautiful today! Please teach this Zeenat also to dress up nicely like you,' remarked Mujahid, coming out after having just woken up, and teasingly pulled a chair to sit close to Shaista.

'Hush! You naughty man! Run away, you lazy fellow!' Shaista said, hitting him playfully on the back.

I insisted that they stay for lunch. They accepted and left for Belagola only in the evening. My days in KRS were no longer as lonely as they had once been. I went to Shaista's house whenever I felt like it. Time flew by when I played with her children. It was the same for Shaista too. She wanted to give her children a good education, especially Asifa, wanting to relieve her of household duties and let her get a degree. Aside from this she had no other wants. She looked hale and hearty; her face glowed.

The lady doctor who examined Shaista that day said that she still had some fifteen-twenty days to go before she was due. That was why I invited everyone to our house that Sunday, and insisted that they bring Asifa with them too. It was a happy day; I had a lot of work and not a moment to spare. As usual, Shaista and Mujahid were teasing each other; Iftikhar trying to convince her of his eternal love; the noisy children; Asifa's silence, and her loneliness. By the time we had had a grand feast amidst all this and said goodbye to them, it was past nine.

Although I woke when the alarm rang at five, I felt like wrapping the blanket tighter around me and sleeping some more. Then I heard the doorbell ring. Having no choice now but to get up, I came out, wrapping a shawl tightly around myself, and saw that it was Iftikhar.

'Arey, Iftikhar Bhai! Come, come, how come you are here so early?'

'I don't have time to come and sit, Bhabhi. After we left here, Shaista got labour pains in the night, at around one. I took her to Mysuru immediately in the factory jeep. She is at Shilpa Maternity Home. She gave birth at three. It is a baby boy.' I felt like Iftikhar blushed a little when he said this.

I felt very happy. Oh! It had been years since I last saw a newborn and participated in all the festivities around a birth. I left Iftikhar right there and rushed to Mujahid, the sleeping Kumbakarna. I threw away the blanket, trying to shake Mujahid awake. 'Get up – get up quickly, please – Shaista has given birth to a baby boy. You are still asleep!' Mujahid pulled me into a tight hug and murmured, 'I promise, Zeenat, whether you have a boy or a girl, I will certainly not sleep all night. I will just sit and stare at your baby.'

'Thoo, how shameless you are. Iftikhar Bhai is outside. Get up and go talk to him.' By the time I brought a cup of tea, Iftikhar had already smoked four-five cigarettes. Handing him the cup I asked, 'Shaista Bhabhi's health is fine, I hope?'

'Hmm. It is OK. But there was some problem. The doctor had said that she might need a blood transfusion. Later there was no need for that. Shaista is very weak though. I will take your leave now,' Iftikhar said, setting the cup down and getting up even before lazy Mujahid could come out.

Mujahid and I left for Mysuru. He continued teasing me all the way, saying that if it was my baby, he would do this, he would do that, he would raise the child himself, and so on in that vein.

When we reached the nursing home, we saw that Iftikhar's entire family had gathered there. Asifa had collected all the children outside, since they had been making noise indoors. She smiled, seeing us. When I asked her, 'How come you are looking so happy?' she replied, 'The baby is very cute, Bhabhi. You will also be very happy when you see him.'

The baby was really very cute, soft and pink like a rose. He was sleeping with his eyes tightly shut. Shaista's lips had lost their colour, and she smiled weakly. I sat next to her and picked up the baby. 'Shaista Bhabhi, the baby might catch the evil eye. How have you managed to produce such beautiful children?' I teased her.

'Don't worry. If you tell Mujahid, he will place a baby much cuter than this in your hands,' she replied.

Just then, Mujahid came inside with Iftikhar. He picked up the baby from me, stared at it for a second and hugged it to his chest. When he asked, 'Bhabhi, I will steal the baby and run away, and then what will you do?' she did not miss a beat.

'What kind of a man are you to steal someone's baby and run? Get your own army ready, then we will see,' she teased him back. Iftikhar laughed loudly.

We stayed there till evening, and when we were getting ready to leave, I spoke to Shaista. 'It might be difficult for Asifa to look after all the children and also manage to send food for you at the maternity home. Shall I keep Sallu, Immu, Naveen and Kamal with me until you come back home?'

'It is OK, Zeenat. Asifa is not my daughter; she is like my mother. Not just now – ever since she left school, she has been managing all the household chores and looking after all the children. I won't be here long. I will go back home the day after tomorrow,' she said.

'Then . . . the operation?'

'I am a bit weak now. The doctor has told me to come back after fifteen days. I will get the operation done then.'

'OK. Then I will go and come.'

After Shaista returned home, I went to visit her a couple of times. But what most surprised me was something we saw when Mujahid and I were on our way to Mysuru one Sunday.

That day, we were travelling by train because we had to stock up on groceries for the house. The train halted at Belagola. How surprising: Shaista was standing with Iftikhar at the station platform, wearing a full-sleeved sweater and a scarf on her head. Mujahid stood at the door of the bogey and waved at them. They hurriedly boarded the compartment we were in.

I stupidly asked, 'How come you're going to Mysuru?' Shaista had regained her old vivaciousness. A mother in confinement for only fifteen days, someone who was not short of anything and lived an easy life, did she have to go to Mysuru herself to run errands? As if she had read my mind, Shaista said, 'Oh, I have never been in confinement for more than fifteen days. I just stay warm, that's all, and if I am not with him, he becomes very dull. I am healthy. Why should I remain lying down all the time? Even when my first daughter was born, I was in bed only for fifteen days.'

I did not dare ask her anything else after this. I had seen my elder sisters and sisters-in-law go through confinement. They did not get down from their beds for three months after delivery. They were not allowed to touch cold water. When they woke up in the morning, Amma would pour three big pots of hot water on them, make them lie down immediately after and cover them with ten blankets. Eventually Amma would decide that ten blankets were still not enough and lay out a whole mattress on each woman. After fifteen minutes the new mother would begin to sweat profusely. Amma would make her get up, wipe away the bad water – that is what Amma called sweat – and give her mutton heart or mutton leg soup. She would dry her hair with sambrani smoke, make her lie down, gather the folds of her stomach in one fist and tie a big voile saree tightly around her waist so as to keep it flat. Then she would make the new mother swallow some fenugreek powder with a plate of ghee . . . but since their husbands had ordered them not to eat ghee and put on weight, they would cleverly push the plates under the bed without Amma noticing.

Later, after feeding the baby, the confined mother would wake up around one in the afternoon. The moment she awoke, rice, pepper saaru and four pieces of the softest meat fried with chilli would be ready. She had to drink only boiled water. In the evening, shavige made with copious amounts of ghee, almonds and cardamom in it, or some sweet dish, and in the night, bread or wheat rottis with

19

meat melogara curry. Forty days of this strict diet later, the new mother could wear jewellery and a new saree; she would look just like a bride.

When my brothers or brothers-in-law spent too much time with their wives during confinement, Amma would grumble. 'What is this shamelessness! If I let the husband and wife spend some time with each other . . . they want to take advantage . . . what do I care . . . if you are all healthy, then your husbands will stay with you . . . if you spoil your young bodies, you are the ones who will suffer . . . look at the Brambra, the Shettru women! Even five months after they give birth, they are still in confinement. Can we do what they all do? Can we take so much care? That is why they are all so strong and healthy.'

She would pass comments like these. If the new mothers sat up, she would tell them that bad water would get to their waists, and if they stood up, she would try to scare them, saying that they would faint and fall down, advising them to lie down instead. 'For forty days after the birth, forty graves have their mouths open for the baby and the new mother. With every passing day, one grave closes its mouth. Is it a small thing for a new life to be born from a body? It is like the mother getting a new life herself,' Amma used to say.

If Amma's words were to be believed, there were still twenty-five graves waiting open-mouthed for Shaista. And she was already roaming about like this! All these thoughts crossed my mind in an instant.

But the mouths of those twenty-five graves closed shut. At the end of the forty days there was a ceremony at Shaista's house. I was getting ready to go there, with silver anklets and a baba suit for Shaista's baby boy, a blouse piece for her, when a telegram arrived.

'Mother serious. Start immediately.' Mujahid and I did not know how to make any arrangements. We stuffed a few clothes that

20

were within arm's reach into a suitcase and immediately went to Mysuru. From there, we left for our village. Amma's condition was not good at all when we reached home. Severely weakened after a massive heart attack, my mother was pale. When she knew that she would not live much longer, she had yearned for all her children at her side. I was the youngest and the last to arrive. On the third day, Amma took her last breath, looking as if she had just gone to sleep. My mother. She who had raised and loved me, she who had cuddled me, was lying in front of my eyes like a stump of wood. I do not know how I tolerated that sight.

Amma's last rites were done. I felt numb. Thinking that I would be alone if we went back to KRS and slip into a deeper sadness, Mujahid took a month-long leave from work and stayed with me. Four-five days after the fortieth-day ceremony for Amma, we returned to KRS.

That day, I could neither sit nor stand in the house. I felt some kind of distress, a sense of agony. I thought it was maybe because I had been in a house filled with people and suddenly found myself alone. Since Mujahid was still off work, we both got ready to go to Shaista's; I picked up the gifts we had bought for her and her baby.

When we reached the house, it looked like the garden was not being maintained. There were no signs of the children in the house. I sat on a chair in the hall and looked around; the door to Shaista's room was closed. Mujahid sat down and, not knowing what else to do, picked up the newspaper. I banged on the door, wondering what kind of nap she was taking till four o'clock in the evening.

'Bhabhi . . . Shaista Bhabhi . . . it is me, Zeenat. Come out in two minutes. If not, I will break the door down!'

I heard the sound of the bolt. Iftikhar followed the sound. I had assumed he would be at the factory, and felt a little embarrassed. I took a couple of steps back. Iftikhar walked out towards Mujahid.

I went into the room. That was all! I felt giddy. All the windows and doors were shut; inside the room the woman standing by the dim light of the bed lamp wearing a peacock-blue saree was definitely not Shaista. The woman, who did not look more than eighteen years old, who stood with her head bent, wearing new mehendi on her hands and legs, a full veil on her head, and adorned with green and red bangles on both her arms, was definitely not Shaista. Before the tears could fall down my face, I came out of the room and asked Iftikhar, 'Where is my Shaista Bhabhi?'

'She is no more. Before we could understand what happened, she had gone very far away from us.'

'Who is *she*?' I asked mercilessly.

'I married her the day after Shaista's fortieth-day fatiha was over. She is from a poor family. I need someone to look after the children after all, that is why.'

'Oh, of course . . . she . . . she is looking after the children well, that is *very* evident. Iftikhar Bhai, no matter what you do, it is all right. But do not repeat the declarations of love you made to Shaista with her. It is OK if you do not get a Shaista Mahal built, or make arrangements for stone slabs to be put all around her grave . . . but if your eternal and intense love reaches her where she is and she were to wake up and come back, you will be in trouble.'

Afraid of what else I might end up saying, I ran out of the house. Asifa had picked up all her brothers and sisters from school and sat them down in the garden, perhaps because she did not want to disturb her father. I saw her and stopped for a second.

'Zeenat aunty!' All the children surrounded me in an instant. Asifa came and stood near me, a group of small children around her, a two-month-old infant in her arms. Her eyes overflowed with tears. Somewhere in the distance, Shaista was probably whispering, 'She is not my daughter, she is my mother . . . '

FIRE RAIN

Just as the azaan for morning prayers began sounding from the mosque, mutawalli Usman Saheb sat up on his bed. Noticing that his wife Arifa was not beside him, he stepped out into the living room and saw that she and their son Ansar were fast asleep on the rug. Even a casual glance made clear there was something uneven about the three-year-old's breathing. He understood what was happening when he saw the wet cloth on his forehead, the scattered milk bowl, cup, spoon, water jug and flask of hot water. Arifa must have stayed up all night, and now lay sleeping, clearly exhausted, in the hall no less . . . he felt a stab of guilt. He suddenly remembered, however, that his youngest sister Jameela and her husband were sleeping in the next room and became agitated. He wondered whether he should drape a blanket over Arifa, but then he thought of Jameela's husband, furrowed his brow and body, and shook her roughly awake. She didn't wake immediately from her exhausted sleep and his temper rose.

A little song that a fakir used to sing came to his mind:

> Handi yendeke heegaleyuve
> Manadalli handi, maneyalli handi
> Maiyalli handi hottavane . . .

The meat of a pig is haram. Likewise anger. Devout Muslims believe that they become impure if they even see a pig. The song equates the anger that slides across their minds, bodies and homes with pigs; the mutawalli had sung it several times too. But that morning, the song disappeared in the face of his unreasonable anger. Impatiently, he fidgeted about and, as if suddenly realising something, roughly kicked Arifa's legs. She woke and sat up straight.

'Why can't you sleep inside?' he asked hoarsely, and walked out without waiting for her answer.

The mosque was a furlong from their house. He walked swiftly, piercing the veils of the dawn mist with his long strides. Although his body moved towards the masjid, his mind kept moving back home, especially to what had happened the previous night.

His most beloved youngest sister, the sister he had tenderly educated till she finished secondary school, the sister to whom he had given eighteen silk sarees, gold jewellery, a motorbike for her husband on her wedding five years ago, that sister had come and asked for a share in the family property, and made the biriyani and shavige payasa prepared in her honour taste bitter. Hmpf! What sort of behaviour was this? His body burned with anger again.

On top of that she had started arguing too! 'Anna, this is the share over which I have rights according to Allah and the Prophet's Shariat; I am not asking you for a share in the property you have worked hard and earned yourself.'

What was the property he had earned? Wasn't he only managing the property his father had accumulated?

'One-sixth of our father's property belongs to me.'

Oho! She had calculated everything before coming. He wanted to say, 'Take your one-sixth share,' and give her a slap. But he tried hard to control the pig that had taken over his body and was restlessly jumping around. Her six-foot-tall husband was also sitting on a chair nearby like a bodyguard.

'You take so many decisions for problems in the mohalla. You should have called me and said, here, take your share. Forget my situation; take Sakeena Akka's case. She has neither a husband nor children old enough to work. How is she to arrange marriages for her two grown-up daughters?'

The mutawalli saheb kept staring at the floor. How surprising it was that Jameela was talking so much. Why was he remaining silent? Images of mango groves, coconut groves, fields, places where they raised silkworms, and resplendent houses in the city passed before his eyes. Which of these could he share with his four sisters?

Jameela continued to croak like a frog. 'Anna, you got me married into a good family, I am not saying you didn't. But please, think. It has been ten years since Appa died. If you had given me my share then, by now I would have earned ten times the money you spent on my wedding. I am not asking for all that money now. But . . . '

The dam of mutawalli saheb's patience burst. Arifa was standing by the door and listening to all this anxiously. She thought Jameela's words, her voice and her argument were all unfortunate. But her demand was fair, wasn't it? Who could refute that? The house from which the mutawalli got four thousand rupees in rent every month, and the coffee estate, weren't they both from the share she had received from her parents' house? Arifa had got her share without having to ask. Her parents had invited her and the mutawalli to their house, fed them well, gifted her a new saree and blouse, handed over the registration papers for the property they had transferred to her, and lovingly sent them home. Jameela had to fight for this right now.

The mutawalli saheb didn't say a word. He grunted and stood up and stared at Jameela. Seeing her elder brother that way, she was a little scared. But she glanced at her husband, gathered a little courage and, as if she had learned it by heart, hastily concluded: 'If you don't give me my legal share, I will have to get it through the courts.' Speechless, the mutawalli saheb walked hurriedly to his bedroom; Arifa, scared by his angry strides, quickly slid to the side and gave way.

He sat like an idol, not even bothering to remove his cap. Beads of sweat formed on his forehead. Arifa switched on the fan.

All these details of the incident passed through his mind. Since it was winter, there was water boiling in the bathroom behind the mosque. By force of habit, he finished all his ablutions. The namaz also. Although he had cleaned his body, the agony remained in his mind. Jameela's audacity nagged him on one side, and the pain of sharing the property on the other. His main concern was to see how he could punish her and retain the whole property for himself. The masjid was large, its grounds extensive. The number of people who came for the morning namaz could be counted on his fingers; there was no one from his close circle among them. He was thus forced to turn back home.

But he did not want to go home just yet. By the time he walked very slowly and reached the circle in town, the doors of Madina Hotel had opened. He walked in and drank a cup of tea, but did not feel relieved. Walking out of the hotel very unenthusiastically, he came to the middle of the circle and stood where a policeman might stand. He didn't blow a whistle and direct traffic. He looked in all four directions, unable to decide which way to go, his manner pitiful. Then the impossible happened.

Dabb! He heard a sound. Before he realised what it was, a crow fell from the electric wire above the road like a dry leaf from a tree. The mutawalli saheb saw this from a few yards away and was about to leave, when another crow came out of nowhere, cawing, kaa kaa. The sound began to echo. Crows began to gather as if by magic. He felt that some of their cawing was woeful. Some, he thought, sounded violent, angry. Some sounded lazy, as if they were cawing out of obligation. Others sounded like the deep sigh of a curse, some like a trumpet celebrating freedom, some like happy calls. He began to feel all kinds of things and decided to get away. Crows began circling his head like they were going to strike. He took a step forward, confused. In the corner of his eyes, the unmoving crow. Arey! Were there so many rainbow colours within the impenetrable black?

By the time he returned home, still absent-minded, and got to his bedroom, the mutawalli saheb was feeling sleepy. Arifa was occupied with household chores, busy with looking after her sick child while getting breakfast and lunch, school bags, shoes and socks ready for her other children, and also preparing special dishes for Jameela and her husband. She did not want the daughter of the house cursing and leaving home sad. She remembered her mother's words: 'Hakhdaar tarse toh angaar ka nuuh barse' . . . If the one who has rights is displeased, a rain of fire will fall.

She had talked to the mutawalli saheb the previous night in soft whispers. 'Rii, don't hurt a daughter of the house. It says clearly in the Qur'an that a girl child has a right to her share, doesn't it? Call your four sisters and give them what needs to be given and wash your hands of it. Allah will give us prosperity in what we have left.' Arifa did not usually give him advice. Although she was scared inside, she ended up talking about this. The mutawalli saheb had made hundreds of decisions. What was she telling him that he didn't already know? Why should he tolerate the words of a woman, burkha-clad, of little value? 'You shut up and do your work,' he had snapped, and gone to sleep, snoring away.

Arifa was rolling chapattis, extremely agitated. 'Oh parvardigaar, give him some good sense,' she cried in her heart. She had just put a wet cloth on Ansar's forehead. Although she was mechanically rolling the dough and turning the chapatti over on the pan, she felt that Ansar was suffering and rushed to the hall where she had laid him down.

That was when she saw the woman. Although she wore a burkha and had a niqab over her face, Arifa recognised her immediately. A dirty saree was peeping through the holes in the burkha that had once been black and had now turned pale brown from wear. Cracked heels, colourless skin, Hawaii chappals repaired using safety pins, Arifa recognised the woman's condition in a glance and felt embarrassed for her. Nor did the woman come in, but remained in the veranda, along with the many men who had come to see the mutawalli saheb. Seeing her standing in a corner, Arifa felt a lump rise in her throat. She stood behind the curtain separating the living room from the veranda and whispered just loud enough to reach the woman's ears alone. 'Sakeena Akka, I beg you, why are you standing there? Come in.'

Arifa could not see the woman's expression from behind the veil to know if she had heard or not. However, the young man standing next to her replied almost cruelly. 'It is OK, Maami, you go do your work. If Maama comes we will talk to him and leave.'

Sakeena was her eldest sister-in-law, a woman of great self-respect. After she became a widow, she took to tailoring to raise her three children and run her family. She did not desire even a drop of water from her maternal house. She would come once in a while during festivals and take her elder brother's blessings. That day she was standing in line with others like a stranger. Arifa wondered if she too had come to ask for a share in property like Jameela, but she quickly put the thought down and called Sakeena inside again. Her attempt to somehow get Sakeena to at least sit in the living room before her husband came out was in vain.

His body felt heavy, but the mutawalli saheb had had a good sleep. He was perplexed to see Arifa peeping at the people in the veranda, something she had never done before, and gesturing at someone outside. Without realising it, his voice rose sharply. 'Arifaaaa?'

Flustered, Arifa dropped the curtain and muttered, as if to herself, 'Sakeena Akka is standing there with the men, like an outsider. I was asking her to come in.'

'What?' When the mutawalli saheb stepped out and saw Sakeena and her son, the blood rose up his face.

Sakeena joined her palms together and, in a strange tone, put forward her request: 'Bhaisaab, please help a destitute widow like me. Allah will grant you and your family happiness and prosperity. My son is studying, in the first year of his BA. He has an interview at an engineering college for the job of an attender. I heard that you are a member of the committee there. My son's name is Syed Abrar. Please get him this job. The application is here, look. If my son gets this job, he will be a pillar of support for our family, even though he was born to an unlucky woman like me. Everyone says if you put in a word, he will certainly get the job. You share the joys and sorrows of poor people. You must show mercy on me.' Before the mutawalli saheb could say a word, she gave him the job application, fell at his feet and left in a hurry.

Crows began to screech in the mutawalli saheb's mind. His face became redder. Even in the cold weather, beads of sweat formed on his forehead. He collapsed on a thick cushioned chair. Arifa's eyes teared up behind the curtain.

A young woman was standing near the door, a baby held tightly to her chest. Adjusting the seragu on her head, she moved a little away from him and said, 'Anna, this child's father had a bullock cart. He had an operation fifteen days ago. I sold both the cart

29

and the bullocks to get his operation done. Now he needs another urgent operation, it seems! That is what the doctor said. I don't have anything now. You . . . you . . . ' Her throat caught and her eyes became misty. She sobbed haltingly.

The mutawalli saheb asked her the name of the hospital, the doctor and other details, told her that he would arrange for her husband's operation and sent her away. Expressing her gratitude, she left, blessing him from the bottom of her heart.

A schoolboy extended his notebook in front of him. The head-mistress of the higher primary school had written, in her round handwriting, asking the mutawalli saheb to please oblige and attend the school development committee meeting at three o'clock that afternoon. He signed the note and sent the boy away, and was about to turn towards the men to listen to their problems when in like a storm came Dawood.

Dawood was his right-hand man. He had become as necessary to him as involuntary breathing. That their thoughts went in the same direction was proof of their friendship. He was an expert in deducing the mutawalli saheb's moods from the ups and downs of his face, the latitude and longitude of the movements of his eyebrows, the quivering of his moustache, the line of his nose and the lines at the sides of his mouth. He would tailor his words, his behaviour, the bend at his waist accordingly. He also had cunning shamelessness and a lack of self-respect. So then . . .

He had not attended the morning namaz. The bloody fellow arrives now? Wonder where he was whiling away time . . . Although he gritted his teeth, the mutawalli pretended to be calm and asked, 'Where did you go, Dawood saheb? You were nowhere to be seen.'

Dawood understood both his question and his manner. Laughing to himself, he answered, 'Assalamu alaikum, mutawalli saheb,' and in fake politeness sat down.

The mutawalli was not only the president of the masjid committee, but was also involved in politics. He was under the illusion that he had the capacity to get all the Muslims to vote for any candidate he backed; several aspiring electoral candidates believed him and came to visit often. That was why many gathered at his house in the mornings. Even Sakeena had sought his help as a political personality, instead of as her elder brother. She had behaved like an outsider and hurt him as well. He glanced at the people in the veranda.

A lot of people were still waiting for their turn to talk to him. But he had urgent business with Dawood. He glanced again at the fidgeters on the bench and moved to stand up. The aged Saabjaan stumbled forward, trying to see through his misty cataracts and white eyebrows. 'Saab, saab . . . my youngest daughter is getting married next week. I don't have any money. You must show some generosity. Once she gets married, I can peacefully close my eyes. Maai-baap! You are like my father . . . you have to show mercy on an old man like me,' he said, about to fall at the mutawalli saheb's feet.

Aha! You have had so many children. Your last daughter, you say? Did you have her when you were sixty? Finally, you are falling in line. A shaitan sniggered in a corner of the mutawalli's mind. He pictured a large open site with a crumbling house standing in the middle. Every time he passed that piece of land, he imagined building a shopping complex on it.

'What do you need from me now, Saabjaan Chikkappa?' he asked, showing no mercy.

'Nothing much . . . ' Rattled, Saabjaan paused for a second and continued. 'May Allah's blessings be upon you . . . I . . . I . . . I need at least forty thousand rupees for this wedding.'

The mutawalli saheb feigned shock.

'Forty thousand rupees . . . what to do . . . where to get that money from?'

He appeared to be deep in thought. Dawood coughed softly.

'Annavre . . . one matter . . . thought I would bring it to your attention . . . if you have some free time . . . no, when one thinks of it, what the world has come to . . . law, morality, dharma, are any of those left?'

'Hmm. What happened, Dawood?'

'Don't you know about this issue? Really?'

Seeing that no answer was forthcoming from anyone, Dawood continued, 'Islam is being destroyed, Annavre . . . there is no respect left for Muslims . . . '

His preface was lengthy.

'Can't you just say what it is?' the mutawalli saheb asked, irritated.

'Annavre, you know that Umar, the one who makes horseshoes? His second daughter is married off to someone in Nelamangala, isn't it, but the boy had married another girl, remember? In any case, the first girl's elder brother—'

'Who the hell is he?' asked the mutawalli saheb, growing increasingly irritated. He did not have the patience to untangle the web of relationships.

'His name is Nisar, a painter. He said he would paint the masjid and ran away after getting two hundred rupees, remember, during the last Ramzan?'

'Ah, yes, yes, got it.'

Now the mutawalli saheb remembered everything. He remembered getting the painter tied to a tree and having him beaten for eating away the masjid's money.

'He fell into a pond and died. Some month and a half ago they found a corpse, you see. The police took it out.'

'Hmm. What happened after that?'

'What was to happen. Everything was totally destroyed. The police took Nisar's corpse and buried it in the Hindu cemetery.'

Dawood had revealed the news slowly, and it was like being shot with a bullet. Can this really be? Has anyone ever heard of something like this? For a second the mutawalli saheb felt like his heart had stopped. Wrinkles formed on his forehead, and he began to sweat. Everyone forgot what they had come for, even Saabjaan. Even if it was nagging him deep in his heart, he did not mention his daughter's wedding. The news made everyone tremble.

To think that a Muslim corpse, without a shroud, without the ghusal, without even the janaza namaz, could be buried unceremoniously in a smashana instead of in a khabaristan! A Muslim cemetery! The mutawalli saheb thought of something. 'But, Dawood, wasn't Nisar circumcised?'

Dawood did not have an answer for this technical question.

'Che, che . . . wouldn't it have been done? But why will the police think of all that? They must have wanted to finish the burial and wash their hands of the whole thing, that's all.'

There were more questions. Things that aroused curiosity. 'How did they know it was Nisar's body?'

'Many days after he went missing, his wife went to the police to register a complaint. The police showed her the clothes they found on the unidentified body, and she recognised them. Then they showed her the photo of the corpse. It had bloated, but it was Nisar's.'

'Or . . .'

'Or the police must have done this deliberately. As if they don't know! If they had come to this masjid and told us a body of one of ours was found, we would have brought it here in an instant and given it a proper burial.'

Dawood said, a little suspicious: 'As far as I know, it was that troublemaker Shankra who told the police and made sure they buried the body in a Hindu cemetery.'

Everyone there was devastated. 'Che! What terrible times. When some people die, there are thousands ready to shoulder the body to the graveyard. And then this poor fellow doesn't even get a shroud and a decent burial.'

Except for twice a year, for the Ramzan and Bakrid namaz, Nisar never stepped into the masjid. He had cheated hundreds of people by taking advances to paint their houses and then disappearing. He would drink away the money and totter about. He had once even eaten the jama'at's money, saying he would paint the masjid. Now giving him a proper burial seemed like the holiest of duties for the same people he had cheated. His corpse began to attain a martyr's status. And above all, the task of ensuring proper burial rituals for Nisar's body appeared to be the solution for the mutawalli's many problems. He pretended to be agonised, lamenting. 'What can be done?' he said. 'People have to suffer for the sins they have committed.' All the people gathered there, including Dawood, thought of the tragedy that had taken place and felt disturbed.

'Tauba, tauba.' Saabjaan slapped his cheeks. 'Death is inevitable for everyone. But no one should get a terrible death like this. No praising of the Prophet, no salutation. Tomorrow someone will bury our bodies too, wherever they want, however they want. They might just throw our bodies away on a whim.'

Dawood did not miss the chance to add his two bits either. 'Mutawalli saheb, somehow – you are there to give us direction, that is why we still remain human – one day they go to the court for something related to the Qur'an, that woman, Shah Bano's case, they made it a big deal and insulted us repeatedly. And now they take Muslim bodies and bury them in Hindu cemeteries? What greater injustice do we need?'

Dawood began to see this as a grave problem. Everyone was restless, even the mutawalli. He plucked at his beard, shoved a finger into his nose now and then, and sat deep in thought. He suddenly became alert and looked at the people. Crumpling his face as if he was immensely sad, he opened his eyes a slit and coughed, clearing his throat.

The issue was so complex that even Arifa came and stood behind the curtain, instead of getting her children ready for school. Having woken up a little late, Jameela spoke to Arifa in whispers and heard what had happened and joined her sister-in-law behind the curtain. Their female hearts were beating fast.

'Ya Allah! No matter who it is, may the poor man rest in peace. May he be given all the rites a Muslim corpse deserves and may he get three gaja of land in a khabaristan.'

Jameela's husband also got to know the news and came to stand outside with the others. Everyone was anxious, agitated. Enthusiasm grew for fighting the holy war to save Islam. Finally, the mutawalli began to speak. 'Now we have to put in all our efforts to have Nisar's remains exhumed from there and buried here. We must be ready to face any obstacle, any problem, do you understand?

'Dawood, inform our youth committee about this as well. Once they arrive, we can go together to meet the district commissioner, the superintendent of police. Let's start work on this today,' he said, quickly adding: 'Tell them not to worry about anything else. There is no money in the jama'at right now. Tell them I will pay whatever expenses are incurred myself.'

He knew that the money to be spent was nothing compared to the popularity and support he would get because of this. It was also in keeping with his status as a mutawalli to say such things. Where would the money go, after all? In his experience people would fall over themselves to donate money for these sorts of causes. He also saw it as a great opportunity to bring the youth committee closer, after they had previously accused him of all kinds of things and distanced themselves.

Everything happened as he expected. Before he came out of his reverie, Jameela's husband had taken out two hundred and fifty rupees from his pocket and placed it on the table in front of the mutawalli. 'Bhaiyya, if you use this for your work, I'll also reap the benefits of the good deed. Allah should grant people like you more strength, good health and money.' He spoke from the heart. He felt that it was not right to have his wife ask for a share in the property when there was this great task ahead. Noting her husband's expression from behind the curtain, Jameela heaved a big sigh of relief.

She had asked her elder brother for a share in the property only because her husband had forced her to, not because she herself wanted it. Like the proverb went, 'If the striking pole misses, a thousand more years of life.' She was glad that they could let the matter go, at least for now. Arifa felt very proud of her husband. Worried that he might have to go accomplish this Himalayan task without food, she rushed in to make him parottas as light as flowers. The mutawalli observed his sister and her husband's changed behaviour and beamed to himself, though he didn't express it and instead walked inside gravely, as if deep in thought.

Taking several young men along, he met the district commissioner first; it was a matter of pride for him to do so. The DC was also young, a Bengali brahmin and a graduate of Jawaharlal Nehru University. He was familiar with the messy snarl of community relations within the district, and the emotional outbursts that would sometimes arise. He read the letter the mutawalli handed over and understood the situation. Although he was laughing within, he sat with a serious, dignified face. He listened to the mutawalli's impassioned words and skirted around the matter to question him in Urdu.

'What else is new, mutawalli saheb? You have never come to see me regarding new borewells for your area or for repairs to the school building or for any other such works.'

The mutawalli stopped him mid-sentence. 'I'll make a list of all that and come again next time, swami; for now, if you could just issue an order, that is enough.'

'But still, mutawalli saheb, soil is the same everywhere, isn't it? What is the difference in soil?' he asked, very casually.

The mutawalli had several irrelevant answers for him. Without dragging it out further, the DC issued an order to the assistant commissioner. Fifteen days passed. The mutawalli saheb did not get tired, even when he had to go from officer to officer, from one department to the next. He did not even hesitate to buy coffee and snacks once in a while for the people who accompanied him.

He was disappointed that there did not seem to be much resistance from the notorious Shankar, but then again, the police and officials provided plenty of delays.

The mutawalli roamed around different offices all day. After that, discussions would go on till late in the night, either in the front yard of the masjid, or in the large hall at the Madina Hotel, or in the veranda of his house. He described the hard work he was doing. He planned how and where to curtail the powers of which officers. He described the many dangers to Islam from various quarters and preached to the youth about how these problems could be effectively solved. He did not realise how quickly fifteen days could pass in this way. The whole jama'at was discussing nothing but Nisar's body and the mutawalli saheb's efforts. Several women draped a full veil and offered namaz, praying wholeheartedly for Nisar's corpse to have the good fortune to be buried in the Muslim cemetery, and for his soul to find eternal peace.

A lot of money was collected towards this noble deed as well. Finally Nisar's body was exhumed. The mutawalli and his followers draped the rotten body in the brand new, starched shroud they had brought with them. Since the body was too rotten for ritual bathing, holy water was sprinkled on it. The foul smell made them want to retch, but no one showed it on their faces. The policemen covered their noses with their handkerchiefs. In the end, Nisar's funeral procession began on the shoulders of the mutawalli and his companions. They had poured on copious amounts of scent and covered the top of the bier with a chador made of strings of jasmine to mask the smell of rotting flesh. None of the jasmine buds had bloomed. 'Har phool ke kismat mein kahan naaz-e-aroos, chand phool toh khilte hain mazaaron ke liye': not all blooms have the fortune of adorning a bride; some flowers bloom only for mausoleums.

The funeral procession had to go quite a distance, but plenty of people had gathered. The coffin did not stay more than a minute or two on anyone's shoulder, and kept changing hands. The procession passed through the city and continued on towards the cemetery, which was there, just around the corner. There were maybe another ten steps to go. Just then a man stumbled along, shouting obscenities at the top of his voice in a strange, vulgar manner, as if to shatter the seriousness and the sadness of the whole situation. The moment he saw the man, the mutawalli, who had lent his shoulder to the front of the coffin, was stunned. He turned deathly pale. Several others in the procession reacted in the same way. No one took a step forward. Everyone's throat dried up. The man spilled some more curses loudly, tottered down a small alley and disappeared.

The first to recover was the mutawalli. He looked at the policemen, who were accompanying the procession to ensure there were no untoward incidents, and instantly became alert. Seeing the procession stop a policeman had moved forward to threaten the drunkard with a lathi. The mutawalli slowly took a step. The jama'at followed. Mutawalli saheb's legs began to shake. Someone came and changed places with him at the head of the coffin. Mutawalli saheb took out his handkerchief and wiped the sweat dripping from his face. He glared at Dawood, who bent his head and looked down. A lot of people were communicating with their eyes. No one spoke; instead they all took long strides and reached the cemetery.

The police stood outside and the corpse was duly buried in the Muslim khabaristan. The nerves in the mutawalli's head were about to burst. Whose corpse was it that they had buried?

He had no doubt that the drunkard was the painter Nisar. He was angry enough at Dawood and the painter's wife to want to chop them up. But his one consolation was this: although a lot of people in the jama'at had recognised Nisar, not one of them informed the police. They had all saved his honour. The momentary relief vanished. Thousands of crows crying kaa kaa began to pluck and eat his brain. Was it a Hindu corpse? Was it a Muslim corpse? The body was too rotten to be identified. Should it rot here, should it rot there?

People were filling the grave hurriedly. Without waiting for it to be fully covered, he rushed home. He was alone except for the crows, striking and trying to kill him.

Extremely tired, he sat in the drawing room of the house. When he did not see Arifa, even after several minutes, he anxiously called out, 'Arifaaaaa! Bring me a glass of water.'

He saw his daughter come out instead and asked, 'Why haven't you gone to school today?'

'Amma isn't at home, no? That is why I stayed back.'

'Isn't at home? Where did she go?'

The girl lifted the eyelashes covering her eyes reddened by crying and crying and replied. 'Ansar is very sick, isn't it, Appa? Amma is with him in the hospital.'

'Huh? What did you say? Who is sick? Since when? What illness?'

Heavy drops of tears fell from the girl's eyes as the questions came one after the other.

'Ansar had high fever for the last fifteen-twenty days, didn't he? The doctor was saying it is some illness of the brain. Some disease called meningitis, it seems.' She started sobbing uncontrollably.

The glass of water slipped and fell from the mutawalli saheb's hand.

Slowly, voices began to sound in his ears again. Anna, my share in the property, Anna, please help this poor widow, mai-baap, give me a loan for my daughter's wedding, Hakhdaar tarse toh angaar ka nuuh barse . . . a rain of fire . . . crows, black, grey . . . the rainbow within them . . .

BLACK COBRAS

Just in time for the Isha namaz, Tarannum came running, the Arabic book in her bag, her dupatta on top to shield it from the rain, and yelled, 'Ammi! Ammiiiiiii!' while shaking out the water dripping from her hair. Rafiya, slowly roasting dried mackerel on coals, did not answer. Tarannum rushed in and said, 'Ammi, Hasina and her mother are sitting in the mosque.'

'Oh. Why?'

'Apparently, there is some judgement today.'

'Oh, is it?'

When he was sent to the Arabic madrasa to study, Rafi was in the habit of dozing off in his seat, or he would forget his books, or lose his cap somewhere. When he reached home, he pushed his mother Waseema's hand away as she tried to hold him still to feed him a mouthful and said, 'Ammi, along with Hasina, her mother has also been sitting in the mosque from that time itself.'

'At this hour? Why?'

'There is some judgement today it seems.'

'... Oh. That.'

After distributing matchbox labels, and pictures of actors and actresses to all the madrasa students in exchange for a stick of chalk each, his pockets were full, but when Hamid reached home, he was crying because of a rotten tooth and told his mother, 'Ammi . . . Hasina is . . . '

As they were all conveying the news at home one by one, Majida lifted her shalwar carefully with her left hand to ensure it didn't get dirty, hugged the Qur'an to her chest with her right, and stepped into the house.

She saw her father sitting leisurely in the drawing room and came to a sudden halt. She held the Qur'an in both her hands, pressed the holy book to her eyes before placing it on the table and asked, 'Abba, why haven't you gone to the mosque?'

'Hmm. Isn't it time for the Isha namaz now? There is still some time for the jama'at to congregate. I'll go,' said Abdul Khader Saheb, the mutawalli of the mosque. He picked up his cap from the teapoy and slowly placed it on his head. Majida snapped, 'I am not talking about the namaz. There, in the mosque, Hasina and her mother are sitting and waiting for you. It seems her judgement is happening today.'

'Oh . . . hmm . . . that is . . . wait, what did you say? That woman is sitting in the mosque? Where in the mosque is she?'

Having forgotten about the meeting of the council he had called for, the mutawalli saheb was scratching his thick, black beard with the tips of his fingers, lost in thought.

'Oh, Abbajaan, you – ! Where they keep the janaza, there, they are sitting near there, Hasina, her mother, Hasina's two younger sisters, they are all sitting there. You must go quickly, Abbajaan, poor things! They are all shivering in the cold.'

The rain, the cold. The eagerness to feel warm! What will now make it fun is some Ceylon parotta, phaal made with lots of chillies, chicken kababs, and to wash it all down, to get a barely noticeable high, some . . .

Along with that, the jewel-like Amina, who had borne him seven children in ten years of marriage, her body, her saree smelling of garlic, fresh ginger and garam masala, her breasts round and full since she was still breastfeeding the youngest baby . . .

The mutawalli saheb's imagination was reaching a peak when Amina herself appeared at the door. She wiped her masala-filled hands on her seragu, and as if she was a rooster about to start a fight, she tilted her neck and coughed softly. The mutawalli looked up at her.

'I am completely fed up. No matter how many times I tell you, you don't let it fall inside your ears. Others are not even married at my age. But I am already an old woman,' Amina grumbled.

'What's happened now?'

'What is there to happen? My back is broken. These children, the home, samsara – do I have even a minute of free time? If I bear one child per year, what will I become? Don't you want me to live long enough to be a mother to these children at least?'

'Hush. Why talk about all that now? Have I ever left you wanting for anything? No matter what, the thing you ask for will not happen, understand that very clearly. I am the mutawalli; if people get to know that I got the operation done for a woman in my own house, I will have to be answerable to them, hamm.'

The conversation would have continued, but there was a sound near the front door, and Amina quickly went in.

'Assalamu alaikum, Mutawalli Saab.'

'Wa 'alaikum assalam. Arey, Yakub, you have only come now? But she came and has been waiting for a long time. Should I take a decision or not?'

'You are here. Does she know the law better than you? Let everything happen according to what you decide. If you can have your food now . . . '

Yakub trailed off.

'Food. Well, something of that sort will be done, leave that,' the mutawalli saheb said.

'How can that be? First you must have your food. I have brought the auto. Once you finish your meal, then we can talk.'

'Ohhhh, what food? What does it all matter. Once one becomes the mutawalli, that's it. We have to forget about house and family. Even if someone comes and calls me at midnight, I have to come to your service, what do you say?' he grumbled.

'Che, che! You must not misunderstand me. God's law says get married not just to one woman, but four. Should women give up their honour and dignity and come to the mosque? I waited for not one, but ten years. Did she give birth to even one boy? And the way she runs her mouth! Abbabbaa! Is that a sign of a woman from a respectable family? So I married another woman. So what? Should I not have? Didn't I go visit her every time I felt like it? The other day, I was driving on the road when I saw Hasina. I dropped her off near the house in my auto itself, and placed ten rupees in her hands. Are we not humans? As a woman, if she can't even adjust this much, then . . . ' Yakub said.

Amina was listening to their conversation from behind the door, and cursed him wholeheartedly. 'Ah! Look at him buttering up. For his own satisfaction, he will even bring down God. He will bring up the Qur'an, quote from the Hadith. But if he is told to give something to feed that poor woman, then he begins to shirk his responsibilities. God, when will you give some sense to this fellow?' She quietly slid behind the door and went inside.

44

'OK, leave it now. Once you start, you go on non-stop,' the mutawalli saheb said, putting on his coat. When he had stepped into his sandals and got down to the road, Yakub said, 'Let's go to the Princess Hotel. No one from our community will peep into the Family Room there.'

'Let's go to a nicer place, in case someone sees us. What if there is unnecessary trouble? Who will give them answers? As it is, you know how people behave. This rain, abbaa this cold! Eyy, Amina, I am going out, I'll be late coming back. Close the door,' the mutawalli said.

In reply came the sound of vessels being slammed down, and Amina's grumbling. 'Mutawalli, it seems, mutawalli. But what kind of man is he? After becoming the mutawalli, does he do the namaz properly five times a day? Has he stopped going to the cinema? Fine, let all that be. Has he at least stopped drinking the devil's piss? May his mutawalli position burn in hell.'

They did not hear her grumble, but the loud sound of Yakub's autorickshaw, running down the end of the street with the mutawalli in it, reached Amina. Aashraf was the unfortunate woman sitting like a ghost in the still quietness of the mosque in this cold weather. 'Poor thing! What is her fault in all this? Is it her fault that she gave birth to three daughters in a row? Is that like making rottis, to roll them out as we want? Thoo!' Amina's heart turned bitter.

She went to the backyard and turned south to reach the high wall surrounding the mosque. She had pushed a few large stones against the compound wall to make it convenient for her to listen to sermons at the mosque when she could spare the time, and to have someone pass over a few pots of water from the hauz inside the mosque. She pulled her seragu over her head, climbed on the stones, and peeped into the mosque's inner compound, covering her face slightly. After finishing the Isha namaz people were walking out of the main door of the extensive compound. She bent forward. Oh, there, in front of the hall that had been built to the north of the mosque, there sat Aashraf, shrivelled up. Her seragu covered her head, while the folds of her tattered saree were wrapped around the baby on her lap. Hasina was sitting next to her mother, her legs stretched out on the cold floor. Three-year-old Habiba was half on the floor and half in her mother's lap, struggling to warm herself.

All those who had come to do namaz cast a questioning look in her direction and left one by one. The fragrance of biriyani wafted from one man's house. The smell of fish curry came from another's. Somebody's new wife was waiting for him. Yet another's son had just learned to walk and was tottering forward. This way, they hurriedly exited the mosque, each looking forward to the happiness that awaited them in their homes, or hoping to free themselves from their endless troubles and woes.

Aashraf remained seated. The powdery rain falling relentlessly for the last two days had not cooled the fire in her gut. The cold that had seeped into her bones had not reduced her energy. The hunger that was gnawing at her stomach with sharp nails had not weakened her. She was banging on the grand door of Allah's house. Not for herself – hers was a dog's belly that could be filled somehow or the other – but to beg for justice for her children. She was ready to fight for their right to live their lives. She stood alone to ask why she was being punished for no fault of her own. But the doors of Allah's house had not yet opened for her. The pale faces of her children who sat around her kept her determined. When her voice continued to go unheard, she had resorted to creating a scene.

The baby sleeping in her lap moved a little. Aashraf tried to stretch her stiffened legs a bit, parted her seragu and looked at the baby's face. Illness had made the baby's face dull, and she looked even sicker in the faint light. The child's nose was blocked. When the baby's chest rose and expanded following the rhythm of breathing, two depressions could be seen below her ribcage. Her eyes were closed; rheum had dried on her eyelashes. The baby's body was burning. Aashraf stared at her.

Her child Munni. It was after she was born that Aashraf's troubles reached their peak. When the first two daughters came, Yakub had been disappointed, but he still lived at home. She had saved some money from the earnings Yakub brought home and had some gold ornaments made; not just that, she had bought silver anklets that were two fingers thick, and she enjoyed walking around, her feet making chamm-chumm sounds. When the third was also a girl child, Yakub disappeared. He had not even looked in the direction of the hospital. He did not step inside their house. Instead, he went to live with his mother.

Aashraf boiled and ate pumpkin leaves to survive. She reused tea powder for two, three days and held on to her life by drinking the weak brew. She also tried every means possible to placate her husband and bring him back. She held the infant to her shoulder and went to the market, and fell at Yakub's feet at the autorickshaw stand. She cried, she begged him to show mercy. 'Allah will destroy you,' she cursed. But it was all in vain.

When she could not see any other way out, she began to go to Zulekha Begum's house to work. The housework did not seem like a burden to her. But whether there was something to do or not, she had to be there from morning till night. Zulekha Begum's husband worked in some office. They had two children, both of whom studied in college. Zulekha Begum read one or the other book all day long.

Once, she raised her head from her book and asked Aashraf, 'What job does your husband do?'

'He drives an autorickshaw, Apa.'

'So then his earnings must be enough to run the household, isn't it?'

'It used to be enough,' she replied, dismissively.

All her thoughts were on the infant Munni whom she had left at home under Hasina's care. Her breasts were leaking, and the front of her blouse was soaking wet. 'The baby must be hungry,' she thought and teared up.

'Then why do you come here to work?'

Zulekha was surprised to hear Aashraf's story. In this day, in this age, are there still people like this, she wondered.

'Do you know, Aashraf, if a daughter is born, it is as if the Prophet himself has saluted the house.'

'Oh, leave it, Apa, how many times should the Prophet's salaam fall on a poor woman's house like mine?'

'You are mad! The Prophet himself had only daughters. A son was born, but died when he was still a child. Have you read about how much he loved his daughters? Have you learned about it? Bibi Fathima was his life. They were living proof of the bond that can exist between father and daughter,' Zulekha Begum said.

Aashraf did not understand a word. Her mind still revolved around thoughts of Munni. Finally, Zulekha Begum said, 'This is utter injustice. Why don't you give a petition to the mosque?'

'Arey!' Aashraf leaped up. 'Why didn't I think of it, Apa?' she cried. 'Please write a petition for me.'

She went to the mutawalli saheb's house four-five times with the petition in hand, but she could not meet him. Then one day she ran and placed the petition in the mutawalli's hands just as he was stepping out. He absent-mindedly shoved the piece of paper into his coat pocket and walked away.

The water supply had been turned on in the public taps along the street that morning. Hanifa Chikkamma, who was sweeping half the width of the street with a stick broom in hand, quickly disappeared behind the fat wall. Rafiya, who had come to place her pot below the public tap, noticed Hanifa Chikkamma making 'shh shh' signs and ran inside her home, unmindful of her pot slipping from her hands. All the women in the mohalla who were occupied with their various chores vanished from sight. Satisfied with the respect he commanded, the mutawalli saheb checked from the corner of his eyes to see if any women were continuing their chores without fear, and walked on, donning a serious face.

When the mutawalli saheb did not call for her even after fifteen days, Aashraf went to his house again. As usual he was not at home. While she sat there waiting, Amina asked her, 'They say that those who get an operation done to stop getting pregnant will not reach jannat. Is that true, Aashraf?'

'Whatever that is, Amma, I don't know. I have to ask Zulekha Apa, she is always reading a lot of fat-fat books.'

Amina came very close to her and whispered, as if it was a secret, 'If that is the case, will you ask her and tell me the next time you are here?'

'OK, ma. She keeps talking about a lot of other things as well. But me? I am stupid, will I understand all that?'

Before Aashraf finished speaking the mutawalli saheb came inside, his face fuming.

'Oh. Your petition is lost somewhere. If you want, write another one and bring it,' he said and went into his room.

If I want – oh no – I don't want, not for me, I don't want my husband even – but my children need food . . .

Munni had been a well-fed child even in the middle of Aashraf's mountain of problems, but she had started losing weight and become weak. Her hands and legs were sticklike, and her stomach bloated. Her nose always running, filled with a hunger that could eat the entire world, Munni cried relentlessly day and night, but still Aashraf did not think of her as a burden. She gave Munni more love and more food than she gave her two elder daughters. Yet what Munni needed urgently was medicine. Where could she find the money for that? Injections, pills, tonic, the doctor's fees every day, and on top of everything she had to wait her turn to see the doctor too. The tablets that she managed to give Munni once in a while were of no use and only made her illness worse.

By the time she got Zulekha Begum to write another application and had gone to see the mutawalli saheb at his home four, five times, she heard a rumour that doused the fire burning in her. It was this: 'Yakub is not in town, he has moved away from here.' Isn't he a man? Whether he is there, not there, whether he carries responsibilities, whether he neglects them, who's going to ask? Who does he have to answer to? He is langoti yaar, after all, a man, everybody's best friend. His past does not rise up to dance in public. The present doesn't touch him. The future doesn't move him, nor is it a mystery. He does not have to remain shyly in the shadows. He does not have to say who he belongs to. He does not need to seek forgiveness, not ever at all, because nothing he does is a mistake.

Aashraf was very hurt. Munni, who was melting away in her lap, became closer to her heart. But a mother's love was not enough for her. Treatment. Care. Within six months, Munni was skin and bones.

Just then, like a thin reed clutched by a drowning man, she heard that Yakub had returned. She ran to the auto stand, but Yakub disappeared the moment he saw her. The next time she was smarter. She came from behind his auto and sat inside with her children.

Without a word, he began to drive. He came to a stop in front of her hut and said, 'You pop out an army of girls and roam around like a dog. Learn to have a little bit of decency at least.' He spat and plonked the children on the ground. Just as she was getting out, confused, he drove off, his auto making a 'barrrr' sound. She hugged her teary-eyed children tightly to her chest.

Seeing no other way, she gave dozens of appeal letters to the mosque committee and to the mutawalli. She begged them to make Yakub provide at least a little money for the child's medical expenses. The only answer she got was, come back later, come another day, go away. In the middle of all this, another rumour came flying by, complete with wings and feathers. 'Yakub is going to marry again. He wants a son who can drive the autorickshaw after him, it seems.' Whatever was left of Aashraf's world came crumbling down before her eyes. She cried all night, and went to sit by the door of the mutawalli's house again. The mutawalli saheb came out yawning at around nine in the morning, saw her and asked, 'What?', his face showing his irritation.

Aashraf described her usual complaints in detail. The mutawalli coughed, spat forth loudly. 'What forbidden thing has he done now? He has done another nikah, that's all, isn't it? He didn't elope with anyone, did he? Let him do it. Do you know that there is a Sharia law that says he can get married to four women? Why are you getting jealous of that? These women are like this only, they know only to be jealous,' he said, looking at Amina from the corner of his eyes. Although Amina, breastfeeding her youngest baby, thought, 'Damn these men,' she felt a prick in her heart. She realised that the day when she would have to line up her children and beg, just like Aashraf, was not far off.

In a weak voice, Aashraf said, 'He — not one — let him get married a thousand times. I am not jealous. As long as he is happy, that is enough for me. I am not going to trouble him. But, Mutawalli Saheb, this child is dying. At least medicine for—'

The mutawalli stopped her mid-sentence and scolded. 'Look, don't talk like a fool. Maut and hayat, our death and life, is in Allah's hands. Even if a rock is smashed over the heads of some people, they don't die. That is because it is Allah's wish that they should live. Just like that, if it is Allah's wish that this one should live, then it will live. If not, it will die. Why should you trouble Yakub for that?'

Aashraf was speechless before such questions. It was true! She tried to console herself thinking that whatever happens is God's will. But the child had non-stop diarrhoea, and, looking at her, she could not put all the burden on Allah and sit quietly. Who else could she ask? Yakub had married again and gone to his new wife's village.

The next time Aashraf saw him, there was mehendi on his nails. The watch he wore on his left wrist was shining. He was standing next to his auto wearing new shoes, stylishly combing his hair, looking almost like a stranger. Completely occupied with himself, he stuffed a ten-rupee note into Aashraf's hands as if she was some beggar, and disappeared.

Aashraf became a stone. But the question of Munni's life and death kept her determined. Zulekha Begum lifted her head from her book and said, 'Look, for any man to marry four wives, there has to be right reason for it. If it is wartime, if many men are dying in the war, then a man can marry more than once. If the wife is suffering from a long-term incurable disease, or if she cannot have children, then he can marry again. Else, if he cannot get satisfaction from one . . . ' She couldn't finish the sentence.

Aashraf suddenly exploded in anger. 'I don't fall into any of these categories. Don't I have children? Isn't it wrong that he left me? Isn't it wrong that he made me and our children destitute?'

'Look, according to Sharia, even if he marries again, he has to ensure that he does not make even a little distinction between the two wives and treats them both equally.'

'That means . . . how, Apa?'

'That means if he builds you a house, he has to build a similar house for her. If he buys you a saree, one for her too. If he spends one night with you, he has to spend one night with her.'

Aashraf's eyes welled up. 'I don't want all that, Apa. If he spends a little money for my child and saves her life, I won't even look in his direction again. But still, what he is doing is wrong, isn't it, Apa?'

'Of course. Hundred per cent, it is his fault.'

'Then why doesn't the mutawalli saheb say that?'

'See, that is where the biggest problem is. In a lot of our jama'at, the mutawallis don't know the law themselves. Secondly, they don't have the authority to implement the law. Thirdly, no one listens to them. And then they accept only the parts of the law that suit them. Where this Sharia law remains is in the laps of poor women like you, like this Munni.'

'Is there no medicine for this, Apa?'

'There is. Why won't there be? Why don't scholars tell women about the rights available to them? Because they only want to restrict women. The whole world is at a stage where everyone is saying something must be done for women and girl children. But these people, they have taken over the Qur'an and the Hadiths. Let them behave as per these texts at least! Let them educate girls, not just a madrasa education, but also in schools and colleges. The choice of a husband should be hers. Let them give that. These eunuchs, let them give meher and get married instead of licking leftovers by taking dowry. Let a girl's maternal family give her a share in the property. Let them respect her right to get divorced if there is no compatibility between the man and woman. If she is divorced, let someone come forward to marry her again; if she is a widow, let her get a companion to share her life with.'

'Apa, Apa, what are you saying?' Aashraf felt like she had lost her senses.

'What I am saying is correct, Aashraf. All these rights are available for women in Islam. A girl can go to school, she can go to the shops, go to work. She can have a life outside. But there is a clause too that she should not exhibit her body and her beauty . . .' Zulekha Begum began giving a passionate lecture.

Aashraf nodded her head, disappointed. She did not want any of this. 'What can I ask about my Munni?'

'What will you ask? Your expenses for food and clothing and for your children, a house for yourself, then a night with him every alternate day. You have a right to all this. He has to give you all this. If he does not, hold his collar in front of people and demand them. This mutawalli, take the slipper from your foot in your hands, slap him with it and insist. Do not beg. Demand justice. Do you know who gets justice? Only those who demand it. People like you will not get justice if you don't demand it. Give a petition to the masjid, gather a panchayat around and call me. I will tell your man, and that mutawalli, what the Sharia is, what justice is. Twisting the Qur'an and Hadiths the way they want in front of a helpless woman is not justice.'

Aashraf was very scared, and felt her hands and legs go cold. If it was only the question of her own stomach, there was no need for all this trouble. 'If God has given life, he will at least provide grass to eat, I could stay quiet thinking this way, but – this Munni . . .'

Aashraf was determined and ready to make justice hers, instead of having to beg for it. Munni stirred in her lap. Her breath sounded strained. There were beads of sweat on her forehead. Munni's neck was soaking wet. Aashraf wiped her child's neck and armpits with her saree. She touched her body, and, even in that state of distress, felt relieved that the fever was coming down. Earlier Hasina had cried that she was hungry, hungry. When she looked around for her in that dim light, Aashraf's heart almost stopped. Unable to bear the cold from sleeping on the floor, Hasina had crawled under a mat inside the wooden bier and wrapped half of it around herself. Habiba was curled up on the floor nearby.

There was a quietness to the green light emanating from the mosque veranda. A cool breeze from the heavy rain and a peopleless environment. She felt a strange fear even in the holy atmosphere of the mosque. She did not know what the time was. Thinking that the business of the outside world must have concluded, she felt afraid. From morning till evening, every Muslim chanted 'Bismillah ir-Rahman ir-Raheem' continuously. Here was a situation that would move even the heart of Allah, the most merciful, most compassionate; but at least Munni had some warmth. The other two children did not even have clothes to fully cover their bodies. At once, a thousand scissors flew across her insides, and a deep sigh escaped her. From her heart: 'Ya Allah!' Allah did not reply. Her stomach, once warm and quiet, now felt chilled, as if a ball of snow was turning inside her. Her blood turned cold, her veins, unable even to shiver, turned to ice. She couldn't understand that someone was calling. Finally, she heard Amina's voice from a distance.

Amina was standing on the other side of the compound wall with a plate in her hands. She was calling, 'Aashraf, take this, there is rotti, come, fast . . . hold this . . . ' Aashraf returned to reality very slowly. Rain continued to fall, as if that was the law of this cruel world. On the other side, far away, rotti . . . An extraordinary strength flowed through her. She held Munni to her chest and got up. Just then—

The masjid gate creaked. The mutawalli saheb, seemingly at the height of happiness, was coming in with Yakub. The mutawalli patted his stomach and burped softly. He spat with a 'pichak' sound from his paan-reddened lips, and slowly walked up to the top of the masjid steps. Yakub walked just as leisurely and stood a little distance away. An expression of 'Look at that, she still has not left' passed across his face. Amina's hands that held the rottis slowly slid back.

In the houses surrounding the mosque, most people had finished their dinners. The men were either watching TV or had gone to sleep. The women, on the pretext of finishing their chores, kept going to the end of their own house compounds, keeping a foot on some high platform, or pressing their palms on the wet walls of the masjid to see what was happening.

Aashraf held Munni, the inspiration for her fight, to her chest, and slowly walked up to the men. The mutawalli was sitting on the top step. Yakub was standing to his left, one step below. Aashraf stood to their right, three-four steps below them. Since there was a roof over this part, she was protected from the rain. But the moisture-laden breeze had taken away her ability to even stand. Yakub was ready to charge and gore her like a bull. Water from the roof was dripping down Aashraf's back and dripping from her seragu. Oh! Even this rain does not soak men, and is behaving so softly, with great respect. She was surprised even in that moment.

The mutawalli saheb had reason to hesitate before speaking. A lot of paan juice had accumulated in his mouth. He couldn't pollute those holy steps. He had to walk up to the compound wall at a distance to spit it, like out of a squirt gun. Just when he was about to get up, Yakub spat out, like he was spitting fire: 'Mutawalli Saheb, what does she want, this whore?'

Mutawalli Saheb became alert all of a sudden. Since he had ended up gulping the paan juice down, his head felt dizzy for a second, though his common sense became alert nonetheless. He realised that in the darkness surrounding the compound wall, there were women-shaped lizards standing on their big toes and watching. He was very certain that a lizard called Amina was no doubt stuck to the wall and staring at him as if she would swallow him up. That was why, for their sake, for the sake of a show of power, the rice, paan and other things that Yakub had bought him moved to one side of his throat.

'Eyy, Yakub. You should not speak like that,' he said.

But Yakub was not in a state to listen. This woman, she had made his life hell. Like faeces stuck to the feet! She was the devil who destroyed him by putting the responsibility of those three girls on him. When all he wanted was to find happiness in the lap of his new wife, and, if a baby boy was born, to have an heir to his autorickshaw. She was the demon troubling him. That Gafoor, Idris, Nasir, all of them have two wives and are having fun, but none of their wives are causing trouble like this. They have quietly gone to their maternal homes, or else they are working as coolies or something. This bitch has not only troubled me for two years, but has now climbed the steps of the mosque even. 'She – her –' Yakub burned with uncontrollable anger even in that cold. 'Lei! If you who squats to pee has this much arrogance, how much arrogance should I, who stands to piss, have?' he screamed, in his very dignified manner.

Not a word came out of Aashraf's mouth. She had become still. Zulekha Begum had not told her what to reply to such questions. She had not even expected such a question. In her confusion she held Munni even more tightly to her chest. By then, Yakub, boiling with rage, came swiftly towards her and, gathering all his strength, kicked her. Aashraf fell to one side. Her attempt to protect Munni even as she fell was in vain. When her forehead smashed to the ground, Munni flew out of her hands. A terribly painful sound never before heard in any masjid escaped Aashraf. Both her children woke up, even Hasina, who was sleeping inside the janaza. Perhaps even the innumerable corpses, carried on that bier before melting into layers of soil, had woken up too. Aashraf fainted.

The mutawalli was in shock. His intoxication vanished. Piercing through the veil of darkness, facing the onslaught of cold and rain, shaking off the dirt that stuck to their feet, with their heads covered, those innumerable women, where were they, who are they, where did they come from, here, is Amina among them? Some lifted Aashraf up, others moved towards Munni. Munni's fever had come down. Her breath was no longer ragged. There was no suffering. She had become free from all the pains of this world. Her life of agony had ended. Her body had fought, determined to live, but had now slipped under death's black chador.

The mutawalli saheb remained sitting, unable to move. Hanifa Chikkamma took Aashraf and her children to her home. Munni's corpse remained in the mosque. All the lights were turned on. Water in the pot behind the masjid started boiling. All the sleeping men slowly woke up and came out. Without saying a word, the cloth-shop owner Mateen Saheb opened up and brought red cloth for the shroud. They bathed Munni, draped the red cloth on her, cried, dabbed attar and abeer on the body, and shifted her to the khabaristan.

At the cemetery, Aashraf hugged Munni and cried ferociously, but in some corner of her heart there was a thread of quiet peace.

There was no happiness for Munni here, no reason for her to have stayed back. Munni is free from pain, and has freed me from pain too; now I don't have to go behind Yakub begging; I don't have to chase this mutawalli, begging; I don't have to answer inhumane questions; there is me, and my two children; but still, poor Munni, she didn't wear new clothes even once, she didn't hold a doll in her hands to play. From the time she was born, she only got injections and bitter medicines to swallow. Her maternal instinct rose up, and she shed innumerable tears again.

After laying the egg of light at dawn, the black hen of ignorance exited, rushing into the darkness to peck at grains and sticks.

Mutawalli Saheb began to walk slowly. Hanifa Chikkamma, sweeping half the width of the road with a stick broom in her hand, brushed the slush here and there furiously. Unbothered that a few drops had splashed on the mutawalli, she held up the broom in her right hand, like a fan, pounded it on her left palm and, staring at the broom, addressed the wind: 'May Allah's curse fall on you. It feels like I saw Shaitan in person.' Rafiya, who had come to place a pot under the water tap, put her pot down, picked up a stone, and, addressing a non-existent dog, threw the stone into a slush-filled drain nearby. 'A dog, just a dog!' she said, sniggering.

Naseema chased her hen, the one with wide grey and white feathers on its back and fat thighs, which sauntered even on its short legs. She caught it by its comb and beak, glared with hatred at the cock perched on its back and said, 'Hey Allah! May your benevolence destroy this damned cock's lineage. It has no shame or dignity. No fear of Allah. Have you been getting fat to feed the worms in the grave? Donkey-face, get lost.' She cracked her knuckles and cursed the cock she herself had reared.

At the corner house, Qazi Saheb's daughter-in-law, who had not so much as come to the main door even though it had been two years since her wedding, walked up to the compound gate and stood watching her husband get on his scooter. Seeing the mutawalli saheb, she addressed the child in her arms and asked, 'Do you want to see a gorilla, my love? Look, there, a gorilla!' When the mutawalli turned back to look, she giggled and slammed the door.

From a distance, Jameela Athe scolded loudly, as if she was addressing someone: 'Nothing good will come your way. You will be born with a pig face on Judgement Day. May black cobras coil themselves around you. May you not remember the Kalima on your tongue when you die.' She tossed a string of curses around like dynamite.

Asifa came out with an overflowing garbage basket, not caring about the seragu that had slipped off her head. She dumped the trash and spat 'thoo, thoo,' loudly, hard enough to fully dry her throat, as if she had seen something utterly disgusting. Her spit might have fallen on him too.

The mutawalli saheb could not forget Munni's face wrapped in that red cloth. Her eyes were shut, but he felt as if she was staring at him. Voices surrounded him from all sides. His heart was heavy, his legs refused to move; every morsel of the biriyani he had eaten felt like it had turned to iron and was punching him from inside. Everything he had drunk . . . like Amina said, it felt like Shaitan's piss, he felt assaulted by its stink, as if he was going to drown in the smell; he was afraid, there was a bad feeling in his stomach.

Just as he was struggling up the steps to his house, he saw the blurry sight of Amina with her mother, getting ready to go somewhere. He wiped his sweat, and, dry-throated and unable to speak, gestured to ask where to.

'Where else to?' she exploded. 'I have given you seven already. At least now I am going to get an operation done.'

Without the strength to stop her, without any words to say to her, just as the mutawalli was about to sit down, Amina spoke exactly like him.

'Look, close the door and look after the children. It will be more than a week before I return.'

A DECISION OF THE HEART

Yusuf would get out of the house by seven o'clock without even having breakfast, and come home only for lunch. In the evenings dinner was at his mother's house, which was not far away. The front of Yusuf's house had a large room. He blocked off the door to the rest of the building, knocked in a new entrance facing the street, designated some space as bathroom and some space as kitchen, and called it a home. The left side of the house was his wife Akhila's; the right side was his mother Mehaboob Bi's. Widowed at a young age, his mother had spat fire on anyone suggesting she remarry, had carried her only son Yusuf on her back, and raised him with a lot of love. There was no struggle she had not gone through; there was no job she had not done.

Yusuf had been forced to sell fruit from early on. Initially he harvested the papayas that had grown in the front yard, carved them creatively, each slice as thin as paper, and sold them. Thin slices of cucumber with salt and chilli powder sprinkled on top danced in the hands of customers. Each piece of cucumber would melt in their mouths. A fruit-selling business that starts like this will grow more prosperous by the day. He set up a fairly large fruit shop. Whereas earlier he used to struggle for every mouthful of rice, he was now in a good position. He did not have many worries. But . . .

His wife was his only source of stress. Akhila was irritated at seeing him jump like a young calf every time his mother was nearby. She knew he didn't like the lunches she made him in the afternoon. If she made fish or meat curry, he never asked, 'Did you give some curry to Amma?' She would not spare him if he did that. Instead, he would mix just the curry with rice and push the fish or meat pieces to the sides of the plate before washing his hands. He would eat dinner to his heart's content, sitting in front of his mother. Some days, he would eat till his stomach was so heavy that he had to lay down there.

This was why her mother-in-law Mehaboob Bi was the arch-enemy of Akhila's life. When she and Yusuf got married, all of them lived together at first. Yusuf could not have imagined even in his dreams that his mother would live away from him, in a separate house. But Akhila's anger, her temper, worsened day by day. She had four-five brothers; all of them lived close by. One day, the fight between husband and wife over Mehaboob Bi got so bad that one of Akhila's younger brothers got in the middle and ended up thrashing Yusuf properly. After this incident, more so than to the witch Akhila who had been responsible for his humiliation, he became closer to his mother, who had hugged him to her chest, consoled him, fanned him with her seragu and shed tears over his condition.

The very next day, seeing his mother getting ready to leave for her younger brother's house in Tumakuru, he became like hot coal. After he swore, 'If you step out of the house, I am going to leave Akhila,' the whole jama'at, Akhila's brothers and some neighbours came to sort things out. They decided that the door to the front room of the house would be walled up from the inside, a new door would be installed from the front and that Mehaboob Bi would live there.

Yusuf worked hard. If he bought a small TV for Akhila, the same kind of TV would grace Mehaboob Bi's house too. If he bought a kerosene stove for Akhila, a similar one for Mehaboob Bi; if he bought a watermelon for this house, a watermelon of the same size for that house too. Although she was the mistress of her own house, Akhila used to boil with envy. Among all this, Akhila's four sons, Raja, Munna, Babu and Chotu, took great advantage of the enmity between the two women. It is possible that if Mehaboob Bi had stood up to Akhila just as much, maybe Yusuf would not have taken his mother's side so often. But the fact that she kept quiet no matter how much Akhila shouted or created scenes was painful to Yusuf, and he naturally became partial towards his mother.

Once, ten-year-old Munna had not only sat by his grandmother and filled his stomach with biscuits dip-dipped in tea, but also described to Akhila how crispy the biscuits had been. Yusuf had not bought those biscuits for either Akhila or his mother. Mehaboob Bi's nephew had visited her and given her a packet. Instinctively Akhila had shouted at Yusuf and cursed his mother. She went to the front door so that Mehaboob Bi could hear, called her a homewrecker and cracked her knuckles. When none of this got a reaction, she began to beat her chest and cry, 'You are making my stomach burn by behaving like a co-wife.'

Her four children surrounded her, scared. Seeing them, she began to sob harder. She could not tolerate the fact that her husband loved the old woman the most, more than her or these pearl-like children. She believed that he treated them like dirt under his feet. In the middle of all her crying, shouting and scene-making, she did not notice Yusuf standing behind her. Once in a while, Yusuf would lose his mind and wonder if he should thrash and kill her. This was one such insane situation. He had inherited a little calmness from his mother, so he remained silent. He sat down on a chair and trained his eyes on the gold rings he wore on both his hands. He loved wearing rings; seeing his attire, his Muslim friends used to tease him. As per Islamic tradition, silk clothes and gold were forbidden for men. But Yusuf wore a Kapali ring and another large ring with a green stone every day.

He sat there, deep in thought, absent-mindedly twisting the ring on his left hand. Although Akhila closed her dictionary of curse words when she saw him, she kept muttering under her breath, 'My savathi, my co-wife . . . '

The dam of Yusuf's patience burst. He abruptly stood up and asked, 'Who is your savathi?' She was not willing to answer directly. 'The one who is ruining my house, the one who is snatching my husband away from me, the one who is stabbing me like an old vulture . . . I will call her my savathi only,' she said, stubbornly. Thinking that it was useless to talk to her, Yusuf walked towards the door. Yet seeing him ignore her protests and retreat to his mother's house in front of her, Akhila's anger rose to the crown of her head.

She rushed and pulled at the back of her husband's shirt and screamed, 'You should have kept her! What did you marry me for?' Yusuf fully lost his temper. 'Shut your mouth. If you talk such filth again, I will knock down all your teeth,' he said.

She widened her eyes frighteningly and began to tug more at his shirt, shouting, 'Are you going to hit me? Hit me. That whore must have told you to.' Losing control, he beat her a few times and walked out of the house.

He did not come back home that night, and instead had dinner at his mother's and slept there. In the morning, he called his eldest son Raja and gave him fifty rupees for Akhila's daily expenses and went out. Akhila waited for him that afternoon, but Yusuf did not come. Her second son Munna was a very smart boy. She made him skip school, told him to sit in his grandmother's house and report back on what was happening there. She waited and waited for him to return but got tired and dozed off. Yusuf went to his mother's house to sleep, handed his son some money for Akhila's expenses the next morning, and left for work. She stubbornly refused to send Munna to school for a whole week and made him stand guard. But it was no use.

Finally, it was she who admitted defeat. She took Babu along and went to Yusuf's fruit shop one afternoon. His anger had also cooled by then. He was a little anxious too, wondering if Akhila had brought her brothers along. But when she began to sniff loudly, making sarraa barraa noises, he understood her tactic was different altogether. Worried what the neighbours in the marketplace might make of this, he used his brains and quickly handed a packet of fruit to his son, saying, 'I will come home in the afternoon, go home now,' and sent them away.

He came to Akhila's house for lunch. She had fried mackerel especially for him. He didn't push them to the side of his plate and burped in satisfaction after eating one or two pieces. The affection of a slight smile, never seen before, was present between husband and wife. Both acted as if nothing had happened.

But when Yusuf went to his mother's house for dinner, he brought two mackerel from Kaka's hotel, packed specially. He placed them in front of her and said, 'Amma, you cannot clean these and cook them, that is why I got some packed for you. Akhila had made mackerel in the afternoon, it was very tasty. But I couldn't eat – it was as if they got stuck in my throat – what would have happened if she had sent you some too?'

Mehaboob Bi replied, 'Let it go. What is important is that you both live peacefully. Fish, meat, chicken, none of this is a big deal. Hands and mouth, all of it is meat too, isn't it? Why should you take it to heart so much? If she doesn't have such courtesies, you should adjust and live with her. Otherwise it just leads to a scene on the road and in the streets, that's all,' biting into the fish between morsels of advice.

Munna was sitting right there, pretending to read the book in his hands, but his ears were trained on what they were talking about. His father did not notice him. If his grandmother had given him a bite of the fried mackerel that was making him drool, he would have gladly shifted allegiance. When mother and son completely neglected him, however, and were interested only in each other, Munna slipped out and went to his mother. Akhila had spread out the mattress and was waiting for her husband to return, chewing betel nut in the meantime. She laid Munna down on her lap and ran her fingers through his hair, and asked with special affection, 'What is happening there?'

He had by then learned of the situation between his mother and grandmother. Not only did he report every detail of the fried mackerel incident at his grandmother's house, but also added, 'And then they said, and then they said, they said you don't have any sense, it seems, it seems you are mad,' applying salt and chilli on the whole thing.

Akhila wanted to make up with her husband and was ready to go to great lengths to do it, but what her son said disturbed her. She pulled the door open with great force, came out, spat the betel nut into the drain and screamed at the top of her voice, inviting her enemy to come out, and thus declaring war. In her current state she could not decide whether it was her mother-in-law who was obstructing her, or if it was her husband who was denying her love, and began to curse both of them non-stop. Yusuf came out, bewildered. Neighbours too had slowly begun to come out of their houses.

Akhila, like a fool, was creating a scene. Since her shouting included the words mackerel, fried masala, Kaka's hotel, brainless person, and madwoman, and seeing Munna closing his eyes like the picture of innocence, it did not take Yusuf long to figure out what had happened. He dragged Akhila inside and slammed the bolt. He was fed up with the commotion. He made Akhila sit on the bed, sat down next to her and tried to calm her down.

'Look here, Akhila, no one said anything about you.' He wanted to tell her not to behave like a crazy person, but bit his tongue with great effort and instead said, 'Isn't she my mother? Look, you have not one, but four sons. Amma has no one else to look after her. If she had another son to take care of her, I wouldn't pay her any attention. If your own children ask if you have eaten, if you are well, what is wrong in that? Tell me, what do you want? I do not want to hurt you; even if I become a pauper, I will not leave any of your wants unfulfilled. But please don't shout at Amma.' He tried to console her in many ways.

Akhila did not speak, and began to sob continuously. 'I don't want anything, rii. Did I ask for jewellery, for new clothes, for a big bed? If I have your love that is enough for me. But that is what I don't get,' she sobbed. He tried to calm her down. He removed the rings from his fingers and made her wear them, hoping that would make her happy. Eventually, they made up.

Morning. Akhila was still sleeping. The moment Yusuf woke up, he removed the two rings from her fingers, slipped them onto his, and left for the shop. Akhila did not stress about anything too much, sent Munna to school, and became occupied with her chores. However, one eye remained trained in the direction of Mehaboob Bi's house. Her ears would prick up at the slightest sound. Her nose twitched at the slightest whiff of masala. She waited for her husband to return.

At around eleven o'clock, Mehaboob Bi came out, fresh from a bath, wearing a clean voile saree with chappals on her feet and a bag in hand. Akhila was curious. Where was she going?

Just as she had finished cooking and went up to the door to see why her husband had not yet come home for lunch, she saw mother and son getting out of an auto. She became angry. Yusuf took out a watermelon and brought it to Mehaboob Bi's house, and then got another watermelon of the exact same size for Akhila's house. When he handed it over to Akhila, she carelessly let it fall to the ground. Before Yusuf understood what was happening, she used all her strength to kick the fruit, as if it were a football. The fruit hit the wall and broke into pieces, its flesh scattered across the floor. His nerves were shattered. Although his fist was closed, he calmly sat on a chair without saying a word. His silence riled her further. Unable to decide if she should shout or pick a fight or cry, she began to hit her head against the wall. Even then, he sat there, indifferent, as if it was a film playing in front of him. It was not evident whether his level of comprehension had reduced, or whether he was deliberately silent, or if he was just ignoring her.

She fell on the floor and started screaming. His great silence continued. After crying for a while, she started beating her chest and abusing him and his mother. She placed a litany of questions before him. 'Have you ever taken me anywhere even once? You were showing off that whore from morning till now. Aren't you ashamed?'

Even though he seemed frozen, he stirred when his mother was mentioned. 'Look here. All that you are doing, none of it will end well. You kicked the fruit. Kick me instead, it's OK, I won't mind, but don't say anything about Amma. She has a lot of problems, do you know? She has knee pain, and did not sleep from the pain all night, that is why I told her to go to the hospital. She went to the hospital in the morning and then came to the shop. Can I ask her to walk when she has knee pain? That is why we took an auto. Was that wrong? I'll get some people together, let them tell me if I have

69

done anything wrong. You shouldn't do all this,' he explained. Her heart was burning. Even if the greater share of her husband's love was for his mother, she was not willing to share him. She felt that his attempt to console her was filled with treachery. This matter would have ended there, if only she had given it some thought. But what she had ignored as a spark had turned into burning coal. She spat out the coal balls burning her chest, adding more poison to them. 'Ahaa. Look at how you are buttering me up. You explained, and now I have to believe you? She is equal to four men if you divide her up. What great disease will she get? She is standing like a Chandali, to swallow my family and drink water on top of everything else!' Akhila screamed.

Yusuf stood up, defeated, and got ready to go out, saying, 'People who talk to you don't have sense, do what you want.'

Akhila knew his weakness. His calm personality irritated her further. Still itching for a fight, she said, 'Riii, you keep the company of worthless whores, I will not say no. Feed them, buy them clothes, do whatever you want. But this whore of a savathi—'

He slapped her when she was still in mid-sentence.

'What! How arrogant are you! If you ever speak Amma's name again, I will make it seem like you were never born. What for you. What do you care. She is my mother. After my father died, she brought me up with so much love. I could get ten bevarsi no-good people like you, but will I get a mother like her? Who are you to come between a mother and her son? You die of envy if I buy her just one saree! You wait and see. I will get her to wear a Panjabi dress in front of your very eyes. I will have her wear gold jewellery all over her body. I will put up a shamiana covering the whole street and get her married.'

He understood her weaknesses just as much as she knew his. She got riled and mocked him. 'You will get Panjabi dress stitched? You will get her married? Do all that if you are a man, let's see.'

'Look, if I don't get her married like I said, I will shave off my moustache,' he said, accepting her challenge.

Poor Mehaboob Bi thought her son and daughter-in-law were fighting as usual and calmly continued rubbing balm on her aching knees in her house.

As was usual after a fight, Yusuf slept at his mother's house. It is said that a woman does not have a permanent house: she has to live in her father's house, her husband's house or her son's house. But here it was Yusuf without a home of his own. Both Mehaboob Bi and Akhila had houses. He, strangely, was stuck between them, running to his mother's lap when he was upset with his wife, and sliding up to Akhila when he needed her. He had to find a solution.

The first option was to give talaq to Akhila. But given that he really loved her, and that they had four small children, he decided that was no answer. Apart from her intense irritation with Mehaboob Bi, Akhila was a good woman. Also, if he gave her talaq, there was no way he could stay in town. Wouldn't her brothers break his arms and legs? So he pushed away the thought of leaving her.

The second option was to marry another woman to punish Akhila, but he began to sweat profusely just thinking about it. He had no doubt that Akhila would murder that woman and go to jail. He worried about Mehaboob Bi. These worries began to eat at him. When he sat, when he stood, when he was in his shop. Everywhere. He had no peace of mind. Sleep had flown. He came to a decision by the time a week had passed.

He swore to do what was first uttered as a challenge. The face of marriage broker Hayat Khan came to his mind. Although he had arranged a lot of weddings, Hayat Khan found Yusuf's proposal shocking. He considered Yusuf's request very carefully and wondered how it might affect his business. He thought there was nothing wrong with it per se, but still consulted with the maulvi at Jamia Masjid. The maulvi cleared his throat and stroked his beard. 'Arey miyan, what better job is there than to get a widow remarried? We will get this nikah done, call us,' he said, encouraging him, making it clear that there were no objections from dharma's side. Hayat Khan began to look for a groom for Mehaboob Bi with enthusiasm. He had not yet opened his mouth, but the news spread the length and breadth of the town. Many laughed slyly; many displayed their generosity, saying, 'So what? Don't men do this? But still, this woman is something.' Many also passed judgement, saying, 'He has lost his mind.' Yusuf and his mother thus became the subject of many discussions.

Yusuf had arranged for a great colour photo of his mother to be taken when she'd stepped out to go to the hospital. Just like Akhila had said, she looked quite hale and hearty that day. On the edge of fifty, she was a handsome woman, which was why there weren't many obstacles to Yusuf's groom-hunting endeavour.

Yet there was a creeper stuck around Yusuf's feet, and his name was Hashim Saab. Yusuf carefully trawled through his history. Of a fairly well-off background, Hashim Saab's six children were all married and lived separately. His wife had been struck by paralysis and become a bedbug. His last son and daughter-in-law lived with him. Hashim Saab urgently needed a woman to look after his wife. Via the marriage broker, Yusuf invited him to Akhila's house on some pretext. He did not give a clue to anyone as to who Hashim Saab was or why he had come. Akhila had cooked well, but since it was the meat of an aged goat, Hashim Saab struggled to chew the pieces. Seeing his scraggy beard and the mutton pieces he had pushed aside, Yusuf realised that no real teeth remained in his mouth. Nor had he any intention of sending his mother to clean the urine and faeces of Hashim Saab's wife, like an ayah. He sent word that he did not like the groom, and continued to look for a man for his mother.

Yusuf was thrilled. What had begun as a challenge, and as a sort of revenge against his wife, became a task he happily pursued. He became so occupied with finding a groom that he had little time for his mother. Noticing this, Akhila stopped fighting with him, and there was peace all around.

Then came Kareem Khan, determined to make an impression, wearing a good pair of trousers and a crisply ironed full-sleeved shirt that went down to his knees, smelling of strong scent and riding an old Jawa motorbike. It was evident right away that he was quite the shokhi-lal and Yusuf rejected the proposal. Kareem Khan already had two wives and a house full of children. He was a dandy and had the womanising disease. There had been many incidents, and news of these had travelled from mouth to mouth; his infamy had spread extensively among women, and no decent people invited him home. When women passed him, they pulled their burkhas a little tighter around themselves.

He seduced the peanut-seller Razak's wife once. He had gone to their house when Razak was not around and had been caught in a compromising position by Razak himself, who was ever vigilant; Kareem had tried to escape through the back door, climbed up the compound wall and fallen into the septic tank. It was a disaster. Now, the faecal matter there – a large pit had been dug and covered haphazardly with granite stones. Some twenty families in the neighbourhood used the pit, so it always remained full. Since no one was willing to touch his shit-covered body, people had chased him away by beating him with long poles. Yusuf had heard a couple of his friends describe this incident in great detail and they had all

73

laughed till their sides hurt. He felt disgusted by Kareem Khan. It would not do to give his beloved mother to a beast like him.

After many such rejections, he thought he'd found a suitable groom in one Abdul Ghaffar. Both he and his wife had been teachers at the upper primary school. They had had three daughters and were a contented family. Abdul Ghaffar's wife had been caught by the cancer demon and passed away suddenly. Two of their daughters had been married off before her death. Now Abdul Ghaffar and his daughter Roshni were each other's only company. This proposal gave Yusuf a lot of peace of mind. Abdul Ghaffar had seen Mehaboob Bi's photo and agreed to the match. After fixing the wedding date, Yusuf had endless work. Abdul Ghaffar informed his married daughters and sons-in-law about this very hesitantly. None of them raised any objections and agreed to attend the wedding, but Abdul Ghaffar continued to feel awkward. He told Yusuf in a soft voice, 'Just appoint a day and get a nikah done. There is no need to call a lot of people and make it a big deal.' But would Yusuf be quiet about it? He had started making special arrangements already.

First of all, he got the vanki ring on his finger polished, and locked it away in his cupboard. He got some four-five other rings melted, added some money on top, and got a necklace made for his mother. He added that too to the cupboard. Akhila was surprised to see him bring all kinds of things in carton boxes every day and store them there. She had no chance of peeking in the boxes when he was not around because the key to the cupboard remained in Yusuf's pocket at all times.

When the marriage talks were going on with Abdul Ghaffar, Yusuf had brought along just two friends for support. But the news had spread across town, and it didn't take long for it to reach the ears of his mother and her daughter-in-law. Both had noticed

Yusuf's strange behaviour. Both were upset to see that his beloved rings no longer adorned his fingers. Akhila was scared these days to start any debate with him. Mehaboob Bi understood where her son's dangerous thoughts were headed and wept all day.

That morning, he brought four goats and tied them up in front of the house. All three people were playing hide-and-seek with each other. No one asked any questions about the goats; Yusuf did not say anything either. He was agitated while making the arrangements because he had not found the right time to talk to his mother. 'The daughter-in-law has finally managed to fill her husband's ears and has succeeded in distancing me forever. Thoo! What an embarrassment this is,' she lamented. Akhila was worried too. 'Che, I've made a mistake. I should not have let it get so out of hand.' She had become speechless in front of her husband. Although she was deeply upset about having called her mother-in-law a whore and a savathi, she also knew that there was no use feeling bad about it now. She was sure that her husband had got a necklace made for his mother, and stubbornly bought at least one or two Panjabi suits for her. The thought of the old owl being more fortunate than herself was disgusting to her, but she did not express it. Scared of what disaster might happen if she said anything at all, she almost forgot how to talk.

This way, each wallowed in their own pain. When the goats were tied in front of the house, the only ones who rejoiced without a care were the children, Munna especially, who not only gathered the neighbouring children but also, who knows who told him, chanted, 'Ajji's wedding goats, Ajji's wedding goats,' and rode them around. When his little song fell on Akhila's ears, she dragged him inside and thrashed him mercilessly, taking out all her anger on the boy. He – his voice loud enough to make the roof fly off – he screamed loud enough for some ten houses to hear. Munna's voice reached Mehaboob Bi too. Under other circumstances she might have gone and hugged him tight, but that day her heart was hard as stone, filling with bitterness in a damned world where no one was there for anyone else. She did not rush to Munna's rescue. Instead, she latched the front door and disappeared into an empire of darkness, forgoing even food. Yet while she had bolted the door to her house firmly, the doors to her mind were slamming against each other; even in the middle of unimaginable pain, even amidst intense contempt for her son and daughter-in-law, Munna's pitiable cries saddened her deeply. For several minutes she was still, devoid of emotion. But the lull lifted slowly and the dark clouds in her mind scattered. Her sense of motherhood took over even in her distressed state.

Not caring for her aching knees, or her half-untied saree, or bothering to pull back up the seragu that was slipping, she hurriedly walked to Akhila's house. Seeing Munna sob in a corner of the living room, accompanied by the other children who were also crying and giving him company, Mehaboob Bi's eyes welled. She pushed her daughter-in-law to the side, screaming, 'Are you a human being or are you a rakshasi? What do you want to do to the child?' and she gathered Munna within the folds of her saree. She became a little anxious, wondering 'What if she creates a bigger scene and gathers all the neighbours?' But contrary to her expectations, Akhila loudly sobbed and fell into her mother-in-law's arms. Her throat caught. 'Bi Amma, Bi Amma, what is happening? All our honour is gone. It is all my fault, hit me with your chappals, I have done grave injustice to you,' she said, shedding copious tears.

Mehaboob Bi had the surprise of surprises. What was this? Could this be? Was it possible for her to shed such tears now, after she had talked her husband into arranging his mother's wedding? After cursing her, calling her an old vulture, hemmari, a plague, calling her savathi – this sudden change – Mehaboob Bi could not decide whether it was for the good or for something worse, and sat down. Making full use of this opportunity, Akhila spared no effort to paint herself innocent. She took back all the ugly titles she had bestowed. Listening to her lovingly call Mehaboob Bi 'Bi Amma' was enough to make even stomach water melt . . . Mehaboob Bi was also melting a little at this display of love. 'Bi Amma, it was some bad phase. What should not have happened ended up happening. It is my fault; I used to behave like a dog. But still, isn't he a man? If he had given me two strong kicks when my madness was at its peak, everything would have been alright. But does anyone get their mother married off in order to take revenge on me? Huh? Have you heard such a story anywhere? Ahaha, I haven't seen such a story in any film either,' she said, promptly shifting blame onto her husband.

Akhila quickly went into the kitchen, made a cup of tea with thick milk, gave it to her mother-in-law and said, 'Chi chi, what does it mean to bring these goats and tie them in front of the house? Disagreements come and go when it is a family. To drag these things to the streets now, how can it be done? Is there a family that never fights? Does everyone make such a big issue of it? Just because someone eats meat, do they walk around with a necklace of bones around their neck? You only tell me, what great disaster has happened? You mind your business, I mind my business, once in a while I scream and shout a little. It is a dog's life, isn't it, that's why. If I am left alone to bark a little, how long will I go on? You only tell me. But I never used to bite, did I?'

The tea in the cup in Mehaboob Bi's hands remained. For some reason she could not drink a sip. She began to feel that Akhila was behaving in a dangerous manner. Even in such a situation, when she was extremely angry with her son, she was not ready to say a word against him. But would Akhila notice such subtleties? Her inferiority complex and sense of guilt were driving her to shrug off responsibility in whatever way she could. Mehaboob Bi thought she understood what was happening a little; otherwise her head was all muddled. All was chaos.

'Bi Amma, you drink tea. I will come back in a bit,' Akhila said and walked out. The tea in her hand got cold. Mehaboob Bi slipped into old memories.

Yusuf was just a little child and he was not as peaceful then. He was always hungry. Unable to find a way to satiate him, Mehaboob Bi used to save him all the stale rice. He ate it gluttonously and demanded more and more. Finally, Mehaboob Bi found a way: she would keep the plate of food in front of him and slowly begin to tell a story. His favourite story was Hatim Taayi. 'Once upon a time there lived a queen in a town. She was very proud of her beauty. A horde of men hung around for love of her, but she did not pay them any attention. She liked no one, and twirled everyone around her little finger. Her job was to give difficult tasks to the men who approached her; she enjoyed watching them suffer.'

Yusuf hmmed and soon all his attention was on the story. Only his hand lay on the rotti. Every time she slowed down, he hmmmed loudly, impatient. She became alert and continued. 'One day, the chief of the army saw her. He immediately forgot himself and became mad about her. He tried many things to win her over, but she refused to glance at him. Instead, she mocked him and said, 'Look, if I have to accept you, you must bring your mother's heart as a gift for me.' The chief went to his village. He looked at his mother's face. Wondering how he could tell her this news, he put his face down and collapsed. His mother got to know what the problem was. She went to her son and said, "Aiyoo, my son, what will I do holding on to this old life? If not for your happiness, what other use does this life have? This heart – take it without any worry – take this heart." Was that not enough to bring that fool to his senses?' By then, Yusuf's eyes had welled up. Mehaboob Bi, chiding herself, blaming herself for not being able to feed her son to his heart's content, tried to swallow the story. But would Yusuf leave it? 'Amma, tell me ma, what happened next ma?' he wailed.

'And then that chief kills his mother, takes her warm heart in his hands and runs to the queen. On the way he trips and falls. The moment he falls, his mother's heart beats in his hands and says: "Aiyoo, my darling, did you get hurt? Go slowly, my son."' By the time she finished the story, Mehaboob Bi's eyes would also tear up, whether for the story's tragic ending or because her son washed his hands with his stomach only half-full. As the story progressed, Yusuf would lose interest in Hatim Taayi, and how he went on to teach the queen a lesson.

Mehaboob Bi was still deep in her nostalgia when Akhila came home with many people: Buden Saab from the shop, Salar Saab from the two-storeyed house, Councillor Mohammed's wife Begum, the mohalla's old woman Hafiza Bi, and others. Mehaboob Bi was yet to come out of her reverie. But she noticed the people and slowly got up from the chair to stand leaning against the wall. Akhila ran around the house, pushing the chairs towards the men and spreading a mat for the women to sit on.

Mehaboob Bi waited for the guests to begin the conversation. Akhila wanted all the confusion to end, but the guests were hesitant about bringing up such a sensitive issue, and the children forgot their regular activities in anticipation of something serious about to happen. Finally, Begum opened her mouth. Although she was elderly, she was famous for her flirtatious behaviour and her taunting words; however, no matter the situation, she was also capable of managing everything. Strong enough to stand up on behalf of all the women and face everyone without any hesitation, Begum smiled slyly and invited Mehaboob Bi: 'Come here, why are you standing there? Come sit here.' Mehaboob Bi stood where she was, a little reticent, and did not answer. The silence deepened.

Given that she was responsible for inviting all of them, it was Akhila who broke the silence. From behind the curtain hanging over the kitchen door, she began to say in a very remorseful tone, 'May Allah forgive me. Shaitan got into my head. I made my mother-in-law an excuse to fight and give trouble to my husband. No one was happy because of all this. Bi Amma never interfered, she minded her own business, but I did not let her live in peace. This was my foolishness, that's all.'

She was not done talking when Yusuf came to the door; he had brought a lot of things in an auto. For a moment – the people gathered there, the suffocating environment, his mother leaning against the wall, Akhila talking, the way she swallowed her words the moment she saw him – seeing all this, he felt it was Akhila's doing. He realised it must have something to do with the wedding and suddenly became alert. He addressed the people softly, 'Assalamu alaikum,' and began to unload things from the auto.

Begum took matters under her control again. When she called him, saying 'Yusuf, come here, we have to talk about something with you,' he calmly took out all the things, counted money to pay the auto driver and came inside. He pretended not to have heard her say 'Come sit here.' He got very angry to see his mother standing, but controlled himself and chose to stand too.

Saab explained his presence there. 'Your wife said there was some trouble in the house, and that is why we came.'

'Oho. Trouble, did she say? If that is the case, let her explain, and you all can solve it,' he said, as if it did not concern him. 'I am doing all this to solve her problem, what is her complaint now?'

he thought, and he was filled with bitterness, though he did not show it on his face.

They noticed the sarcasm in Yusuf's voice, but the guests took it calmly and said, 'Akhila, my dear, whatever it is that you want to say, say it in front of your husband, ma. His heart should become clear, that is important.' Akhila's eyes welled up. She was truly agitated because of all these developments. 'You all know everything. You have all advised me about this several times in the past. But even then, I had not come to my senses. Unable to bear my fighting, my husband is preparing to get his mother married off. Tomorrow is the nikah,' she said, her throat catching at the last words. She paused for a moment before continuing. 'I have made a very big mistake; I will rectify all of it. I will think of her not as my mother-in-law, but as my mother, and look after her. Whatever has happened so far, please put those mistakes in your stomachs and set my family right. You are all learned people.' Tears poured down her face.

Yusuf was shocked. Was this . . . this was Akhila? She who called his mother a savathi, she who said things that shouldn't have been said and set fire to his chest, she the one who chased his sleep away on many nights and destroyed the peace of his days, his happiness? Forget suspecting her honesty. He became incapable of guessing what must be going through his mother's mind. Akhila's drama left him stunned.

His mother was silent while he seemed to have lost his speech. A well of irritation, a furnace of envy, the way Akhila confessed and behaved like a saint, this face of hers unfamiliar to him. The panchayat people who had come thought that they could get a foothold into this family's issues if its members themselves showed cracks in their relationship during such a sensitive time. But both mother and son were symbols of silence, as if they had decided their strategy in advance.

Akhila continued. 'If I make even one mistake from now on, I am ready for any punishment you give me. I have been properly punished for my foolishness . . . '

The rest of her words floated away as inaudible mutterings. Begum looked at everyone very seriously and said, 'Yusuf, when it is a family, a household, something or the other comes and goes. Does anyone create such a big scene for that? You should know how to manage your wife, how to look after your mother—'

Buden Saheb interrupted. 'Isn't that the case? The rider must be right first. If he is alright, he can tame any horse at all.' Mehaboob Bi lifted her eyes and glanced at her son. He had beads of sweat on his forehead. She felt that he was sweating too much. Yusuf was feeling helpless; anger had vanished somewhere, and it was misery that was standing out on his face. He had given his word to get his mother married, without her knowledge. Before he could delicately bring up the issue with his mother, Akhila had crudely talked about it and brought his mother to a state where she herself was about to reject the idea. If his mother thought that he had come under pressure from his wife and was trying to get her married to send her away – what if she gets hurt? What if she spits in his face and leaves for Tumakuru? It would feel like a permanent rejection.

He did not even cry, but then tears do not fall from the eyes alone. He was wiping tears from every pore of his body; his face was red. The sweat on his forehead was profuse. His entire being came together to piteously cry out, 'Amma, Amma, please understand me, ma. I am not sending you away because of her torture, ma. It is not even to take revenge on her, instead it is because I want you to be happy, so that you are free from this hell, so you can have some peace, that is why I did this, ma!' He was trying to make contact with her but they had both turned to stone. They were not aware of the world at all. Yusuf's melted heart was flowing away. He was being shattered with every passing second. More than anything else, his strength was diminishing. A fear was engulfing him like never before; his childhood hunger grew like a giant and came before him, its mouth wide open to swallow him whole. He shook his head, trying to escape it; his voice, the strength in his hands and legs, nothing remained. He was going down into the earth and showing no resistance. That was when a strange, very calm voice, a voice very dear to him, said:

'What commotion are you all creating? I don't understand.'

Who was it? Which angel was speaking these words filled with promise?

'Yes, I am getting married. It isn't wrong, is it? I am not ruining anyone's house, am I? You all should be happy. My son is taking the lead and doing this with pride and love. He is making all the arrangements as if I were a young virgin bride. That is my good fortune. There is no need for you all to come and ask about this, and there is no need for us to answer either. For other things we need you and the jama'at; we will never reject the community. So please come to my nikah tomorrow morning. That is enough.'

Her mind had taken a surprising turn. She was aware that if either Akhila, who was showing such audacity, or Yusuf had turned to look at her, in that instant she would have become an exploding volcano. The decision she took in that moment was not for her own life but to ensure peace in Yusuf's.

Understanding that she was indirectly asking them to leave, the panchayat wondered if they could find any fault in her words or in her behaviour; Mehaboob Bi slowly walked into her house.

Yusuf began to recover. Seeing the panchayat members still sitting there, he very softly said, 'Akhila, may you also have the good fortune of having your children arrange your wedding,' and spat out enough bitterness for a lifetime.

Akhila felt like she had been hit by lightning. Shaking, she cried, 'No, riii, please no, don't curse me like that!' She hugged Munna and began to sob, thinking of the problems she would have to face if his curse came true. The panchayat communicated with their eyes and stepped out without another word. There was no one to stop Akhila's uncontrollable sobbing as it pierced the silence of the house. Yusuf left to make the rest of the arrangements for the wedding.

RED LUNGI

There is no end to the woes mothers face come summer vacation. All the children are at home; if they're not in front of the TV, then they're either up the guava tree in the front yard or on top of the compound wall, and what if one of them falls and breaks a hand? Or leg? But it's not just that, no: it's all the crying, the laughter, the meting-out of punishments based on some arcane system of justice from another world. That's why Razia's headaches increased as summer vacation began. The nerves in both temples throbbed, her hot head felt like it would burst, and the veins at the back of her neck threatened to snap any time. They came, one after the other, complaining complaining, and between complaints it was screaming and crying. And then the kind of games they played . . . abbabbaa . . . sword fighting, machine gun, bomb attacks . . .

'Enough is enough,' she thought, as she lay on the divan cot in the hall, a piece of cloth tied tightly around her head. She was in no condition to tolerate any kind of noise. The TV was still switched on, albeit at low volume. She had issued a stern warning and was hoping to finally relax and stretch out her legs when one of them screamed: 'Doddamma! Doddamma, she is pinching me!' Then her anger knew no bounds, and she got up, cursing them in her head.

Just as she was thinking 'There are six of the damn things here already, and each brother-in-law has two-two . . . three-three . . . they have all landed on us for the holidays and my younger sisters' children are here also, what do I do, oh god,' her husband Latif Ahmad stepped inside. He became alert when he saw his wife's condition; she had always been allergic to children. First those migraines, and then the children rubbing masala on her discomfort with their noise, he thought, looking at them all from the corner of his eye and counting even in the middle of his helplessness. One, two, three, four . . . eighteen children in total, all between the ages of three and twelve.

Before she could open her mouth, and just as he was scolding them ('Eyy, all of you sit down quietly, I won't give anything to those who make noise'), Hussain came in behind him from the farm carrying a basket of mangoes. When all the children screamed and pounced on the basket, it was Latif Ahmad's turn to be frightened. He looked at his wife helplessly and walked towards the bathroom. Unable to tolerate the pain, Razia caught hold of one or two children within her reach and whacked them. Seeing a summer of continuous torture before her and no other way out, in the end she decided that she'd have to engineer bed rest for some of them somehow. Circumcisions, she decided. She would get khatna done.

According to her calculations, out of eighteen children, eight were girls and would be spared. Of the remaining ten, four were of even ages, at eight, six and four; those little devils would have to be spared too. Latif Ahmad agreed to her decision to get khatna done for the remaining six without a word of protest.

Theirs was a wealthy family in the district centre. Although half a dozen of Latif Ahmad's younger brothers had government jobs and lived elsewhere, as the eldest, all family functions were conducted in Latif Ahmad's house. Razia did not hesitate to spend money for these things. She thought of it as her duty. And the fact that two of the six eligible boys were the sons of her younger sisters also brought her joy.

Preparations began as per her instructions. Several metres of red cloth were bought. Even the children began to join Doddamma in making arrangements. She cut the fabric to measure and made lungis. The girls had a lot of work, stitching sequins on the lungis and painting them, but making lungis for six boys did not require the whole roll. There was a lot of leftover cloth. When she wondered what to do with it, the solution arrived: 'Arey, there is our cook Amina's son Arif – also our worker's son Farid – let us get khatna done for some other children from poor families,' she thought, and translated the idea into action immediately.

There were five masjids in town: Jamia Masjid, Masjid-e-Noor and others. After the Friday namaz, the secretaries of all these masjids took the mics and conveyed this message: 'Latif Ahmad Saheb has, as an offering to God, made arrangements for a mass Sunnat-e-Ibrahim next Friday after the afternoon namaz. Those interested must register their children's names in advance.'

They could have just said khatna, colloquially speaking. But since the words uttered from a stage and through a mic have to be formal, the secretaries did not, instead calling it a celebration for Prophet Ibrahim. But both mean the same thing: a collective exercise in which children look forward to an event but end up screaming loudly together.

Everything transpired just as Razia had expected. A lot of poor people came and registered the names of their children. Razia cut cloth for lungi after lungi. Only the children at home got to have sequins and zari on their lungis; the others were plain red. On her son Samad's, there were so many sequins one couldn't even see the colour of the cloth. Sacks of wheat and copra were brought in. Ghee made from the finest cow's milk, almonds, raisins and dates were bought for the children at home.

The children were strangely restless, agitated; everyone else was happy; the air was festive. Friday arrived before they knew it. Once the afternoon namaz was over, Latif Ahmad quickly finished his lunch and appeared in the compound next to the masjid. A lot of people had gathered; the parents who had brought their children, as well as the children who were to get khatna done, were all standing in line. An army of young men were in attendance as volunteers. All were dressed in white shalwar and jubbas, with either white topis or white cloths tied on their heads. Since they had taken baths for the Friday namaz, they all looked fresh and clean. Many had lined their eyes with surma and generously dabbed on scent, so the whole atmosphere was filled with pleasant smells.

Arrangements had been made for khatna inside the madrasa close by. Ibrahim, who was built like a wrestler, was the special guest that day. His biceps were prominent under a thin white mul jubba. Doing khatna was his traditional profession; he practised the barber profession the rest of the time. He was involved in necessary preparations in one corner of the expansive madrasa hall. He hurried about and placed his bronze bindige pot upside down. He'd had it brought for the ceremonies. Razia had made Amina scrub that bindige with tamarind juice two-two times to make it shine. A plate, filled with finely sieved ash, was kept on the floor in front of it.

Ibrahim inspected all the arrangements until he was satisfied. He was a very experienced hand. It was said that once he brought the knife down, the khatna would be done perfectly and heal without infection, such was the fame of his healing powers. In another corner of the madrasa hall, a group of young men were spreading out a large jamkhana and smoothing away wrinkles. Ibrahim checked everything over once again and got up slowly. He took a shaving knife out from his pocket, moved it across his left palm and instructed, 'Bring them in one by one.'

Standing next to him and looking agitated was a volunteer named Abbas, who, unable to stop himself, eventually blurted: 'If you give me this knife, I will sterilise it in hot water and bring it back. We can add a little Dettol to disinfect it too, I think.' Having noticed Abbas from the corner of his eyes, Ibrahim understood that his was a brain that had climbed the steps of a college. He looked at Abbas with the disdain reserved for vermin and mockingly asked why. 'So that there is no chance of a septic . . . ' trailed off the flustered Abbas, as Ibrahim was not done mocking, and cruelly asked if he had had such an infection himself. Abbas's friends started giggling, ki ki ki, all around. Abbas, irritated, scolded – 'You are all so uncivilised' – and moved away. Ibrahim smiled triumphantly and called out once again: 'All of you come one by one.'

The volunteers standing outside ordered the boys to remove their underwear. The first in line was Arif. He was a grown-up boy, around thirteen years old. Usually boys had to be circumcised before the age of nine. But his mother Amina had not had money to get the procedure done. Watching him remove his shalwar and pull his shirt down, people around him laughed. A young man who struggled to control the laughter behind his lips punched Arif lightly on the back and pushed him inside.

About four-six people grabbed him and made him sit on top of the bronze bindige. He was confused. Before he knew what was happening, a pair of strong arms came from behind, went under his armpits, rested on his thighs and parted his legs. By the time he started screaming in terror, two people held his left and right arms tightly. His heart was beating loudly; he wanted to escape. But those who held him tightly were smarter and stronger than he was. They held him so tight that he could not even wiggle. He tried with all his might to free himself, failed, and screamed as if his throat was going to tear apart: 'Let go, let me go, aiyo . . . Amma . . . Allah!' Three-four voices, as if they were waiting for just this, said, 'Eyy, you should not scream like that, say deen, deen.' Between gasps Arif repeated, 'Deen – deen – Allah – Allah – Amma – aiyoo . . . '

While all this drama was going on, Ibrahim calmly took a piece of bamboo as thin as paper and attached it to Arif's penis, arranging it so that only the foreskin was in front of the bamboo clip. One of the men turned Arif's face to one side and urged him, 'Bol re, say it, boy. Say deen. Say it quickly, quickly.' Deen has many meanings, belief, faith, dharma and so on, but without knowing any of them Arif tore his throat apart screaming it. Deen! Deen! His tongue dried up; sweat dripped down his back; heat rose in his body; his hands and legs went cold with fear. As if for the last time, he made a futile effort to free himself.

'Why, boy?' asked one of the volunteers holding his legs down. 'Let me go, let me go, I have to pee,' he begged them, only to be told 'Wait for a while, you can go then.' They held him tighter. At that very instant, Ibrahim brought out the razor he was holding behind his back and slid it over the part of Arif's penis in front of the bamboo clip. The foreskin fell on the ash-filled plate in front. Blood spurted from the wound. Ibrahim took some of the ash from the plate and sprinkled it gently on the cut. The dripping blood mixed with the ash, and its flow began to reduce. Arif's face was pale. He was soaked in sweat. Little gasps were still coming out of his mouth sporadically. Two young men lifted him, brought him unceremoniously to a corner of the hall, and laid him on the floor.

The cold plastering on the floor gave his backside some relief. But still, there was a burning pain . . . A few young men caught hold of another boy and ran towards Ibrahim. Abbas was coming near. He poured some water into his mouth from a cup and began to fan him. Right then another voice thundered, 'Deen, deen!' Even as Arif was holding his stomach and writhing in pain, they brought another boy and laid him down on the mat.

'Deen! Deen!' different voices continued screaming. Bodies were thrashing about in pain here and there. As for Asif, even with the searing pain, his eyes were drawing shut. Sleep overtook him but went away just as suddenly as it had come. Before he knew it, he was awake. He drifted in and out a couple of times and was nearing deep sleep when someone started shaking him gently. Although he was still in pain, it was no longer unbearable, and he slowly opened his eyes. Abbas was standing before him, his face sympathetic, and asked, 'Arif, can you walk? Look over there, your mother has come.'

He tried to look at her from where he lay. His mother, wrapped in a burkha that was torn here and there, with holes in many places, could neither come in front of the men nor leave her son alone in such a condition. She stood peeping a little from the other side of the door. The sight of his mother's faded burkha gave Arif a fresh dose of energy. Abbas helped Arif up, and they walked slowly till they reached her.

Just as Arif was approaching the door, Latif Ahmad, who was sitting on a stool, placed a bag in his hands. Even though he was in a lot of pain, Arif peeped into the bag. It was full of wheat and two halves of copra. One packet of sugar, butter in another plastic packet . . . his tongue began to water. A boy who was about to go inside fell at the doorstep and started crying. Arif stood up straight like a hero, looked at the boy and shouted, 'Eyy, Subhan, don't be scared. Deen . . . say that. Nothing will happen.' He had already acquired some seniority. Arif came out limping. Amina took the bag from his hand and made him sit on the veranda outside. He spread his legs out and sat carefully, ensuring that the lungi did not touch the wound. A boy standing in the line asked him loudly,

'Lo, Arif, does it hurt?' Careful not to show any signs of pain on his face, Arif replied, 'No, not at all, kano, it does not hurt even a bit.'

A bearded middle-aged man standing nearby heard him and said, 'Shabash, son, here, take this, for your care,' giving him a fifty-rupee note. All the boys standing in line looked at him enviously. Screams could be heard from within. 'Deen . . . deen . . . aiyo . . . Allah . . . ' Another boy got shoved inside.

The boys kept going in one by one and coming out wearing red lungis. That was when she arrived. She was extremely thin, her eyes set deep in her face. One couldn't see a waist on her body, yet, surprisingly, she carried a child on it. A patched-up blouse hid under a torn saree. She was dragging a six- or seven-year-old boy with her other hand. The boy was wiggling about a lot, but her grip was strong. His cries were heartbreaking. The woman tried to pull her torn saree over her head a little, and it tore some more in the process. In a voice even she could barely hear, she called, 'Bhaiyya!' Engrossed in talking to someone, Latif Saheb turned back to look and asked, 'What is it, ma?'

The boy started crying louder. 'Get Sunnat done for him too, Bhaiyya,' she said. 'No, no, I don't want it,' the boy shouted and was about to flee. The mother held his arm tightly. The veil on her head slipped. Her dried-up stomach, her protruding collarbones, hollow eyes, patched-up blouse, all these offended Latif's eyes. He averted his gaze to the floor and scolded the boy. 'Eyy, stand quietly. Will you not be part of deen? Until you get khatna done, you will not belong to Islam. Will you remain like that?' The boy spat out the truth amidst sobs: 'I have had khatna done.'

Agitated, the mother immediately said, 'But Bhaiyya, it was not done properly, it can be done once more.' Although Latif Ahmad thought something was amiss, he could not be sure. He called one of the young men standing nearby. 'Ey, Sami, catch hold of him and see what has happened.' Some mischievous boys waiting for entertainment lifted the boy up suddenly. One dragged the boy's shorts down. The ill-fitting pair of shorts, made to someone else's measure, slid easily. Everyone held laughter on their lips and in their eyes, and looked on with curiosity.

'The khatna has been done properly.' All the boys let out the laughter they had tried hard to suppress till then. One of the men bristled and said, nastily, 'Bring your husband too. Let's get him circumcised and give you wheat and copra.' There was another wave of laughter.

The moment his hand was let go, the boy pulled up his shorts hurriedly and vanished. His mother pulled the threadbare seragu over her head and walked away, dragging her feet heavily. One of the men spat out in disgust and said, 'Thoo! What all kinds of people there are in the world . . . They will stoop to any level.'

A little while after she had gone, Latif Ahmad began to feel uneasy. When there was so much poverty and misery around, was there a need to be inhumane too? She came before his eyes again and again. 'Che, I should not have sent her away empty-handed.' He began to feel agitated. He looked around, but she had vanished just as suddenly as she had appeared.

The line kept moving forward. Red lungis kept coming out. Latif Ahmad looked at the clock impatiently. It was already five in the evening. The well-known local surgeon, Dr Prakash, had asked him to bring the children from his household to get circumcised by six. What might those children be doing now? Razia had bathed all of them that morning, and Samad, her eldest son, with extra love. She had been telling her husband for the past six years, that is, since Samad was five, 'Let's get the child circumcised, he has become very thin.' She had hoped that at least after khatna he would put on some weight. But Latif Ahmad did not have the courage, and had given one or the other excuse to postpone it. The time had finally come. But he was still a little anxious.

Razia's brothers-in-law had come for the ceremony. Her sisters had also travelled long distances to come home. The house was full of guests; all the children wore new clothes; the boys getting khatna done strutted about. While all the young and old men had gathered at the masjid for the mass khatna event, most of the town's young girls and older women had gathered at Latif Ahmad's house.

After lunch, they made the boys in sherwani, Nehru coats and zari topis sit down in a row. Garlands long enough to touch their feet fell on their necks. They wore jasmine flowers around their wrists. Well-wishers came. They cuddled the children. Someone slipped gold rings onto their fingers; someone else gifted them gold chains. The five-hundred-, one-hundred-rupee notes they received were too numerous to count. Everyone who came performed the ritual of removing the evil eye by cracking knuckles over the children's heads. Betel leaves, bananas, karji-kaayi and other snacks were distributed. No one had the time to talk to each other. The house was filled with confusion, chaos, hurry-burry.

She was standing in front of Latif Ahmad. Tired of standing, he had got someone to bring him a chair and had sat on it to supervise the mass khatna event. Just when he was opening his mouth to yawn aaaa, she came before him. She was thin, but her breasts had not dried up; an old sweater covered them. She had tied an old scarf around her head. Her face was pale. She held something in her hands, a cloth bundle pressed to her chest.

'Bhaiyya! Get Sunnat done for this one also.' Latif Ahmad looked at it. He stared at the one-month-old tender bud, wrapped in that piece of cloth, and looked up at the mother. He became anxious that the young men standing close by might surround him, and each might have something nasty to say. Without another word, he took out a hundred-rupee note from his pocket and placed it in her hands. He began to feel as if it was Razia standing before him and holding Samad. The woman did not stand there a minute longer and walked away quickly without a backward glance. He began to feel again that he should have given a little money to the woman who had come before. But then . . . another woman . . . yet another . . . one more . . . they will keep coming . . . where is the end to this? After the last boy was circumcised and he had sent everyone home, Latif Ahmad began to feel calm. Now he had to see after the children at home.

By the time he reached his house, everyone was ready to go to the surgeon. Dr Prakash had told Latif Ahmad: 'You all come by six o'clock. Let us give the children some local anaesthesia and get the operation done without causing them any pain. If the children go to sleep at night, they will wake up feeling fresh in the morning.' Thus, the whole family had gathered in front of the operation theatre at Dr Prakash's children's hospital in the evening. The operations took place without any problems, though some children cried and fussed.

After they had been brought home, the children were made to sleep on soft mattresses under fans. There were people to wait hand and foot on them. Except for one or two children groaning in pain now and then, there were no other sounds. There was no shortage of laughter, loud chatter and festivities in the house. Every eight hours, the children were woken up, given almond paste mixed with milk and painkiller tablets, and made to lie down again. The next day most of the children had recovered. There was an abundance of good food to aid their healing. Milk, ghee, almonds, dates . . . There was enough of each to eat and even throw away.

The fifth day after the mass khatna event, there was a lot of noise coming in from the front yard. Razia came down the stairs and peeped out and was surprised to see the cook Amina's son Arif up on the guava tree plucking the raw and half-ripened fruits. Two of the servants were shouting at him to get down. His mother was standing below the tree, by turn begging the servants and beseeching her son. After he had had his fill of the fruits, Arif climbed down leisurely. The servants caught hold of him. When they brought him to Razia, he casually took out another guava from his shirt pocket and bit into it. Razia had the servants let go of him and asked, surprised, 'Has your wound healed?'

'Hmm, yes, Chikkamma,' he replied and parted his lungi without any sense of shame or hesitance. Razia could not believe her eyes. There was not even a bandage on his wound. The cut had healed. There was no pus or infection either. The wound had healed! Her son Samad was not even able to stretch his legs out. Even with all the antibiotics he was taking, the wound had become infected. Just that morning, when he had to be bathed, he had not been able to take a single step. They had to carry him and make him sit on a stool in the bathroom. They had used a sterilised steel cup to cover the wound so as not to get it wet and had then bathed him. He was exhausted after that. His body had been dried gently. A nurse sent by Dr Prakash had come and put a fresh bandage on the wound and given him an injection. And here was this boy, playing like a monkey on top of the tree. She could not stop herself from asking: 'What medicine, what tablets have you been taking, Arif?'

'I have not taken any medicines, Chikkamma. That day the ash that they put on the fresh wound, that is all . . . '

In fact, Razia did not know how khatna was done for these poor children. After hearing that ash had been sprinkled on their wounds, she got very agitated. Worrying what might happen if one of these poor children died, she came inside. After looking over all the children sleeping upstairs, she went to her son. Samad was also sleeping. Fruits, several types of sweets, biscuit packets and dry fruits were piled high on the teapoy next to him. She peeped down to the front yard. She thought that if she could see Arif, she would call him up and give him a packet of biscuits at least. But he was nowhere to be seen. She laid a thin blanket over her son, came down and went to the kitchen to supervise the cooking.

Chicken soup had to be prepared for the circumcised children. Pulao and kurma had to be made for the guests at home. It was not even ten minutes since she had come into the kitchen when she began to get very restless. Amina was working swiftly, but even though Razia felt that the food would not be ready in time if she was not there to supervise, she still did not feel like staying. Leaving the chicken that she had been inspecting, she rushed upstairs. She had shut the door behind her to ensure Samad's sleep was not disturbed. When she pushed the door open, a heart-stopping scream fell out of her mouth. It was as if a black screen had fallen over her eyes. When the relatives heard her scream and rushed out of their rooms, what they saw was an unconscious Razia and a blood-soaked Samad on the floor. Samad had woken up and got down from the bed to look for his mother. By the time he reached the door, he had fainted. His head had hit the wall and blood was oozing out. The raw wound from the operation had also opened up and blood was dripping from it. In the end, he had to be admitted to hospital.

On the eleventh day, the children from Latif Ahmad's family were given a ritual bath. That was the day Samad also returned from the hospital. There was a grand function that evening in the house. The whole town had been invited; several goats were slaughtered. Grand preparations had been made for the feast. A shamiana had been set up in front of the house and on the terrace. The smell of biriyani wafted from the backyard in waves. There was a lot of festivity. Samad was still very weak. Razia had not let him out of her sight even for a second. She placed his head on her lap and was talking to everyone from the bed she was sitting on.

As she sat there, she noticed someone passing by the corner of the drawing room and called out, 'Eyy, who is that? Come here.' The passer-by heard her and came back saying, 'It is me, Chikkamma, me.' Razia opened her eyes wide to see – Arif! Although he was wearing a worn-out shirt with a torn collar, his face radiated health. He had already discarded the red lungi and started wearing trousers. This meant that his wounds had healed completely. She turned and looked at Samad. Her eyes filled with tears. She grumbled to herself, 'Khar ku Khuda ka yaar, gareeb ku parvardigaar' – if there are people to help the rich, the poor have God.

Her gaze went to the trousers he was wearing. The threadbare trousers were torn at the knees. Seeing Razia silent and lost in her own thoughts, Arif turned to leave. When he turned, what she saw were two big holes at the bottom of his trousers and shirt. She was appalled.

'Wait, Arif,' she said, getting up. She opened the bureau and cast her eyes over Samad's neatly folded stack of clothes. About ten-twelve pairs of clothes that he had received as presents were still unopened. She placed a pair bigger than Samad's size in Arif's hands and said, 'Take this. Go and wear these clothes. When you come to eat, you should be dressed in these clothes, OK?'

Arif's eyes began to twinkle. More than gratitude, his look reflected a sense of devotion. He moved a hand over the T-shirt tentatively, and Razia smiled. Samad sat up, laying his head on her shoulder. Arif kept looking at both of them and began to walk slowly towards the door, hugging the clothes Razia had given him tightly to his chest.

HEART LAMP

Mehrun had barely moved the half-closed door, just putting a foot inside, when her father, who was lying on the divan cot in the drawing room, and her eldest brother, who was discussing something with him in a low voice, both stopped talking and looked at her. Just as her niece Rabia came running from inside and announced, 'Mehrun Phuppu has come – Mehrun Phuppu has come,' Amaan, her second-eldest brother and Rabia's father, came out of his room, foam from the shaving soap he had applied on his chin, the brush still in his hand, and stood in the drawing room looking at her as if he couldn't believe his eyes. Her eldest, Athige, who was teaching the children the Qur'an in a sing-song voice, came out to the drawing room to stare at her, unmindful of her seragu, the free end of her saree slipping from her head. Her mother, holding the tasbih prayer beads in her thin hands, stood shell-shocked, as if asking: 'Is it true? Is this true?' Her younger sisters, Rehana and Sabiha, peeped from behind the drawing room door, not caring that the chapattis they were making in the kitchen were getting charred on the tawa. Thankfully her younger brother Atif was not at home.

The whole house momentarily stood still. It felt unfamiliar to her. The mother who had kept her in her belly for nine months and raised her did not say 'There you are. Come in, my dear,' and her father, who used to delight in the little girl who jumped on his wide chest, didn't have even a small smile of welcome; neither her eldest brother, who proudly called her 'my pari, my angel', nor Amaan, who had insisted that she must be sent to college, greeted her. Their wives stared at her as if she was from another planet.

Mehrun's heart fell. It was only when the nine-month-old baby girl in her arms let out a sharp scream that everyone came out of their stupor. Her eldest brother asked her, 'Where is Inayat?'

She lowered her head as if she had committed a crime and replied, 'He is not in town.'

'Then who did you come with?'

'I came alone.'

'Alone?' A chorus rose around her as she stayed standing at the threshold.

'Farook, take her inside.' Once her eldest brother's instruction was issued, Mehrun walked in, her footsteps heavy and unsteady. It felt like a courtroom. Her baby began to scream, and, without removing her burkha, she pushed the niqab up, sat on her father's bed at an angle, and put her breast to the baby's mouth. She hadn't washed her face. Her stomach began to burn as the baby drank. She hadn't eaten since the previous night. Except for her mother, no other women could be present at this meeting.

'Meher, did you inform anyone at home before coming?'

'No.'

'Why? Why didn't you tell them before leaving? It seems like you have made up your mind to bring us dishonour.'

'Who should I have informed? Who is there? It's been a week since he last came home – he didn't even tell me where he was going. I wrote to you all, but you didn't reply, didn't care if I ended up dead or alive.'

'You wrote that your husband has gone off with some nurse. And you want us to believe that?'

'If you didn't believe me, then you should have come and enquired. There are people who have seen them together.'

'And what should we do after we come and see him? Say we catch hold of him and ask him about it, and he says, yes, it is true – what can we do then? Should we submit a petition to the mosque? He will say, I have made a mistake, I will make her a Muslim and do nikah with her. Then she will be a savathi to you. And say we scold him some more. What can we do if he says, I don't want this woman called Mehrun, I will give her talaq?'

By now, Mehrun was weeping uncontrollably. Moving her baby to the other breast and continuing to feed her, she pulled her seragu from under her burkha and wiped her eyes and nose. A momentary stillness.

'That means you are all not in a position to do anything, right?' No one spoke. She continued. 'I fell at your feet, saying that I didn't want to get married. Did you listen? I said, I will wear a burkha and go to college. I begged you not to make me stop studying. None of you listened to me. Many of my classmates aren't even married, and yet I have become an old woman. I have the burden of five children on me. Their father is roaming around, and I don't have a life. When a man is doing such a haram thing, are none of you able to ask him why he is doing this?'

'Enough, Meher, enough.' Her mother shut her eyes and shook her head.

'Yes, Amma. I have also had enough. At first people started whispering, and then those who saw them together at the theatre and going into hotels came and told me directly. And then he became bold enough to start going to her house. And after everyone scolded him, he went to Bengaluru, spent thousands of rupees, and got her transferred. Now he has been living with her for the last eight days. For how many more days can I tolerate this? How will I survive?'

'Have patience, my daughter. You should try to bring him back on the right path with love.'

'Amma, don't I have something called a heart? Don't I have feelings? I cannot respect him as my husband when he has gone off like this. My body fills with disgust when I see him. Loving him is a very distant idea. It is not about him giving me talaq – I will get it from him. I will not go back to that house.'

'Meher, what are you saying? This is too much. He is a man, and he has stamped on some slush, but he will wash it off where there is water and then come back inside. There is no stain that will stick to him.'

Before she could reply, Amaan cut in. 'Look how she is behaving in front of us. She must have talked like this in front of him too. And that is why he must have got angry and left.' He paused and softened his tone. 'If the daughters-in-law of this house learn these kinds of things, that will be just great, won't it?' Mehrun's sadness morphed quickly to anger and then disappointment.

'You argue very well, Anna. May God keep you well. It is true: I am the bad person. I have learned what my bad nature is. I did not go out without a burkha. He told me to discard it, and wear my saree below my navel and strut around holding hands with him. But you covered me in a burkha and brought me up such that I would not even let my saree seragu slip from my head, didn't you? I feel naked if I remove it, now. You filled me with the fear of Allah. I did not agree to do what he asked me to, and so he took up with someone who dances to his tunes. And now you are all afraid that I'll become a burden to you if he leaves me – that is why you are telling me to bear with it. But that is not possible now. Rather than burn in that living hell, I will take my children and work as a coolie somewhere. I will not be a burden on you all – not a burden at all.'

'Is the fruit a burden on the creeper, Meher? Don't talk non-sense,' her mother protested.

'Amma, take her inside and give her something to eat,' her eldest brother said gravely. 'We will leave for Chikmagalur in ten minutes. If there is a bus, we will take the bus. If not, we will get a taxi. We cannot dance to her tunes either.'

'I will not drink a drop of water in your house. Nor will I go to Chikmagalur. If you take me there by force, I promise you I will set myself on fire.'

'This is too much, Meher. Those who want to die don't walk around talking about it. But if you had any concern for this family's honour then you would have done that instead of coming here. The house that your dholi goes to should be the house from which your dhola comes out. That is the life of a decent woman. You have a daughter studying in high school; you have two younger sisters who are of marriageable age. One wrong step and you will come in the way of their future. You say that we must listen to your childish words, and go and fight with your husband, but we also have wives and children. So go inside and eat something.' He turned briefly to his brother, and then back to face her. 'Amaan, run and get a taxi. And you, Meher, if your children or the neighbours ask, tell them you took the baby to the hospital, or something. What time did you leave to come here?'

She did not speak.

'It is now nine thirty,' Amaan said. 'She came at nine o'clock. The journey is three hours long. She must have left at six o'clock in the morning. If we leave right this instant, we can get there by twelve thirty.'

Mehrun did not stir from where she sat. Her mother and her younger sisters took turns begging her to eat, but she did not put a crumb of food or a drop of water in her mouth. When the taxi came, she did not talk to anyone. Stepping outside, the baby held tightly against her chest and her older brothers beside her, she said goodbye to none of them. Only as she walked down the last few steps did she look back to take in the house in which she was born and raised. Her eyes filled with tears. Her father held his chest, coughing. Her mother was sobbing, turning to her daughter, then to her husband, making him lie down, fanning him, sprinkling water on him, and saying to herself, 'Oh God, if I have earned any bit of punya, any virtue, any merit in my entire life, let my daughter's life be sorted.'

Amaan opened the car door, indicating to Meher with his eyes that she should sit inside as he grumbled under his breath. She used to boast, sometimes, about her pride in her elder brothers. When she was angry with her husband Inayat, she would say, 'My brothers are standing like sher-e-babbar, and if you keep acting like this, one day they will chop you up and throw away the pieces, hushar!' But this pride had been completely erased. Her brothers' words rang in her ears: 'If you had the sense to uphold our family honour, you would have set yourself on fire and died. You should not have come here.'

She didn't turn to look at her home as she got into the car – neither at her mother, who she would have seen peeping through a window, nor at her sisters peeking from behind a curtain, nor at her sisters-in-law, who were probably busy inside with their chores anyway. But tears cascaded down her face from under her veil. She sat biting her lips and swallowing little sobs.

The car was running fast. No one spoke. Amaan was sitting in the front seat, next to the driver from the mohalla. Could one discuss family secrets in front of him? Their journey continued in silence. She had been dice in Inayat's games of love and lust for sixteen years. And after sixteen years, he had then insulted her womanhood. 'You lie there like a corpse. What happiness did I get from you?' he had taunted her. 'What have I not given you – to wear, to eat? Who is going to stop me? I am with a woman who makes me happy.'

She didn't notice the trees or the sights or the road. It was only when the car came to an abrupt stop and she looked out disinterestedly that she saw the house they said was hers. A young girl with a withered look on her face came running to the car from the front door, saying, 'Ammi! Finally you are back. I was so worried.' She picked up the baby from her mother's arms, held her to her chest and ran back inside.

Mehrun took slow steps into the house. It felt empty. The other children had gone to school, and her sixteen-year-old daughter Salma, who suffered her mother's pain alongside her, was the eldest at home that day. Salma had sent her siblings off to their studies, anxiously waiting for her mother to return. Seeing her uncles with her mother, she had let out a sigh of relief. She was excited to see her uncles. They will drag that other woman by her hair and chase her away, she thought. She ran about like a deer, bringing her uncles snacks, boiling the tea.

Mehrun was lying down in her room. Salma walked in, wiped the tears from her mother's face, fed her some mouthfuls of food, and was coming back out with the plate of leftovers when she heard a familiar voice.

She ran back to the bedroom. 'Ammi, Ammi, Abba has come.' Mehrun pretended not to hear her and sank further into the blanket she had covered herself with. The nerves in her head were throbbing as Salma walked out to the living room. Her uncles had gone back outside, and Salma could hear the men talking. There was conversation, laughter, salaams.

'Arey, Bhaiyya! What time did you come?' Inayat was asking.

'We came just now. How are you?'

'Oh, I am fine, thanks to God. And all your duas.'

Amaan's voice: 'Where have you been, Inayat Bhai?'

'Just here. Some work, doing this and that – you know how it is. After all, we cannot just sit at home after waking up. Salma,' he called. 'Salma, where is Ammi? See who has come. Tell Ammi to come out.'

There was no sound from inside the house. 'Wonder where she is,' Inayat said. 'She must be inside with the baby. Let me call her, hold on.' He came in and saw Salma, and asked her in a low voice: 'When did these people come? Where is your Ammi?' A thread of suspicion began to unspool in his heart.

'Uncles came just now. Ammi is still sleeping,' Salma answered cleverly.

A sigh of relief escaped Inayat.

'She has not woken up yet? What has happened to her?' He came to the door of the bedroom. The sight of Mehrun curled up and sleeping disgusted him. Her only claim to importance was that she was the mother of his children. Although he wanted them to, his legs did not carry him inside.

She imagined how he must be standing at the door. His clothes, the stench of cigarettes, the smell of his sweat, his ageing body, his large eyes. The man who had left his mark on her every nerve was a stranger to her. She stayed with the blanket wrapped tightly around her, hearing his voice.

'Salma, come here. Tell her to stop with all this drama. That if she has called her brothers here to advise me, she will be tying a noose around her own neck. In one single breath – one, two, three times – I'll say it and finish this off, tell her. And tell her that after her talaq, see if she is able to get her younger sisters and her daughters married off. Tell her this – that she is ruining the family honour in front of guests. Tell her, your mother. Let her greet her brothers – ask her whether she wants chicken or mutton, because it is almost noon now, so tell her to start cooking lunch soon.' Salma was not even there, but he spat out everything he had to say, imagining she was.

Inayat and brothers-in-law talked as if nothing was wrong. They talked about coffee prices, about the elections in Kashmir, about the investigation of the murder of an elderly couple in the neighbourhood, about the Muslim girl from the mohalla who had married a Hindu boy in a civil ceremony, about this thing, about that. The conversation continued as the pressure cooker whistle went off, and the blender whirred, and the strong smell of masala wafted in, and the chicken was brought in, and the food was ready because Mehrun had made it, and Salma ran around serving them all lunch. Mehrun came out from the kitchen only once, only briefly.

A heavy meal later, their mouths full of tambula, Mehrun's brothers got ready to leave. Before they went, Amaan came and stood near the kitchen door. 'Use a little bit of smartness and manage all this,' he said. 'I will come and visit next week. He will behave like this for a few days and then come back by himself. You must be responsible. What problems some women have to face – husbands who are drunkards, mothers-in-law who beat them. Thank God you are in a good situation. He is a bit irresponsible, that is all. It is you who must balance all that.' Her brothers left, and as soon as the sound of the car disappeared, Inayat flew out of the house too.

Salma turned to look at her mother. Her uncles had neither consoled nor helped her. She began to pulsate with her mother's grief. Her eyes had welled up when her father walked out. The house was veiled in gloom, and when her siblings returned from school they were not able to lift it. Each had their own chores to do, each their own burden.

As evening started to lose its light, lamps were lit around the house. But the lamp in Mehrun's heart had been extinguished a long time ago. Who should she live for? What was the point? The walls, the roof, the plates, bowls, stove, bed, vessels, the rose plant in the front yard — none of these were able to answer her questions. She didn't register the pair of dull eyes that hovered around her, standing guard. Salma wanted to be buried in her books; she was supposed to be preparing for her looming SSLC exams. But a great anxiety that could not be named kept her mother constantly in her line of sight.

In the quietness of the night, Mehrun stared into the darkness. It was as black as her life. The children were asleep. Only Salma was still up, studying in the drawing room, her eyes trained on her mother's room.

Mehrun's sleep had vanished. She wondered: had her battles in her family house been any easier? Her wedding to Inayat had been a month before her second-year BCom exams. She had cried, begged to be allowed to sit them, but everyone had been deaf to her pleas. A week or so after the wedding, she had hesitantly talked to her husband about it. He had laughed, called her 'love', 'darling', 'my heart'. 'If you are not here,' he had said, 'won't I stop breathing?' Mehrun had believed that if she was not with him, maybe he might. She was happy. She had followed his every wish, and she had been the lamp that lit up his heart.

Only when her parents-in-law had passed away a year ago did Mehrun finally get her husband all to herself. Her sisters-in-law had gone to their husbands' houses; her brothers-in-law had gone their own ways. This old dream, of having a house of her own, had been fulfilled. But now that it had, her face had become wrinkled, and the veins on her hands stood out, and there was a thin shadow under her eyes, her heels had cracked, and dirt had settled permanently under her chipped, uneven nails, her hair had thinned – and she had noticed none of this. And maybe Inayat would not have noticed either, if it weren't for his appendectomy, and that nurse, working too much for too little pay at a private hospital, with a thousand dreams in her eyes, who walked or maybe floated on air – one couldn't tell – with her glowing skin and honey-coloured eyes that drew one in like a whirlpool, who was sliding down her thirties, and was ready to do anything, anything at all, to secure her future and satisfy her dreams.

Inayat hadn't addressed the nurse as 'sister'. From the first day of all those days he spent in hospital, he had called her by her name instead.

And then he had insulted the womb that had given him his many children. He had criticised Mehrun for her loose stomach, and her sagging breasts that had sated their children's hunger. He made her soul feel naked too. One day he had said, 'You are like my mother,' and with those words had pushed her alive into hell. In the few months since he had uttered these words, every morsel of food she ate in that house felt like a sin. The feeling of being a stranger in her own house nagged at her, and the fire of insults ground her down, and so she had sought the help of her family.

The night was getting darker, and the agitation in Mehrun's heart was hardening. She had never felt this lonely. She had no desires. She sat up on the bed. There was no one to ask after her. There was no one to tease her, hug, kiss her. The person who had done those things belonged to someone else now. There seemed no end to life. And even the loud noise from behind didn't stir her. She knew that a framed photograph had fallen and the glass had shattered, and the frame had broken into pieces, and the photograph had fallen out, but a kind of anxiety had set up home in her and she had no desire to sort out the mess. She slowly got out of the bed. She stared at her baby for a long time, and then walked out of the room. Her little children were sleeping peacefully.

When she walked quietly into the drawing room, she saw that Salma, who had been sitting there studying, had succumbed to sleep, her head resting on the table. She stood there, next to her sleeping daughter, and began to shake. She had thought that all her feelings were dead, but the surge sweeping through her as she looked at Salma made her want to collapse. She restrained an overwhelming desire to touch her daughter and said to her, in her heart, 'You must be a mother to these children, my dear.'

Her feet slowly began to take her forward. She opened the door and stepped into the front yard. The few plants she had nurtured looked like they were weeping. They seemed to nod in agreement with the decision she had taken. She came back inside, locked the door behind her, went to the kitchen, picked up the can of kerosene and went around the house, unable to decide where she should be when she poured it on herself. She stopped to look at her sleeping children once again before coming back into the drawing room.

She didn't look at Salma.

She walked quickly to the kitchen, picked up the matchbox and, holding it tightly in her right hand, quietly opened the latch of the front door and stepped into the yard again. She stared into the darkness and made sure she thought of how she had nobody, how no one wanted her, as she poured the kerosene on herself. She was in the grip of a force beyond her control. She looked around, and no sounds reached her, and she could feel no touch, no memories were left, no relationships could pierce her. She was beyond her consciousness.

But everything was happening inside the house, where the baby's shrieks of hunger had woken Salma with a start, and made her rush to hold the baby to her chest, and call out 'Ammi, Ammi,' crossing the room to where her siblings were sleeping and then around the house looking for her mother, before spotting the open door and running out into the yard, and, even in that blurry darkness, seeing her mother's form and smelling the kerosene. Without thinking she rushed forwards, with the baby in her hands, and hugged her mother tightly. Her mother, the matchbox in her hand, looked dispassionately at the girl hugging her, as if she was expecting someone else. Salma put the baby on the ground and cried, 'Ammi! Ammi! Don't leave us and go!' She held her mother's legs.

Salma was sobbing, and the little baby was crying on the ground. Mehrun looked at them, and she fought to be free of the strange force that had enveloped her, and the matchbox fell from her hand. Salma was still clutching her mother's legs. 'Ammi,' she was saying. 'Just because you have lost one person, you will throw all of us at that woman's mercy? You are ready to die for Abba, but is it not possible for you to live for our sakes? How can you make us all orphans, Ammi? We want you.' But more than her words, it was Salma's touch that affected her.

She picked up the sobbing baby and hugged Salma to her chest, and, feeling as if she was being comforted, touched and understood by a friend, Mehrun's eyes became heavy, and all she could say was 'Forgive me, my darling,' as the darkness of the night was thawing.

HIGH-HEELED SHOE

Call the world a small place, or call it big, say that the world is round, giggle hehehe and say the world has become a small village . . . say something! No matter what you say, it makes little difference.

If there was any difference to speak of, it vanished five-six years ago. Then, when someone returned from Saudi, there were no rajas and maharajas like them in a family! No no, there were no emperors like them. From the nappies they stuck to their children's bottoms, to the toothpaste-filled plastic tubes they used, to the frills those women wore, the colourful and tantalisingly thin nighties with delicate lace, the sarees that draped around them like dead snakes and showed off their curves 'as is', the scents that emanated with every beat of their pulses, the dress watches, the Samsonite suitcases . . . and then, the name pendants hanging from their necks, as if they would forget what they were called! Fingers full of rings, gold bangles stacked till their elbows, bracelets – no one had to clarify that it was all real gold – earrings that hung like whispers from their ears, thin cotton underwear the colour of white pigeons . . . was it just one or two things? What all could one describe! And then, and then, lightweight bathroom slippers that looked like peacock feathers, chappals, sandals. When Nayaz Khan's horse of imagination reached this point, it would begin to limp. Like a weak, dried-up horse that pulled a jatka, it would shamelessly refuse to step even one foot ahead. So Nayaz Khan wanted to stop too, at the magical world of that one pair of shoes that always made him forget himself.

Three years ago, his sister-in-law Naseema had returned from Saudi on vacation. The Rado watch that his brother Mehaboob Khan got him sat resplendently on Nayaz's left wrist. It had also sparked jealousy among his colleagues. He was only a second-class peon at the DDPI office, and Rajeeva, a colleague who also ran a moneylending business on the side, expected the watch would fall into his hands someday. Nayaz was not really concerned about having to pawn it eventually. All his attention was on Naseema's shoes.

Around forty, Naseema's beauty had not yet faded, though Nayaz did not notice much about her, training all his attention towards his sister-in-law's feet. Her shoes had stolen his mind. Beads set out like flowers in bloom, a barely-there sparkle in them, sat on a soft black leather sole. The heels were high and tapered. It seemed like the shoes had been designed especially for her feet. When she wore them and sauntered about, it looked like she was floating on air. He had desperately hoped that after wearing those heels she would fall, certainly she would fall, maybe break her big toe, definitely sprain her ankle. He had expected her to then leave the pair of shoes behind, and he could get them repaired and give them to Asifa to wear. But all his calculations had been turned upside down.

A nasty thought appeared in Nayaz's head. He could steal the shoes and hide them away the night before Naseema was to return to Saudi. As if she had sensed this, along with packets of fenugreek powder, ragi powder and chilli powder, she packed those shoes eight days in advance and hid them in one of her suitcases, and began to wear Liberty chappals. He felt guilty, as if he had been caught red-handed, and stopped talking to her altogether.

Finally he decided to bravely bring up the topic the night before they were to leave, and ask her to give those shoes to Asifa. Although they were all up late into the night talking and doing the last of the packing, not a sound escaped his mouth. He felt stuck in a strange situation and all his attempts to escape it were in vain. All his fight, his agitation, all this for a paltry pair of shoes, that too for his wife to wear? Towards the end of the evening he became very agitated and restless. Soon he got so bad that he began to vomit continually, a slight fever spread to his entire body and he did not leave bed for eight days.

Because of this he could not go to the airport to drop his brother off. Since Asifa could not go without him either, he felt sad that his brother and sister-in-law left by themselves. Naseema did not let the matter go and taunted her husband, 'Aha, poor thing, boarding the plane like you are an orphan! What all did you not do for your dear, dear younger brother? You should have poured some more money there now.' Even then, Mehaboob Khan called his brother one or two times from Mumbai without his wife's knowledge and asked after his health.

Although he tried very hard not to think such things, similar thoughts did eventually enter his brain, and Mehaboob Khan began to distance himself from his brother. Two years after he had left for Saudi he was going back to visit his birth village on a two-month-long vacation. He had called to inform his brother as well, and there was only one week left until his flight home. As usual, he had asked his brother if he wanted anything from Saudi. But even then, Nayaz did not have the guts to tell his brother what he really wished for.

Nayaz did not have a moment to catch his breath that day. He had borrowed money from his colleagues and friends and was busy renovating the old house he lived in. So what if it was an old house? His grandfather had built it. It was the house where his mother, as a new daughter-in-law, had stepped over the threshold, dipped her hands in sandalwood paste and left handprints on the west-facing wall of the living room. His elder brother was born in that house; he was born there too. Both his sister-in-law Naseema and his Asifa had, like exact copies of his mother, dipped their hands in sandalwood paste and made prints on the western wall of this very house. His Munni had taken her first tottering steps here, all in this very house. Within a month of each other, his parents had answered the call of the unknown and walked away from here . . . It was from under that pomegranate tree that their bodies had been lifted onto people's shoulders. He was now whitewashing over all these memories.

Nayaz had inherited the old house after his father's death. Mehaboob Khan had never asked him for his share. Whenever he came on vacation, he would sleep on a straw mat, asking for little. He would sit, stroll about and sleep peacefully wherever he wanted. Naseema, however, would not let her bare feet touch the floor. She would wear her bathroom slippers and walk around noisily. The sight of her crinkling her face and taking wide steps, as if the floor was filthy, every time she had to go into the kitchen to pour herself a glass of milk, made Nayaz angry. His heart would become bitter. Asifa, though, would ignore these little irritations and trail behind her, calling her 'Bhabhi, Bhabhi' and treating her like royalty. This so-called Bhabhi Naseema was reluctant but still accepted all the attention.

He would not have felt bad, even if Asifa had stooped lower to cater to all of Naseema's whims. It would have been enough for him if Naseema had given her high-heeled shoes to Asifa before she left. He would have been satisfied if Asifa had walked around like a fairy just once. He would feel fulfilled if he could touch those feet after they had worn those shoes. Dreamily thinking of all this, he came back to reality with a thud.

The big mango tree in front of the house came down. In the beginning, he had got people to chop its branches one by one. It was a Raspuri mango tree, each fruit large enough to fill the width of two palms. Every year after eating his fill, he would give baskets upon baskets of the fruit to his colleagues. Tired of doing even that, for the last four-five years he had been selling the crop to a fruit merchant the moment the tree started flowering, and getting palmfuls of money instead. But now, seeing all the space the tree occupied, he began to get irritated. Between the compound and his house, the tree had, without any consideration, occupied a space large enough to build a whole house.

That year, when he waited for the fruit merchant to come during the flowering season, all Nayaz Khan got was disappointment. When he went himself to meet one or two merchants, they dismissively told him, 'Who wants just one tree, man? It is a good harvest this year. Either you bring the mangoes here yourself, or throw them in the garbage.' But then he got an unexpected offer from someone: if he were to chop down the tree and get a cellar and two shops above it constructed, this man would take the spaces on rent, and even give money in advance for them. Nayaz did not want to lose such an opportunity.

Maybe there was an owl sitting on his shoulder. In the beginning he got the branches cut one by one, and one day had the whole tree brought down. Arifa watched from the window and shed copious tears. She did not have many memories. They were so few she could have pickled them all in a single jar. During her first pregnancy, she had, without telling anyone, brought down a mango with a stick, the fruit a little sour, a little astringent at the top when she bit into it, and the mischievous girl hidden somewhere within her had been a part of this small happiness. She had plonked herself under the tree on summer afternoons in the early days of her marriage. Those stolen moments of love under the tree, that was all. The sourness of the raw mango, the sweetness of the ripe mango, the abundance of each fruit, the expansiveness of the shoots.

Nayaz Khan built it all: the cellar, the two shops, and alongside them his house renovation went on too. He attached a bathroom to the room his elder brother slept in. He set out marble tiles, as white as the feathers of a swan, all over the kitchen floor, to suit his sister-in-law's delicate feet. Since he wanted to exhibit his business acumen and give his brother a big surprise when he returned from abroad, Nayaz hurried through all the work. He did not say anything to his brother, but from time to time Naseema still heard highly exaggerated reports from her maternal house. Based on these, she rode on the horse of her imagination and taunted her husband, poking, cutting and boiling him with her hurtful words, and derived great pleasure from it. She succeeded in creating a divide between the brothers, who had been as close as Rama and Lakshmana.

That was why, although Nayaz Khan was hurrying about to ensure that all the work was completed by the day his brother arrived, Mehaboob Khan quietly returned from Saudi and went straight to Naseema's maternal house. Before, he would have stayed in Naseema's house for a week out of courtesy and returned to his own home to spend the rest of his vacation there. But now, would Naseema let go of such a great opportunity? She reined him in and made him stay on in her parents' house. In the middle of his restlessness, Mehaboob Khan felt intolerably tormented, suffered silently and stopped talking. His laughter, his words began to feel artificial; he felt as if he had lost everything of his own and became distressed. He began to get angry if he was so much as touched. He began to flare up like a mustard seed dropped in fire. He did not get peace of mind in any corner of that house. His irritation began to increase, and he started losing his temper for no reason. That was when Naseema decided the time was right for Mehaboob Khan to meet his brother. If he had to lose his temper, let him lose it with his brother, what do I care, she thought, and convinced her husband to meet Nayaz.

In between all this, Nayaz Khan, worried that he had not received a letter or a phone call from his brother, called Saudi a few times, racking up a bill of thousands of rupees, only to learn that his brother had already come to India. Agitated, he wondered why his brother had not yet come home. Just as he was calling his sister-in-law's maternal house, Naseema was stringing her husband to a bow and getting ready to fire.

Finally, Mehaboob Khan went home. His heart broke. He did not shed tears. But he became a sea of tears himself. Not a word came out of his mouth, though he himself collapsed. He wished he had never seen this sight at all. He wished he had not come back to India. He wished he had burned to ashes in that desert land. At least then maybe the branches of the mango tree would have come and softly fanned him with their green shoots and leaves. The swing that he and his brother played on was going up and down from a branch of the tree. Their father was sitting on a chair below the tree and teaching him and Nayaz verses from the Qur'an; his melodious voice was humming in Mehaboob's ears now. When he remembered how, as a child, he had clung to his mother's waist and she would hold a plate in her hand to climb down the steps one by one, walk to the mango tree and feed him mouthfuls of food, and then make him sit on a branch of the tree and continue feeding him, it felt like someone was running a pair of scissors over his gut. This was the tree in which they carefully, fearfully climbed from one branch to the other, where they later jumped around and played like monkeys. Couldn't they at least have told him they were doing this? How could one forgive this disaster, all for greed, some little money? His brother had not even had the courtesy to ask. On top of that, Naseema continued to nag, saying, 'Riii, your brother has borrowed a loan from the bank. Now it is as if he owns the entire house. Let it go, you poor thing, you don't have to bother about anything now. There is no need to take the trouble to draw up papers and sign off the house to him. Or did you give him everything and finish it all off without telling me either?'

Slowly, Nayaz Khan began to understand the secret behind his elder brother's silence. He realised that his sister-in-law had the upper hand now. But how to get out of this knot? He became restless too. However, even in the middle of his agitation, when Naseema came with her suitcases, his eyes drifted towards her feet; it became difficult to say whether his hungry eyes were satiated or not. This was because, along with a pista-green Panjabi dress with zardozi work, she was wearing a beautiful thin-heeled shoe. Her gait was attractive now because of the shoes she wore. It became impossible for him to peel his eyes off her feet, and he felt strangely drawn.

Nayaz Khan had borrowed money from many people. He had borrowed from his office, as well as a huge amount from private lenders. Rajeeva, who had his eyes on Nayaz's watch, had also lent him money. With all that money, he had ended up buying a second-hand fridge and washing machine, alongside renovating, whitewashing and painting the house. After all, he was very confident that his brother would help him out financially after seeing all the work he had put into the house. But Mehaboob Khan was a broken man. He found his brother's every action, word, activity, everything to be artificial. His thoughts painfully oscillated between wondering whether he should pat his younger brother's back for all the things he had done, or insult him for building a tomb over his memories. He began to feel that it was not his house at all, like he was a stranger there, like an unexpected, unwanted guest. That was why none of the facilities the younger brother had made for his elder brother moved Mehaboob. Why did he not consult with me even once before doing all this? Did I become so distant, so inconsequential? When did my brother become so greedy? For what? There was no place under the cool shade of the mango tree to look for answers to these questions.

The chasm between them grew wider. What voice could possibly bridge the cracks that were caused by silence? They caved in on themselves. Only Naseema's lips carried a small smile of relief. The high-heeled shoes that she wore all the time. A dark shadow of anxiety on Arifa's face. The black clouds that surrounded her eyes shone as never before. On top of that she was five months pregnant. She was not showing much yet, but the pregnancy had sucked Arifa's essence from inside. She was thin and feeble where a pregnant woman should have been happy and glowing. She had to look after Munni, treat the esteemed guests well, negotiate the cold war between her husband and brother-in-law, her co-sister's veiled taunts . . . Was it one or two things she had to deal with? She was exhausted. As if all this wasn't enough, she had an unbearable cough that raked her whole body, as if the wind was scattering dry leaves. Although Nayaz Khan noticed her condition he did not give it priority. Mehaboob Khan noticed it too, and but for his anger towards his younger brother, and fear of his wife . . . If not for these two things, he would have taken her to the hospital himself and ensured she got rest and recovered. But there was that thing called ego. The snake of arrogance had laid many, many eggs.

The sun was blazing high above the house. The wind was shy, and stayed hidden. Naseema, who had schemed like Manthare in the Ramayana, was fanning herself with her seragu. The coals of jealousy were burning brightly. In between all this, that young pregnant woman was trying in vain to draw a common thread between them all. By the time one week had passed by, Mehaboob Khan had had enough. During his most difficult moments he felt the mango tree calling to him. He wilted not because of the heat outside, but because of the summer that raged indoors.

One afternoon when he was lying down, the mango tree came close to him, and all kinds of other relationships too. The tree did not say anything. It rested its cool hands on his forehead. It was that touch that made the volcano within Mehaboob begin to cool down. That was all! He did not know how long he slept like that, he did not know what kind of invisible effect it had. By the time he woke up, it was evening. The sun was busy playing hide-and-seek.

'Bhaiyya, Bhaiyyaji . . . ' He was awake but he kept his eyes closed. When he opened his eyes to this distant call, she was standing in front of him. Like a fruit-laden mango tree with expansive branches, like an abundant harvest of ripe mangoes, like the deep dark leaves of such trees; like a rich, blooming flower bouquet; like a tender mango filled with the promise of life; a prominent forehead, a mix of love and respect in her eyes.

'Have some tea, Bhaiyya.' He accepted the cup as if it was elixir. Lost in thought, he looked at her from top to bottom. She had become weak. All her life forces had dried up. She waited until he finished drinking his tea, and took the cup in her hands. For some reason, it shook him.

'Arifa, why have you become like this, my dear?'

Fifteen days after he had come home, this was the first time he had spoken to her so gently. She did not say anything. Her eyes were full. She looked down. He was moved.

After half a second, he anxiously said, 'You must be ready in fifteen minutes. Let us go to a good gynaecologist. If you trust that useless fellow, this is what is going to happen. He is incapable of bearing any responsibility.' He continued in a low voice. 'By the way, you don't have to worry about dinner. After we see the doctor, let us eat at Mughal Darbar.'

Naseema, sprawled on the bed, woke with a start. There was no other way. The flood kept at bay all these days by sandbags now burst forth, and there was nothing to hold it all back. She leisurely got up, wore her beautiful Panjabi dress with kasuti embroidery and her high-heeled shoes, and came out to the living room. The moment Nayaz heard the message Arifa brought in he was overjoyed. Anna is becoming normal! This was the opportune moment he had been waiting for. He sat on a cane chair in a corner of the living room and began to think. Now he could tell Anna everything. His achievement, or maybe it was his foolishness, he could place them in front of his brother, and maybe get one or two slaps. Where had his common sense gone? Before all this was to happen, he should have talked to his brother, asked him for advice. His aimlessly wandering gaze suddenly stopped. A little above the ground, there were Naseema's feet, wearing the high-heeled shoes that had stolen his heart.

He had forgotten about them in the turbulence of the past few days, but now, when it seemed like his brother had begun to thaw, the shoes reappeared like ghosts. Wherever she walked, his eyes would follow her. He began to think that it would be enough if she could just step on his outstretched palms. He controlled himself with great difficulty. 'Mad, mad fellow, what are you doing? Go to hell. You are crazy about a pair of shoes. You are ready to steal too, even to beg? You'll be destroyed,' he scolded himself. But still, but still . . . high-heeled shoes. They had some special magical power. They not only pulled him in, but had also destroyed his common sense. He had lost himself, his senses, knowledge, consciousness.

He'd become obsessed. He had to get those shoes, and get Arifa to wear them – this desire became so great that he forgot everything else. He sat still, as if in shock. When he came out, Mehaboob stared at his younger brother for a second. Looking at his younger brother's behaviour, a wave of sympathy rose up in a corner of his heart. Not expressing it, he walked out.

Until Arifa's tests were completed at the maternity home, Mehaboob stood there with as much concern as a mother might show. Everything else was normal, but the fact that she was anaemic and suffering from high blood pressure worried him, though he did not show his concern to his wife. Naseema had no doubts that all these expenses would be borne by her husband. Not only did he pay for the tonic and tablets, he carried the plastic cover filled with medicine himself, like a servant. The sight made her fume.

Mughal Darbar was a little distance away from the centre. It was not yet dinner time. Naseema had other shopping to do.

Material things had become priceless, and human beings worthless. Behind those material possessions, people's feelings were on sale. Things decided the relationships between small people with big shadows. A fridge had the capacity to change the life of a young bride. The different colours it came in could play Holi on her young dreams. Such possessions held a prominent spot not only in the house, but also in making life decisions. People were running, having tossed their worthiness and their relationships into the air. Tired, collapsing in exhaustion, sweating, they were running. Aha! The golden deer is more than roaming about, it is making everyone mad too. It has brought everyone under its spell. The tale of its magnetism – no one could grasp it in their hands – this was the grand mark of civilisation!

Naseema and Arifa were at a garments store. Mehaboob sat on a stool and was paying great attention to the furniture, the design of the false ceiling, the way the counters were built and so on. Nayaz Khan was roaming about, stopping before every store, staring at the things displayed in the showcases. Just as he went back and forth and was about to go to the shop where his family was, he felt as if someone had touched him very lightly on the back. That touch! Feeling as if it was the answer to some unending search within himself, he stood still for a minute. When he turned to see who it was, there was no one behind him. But then, just like that, the moment he turned back, in a giant showcase in front of him, among a pile of imported products . . . His heart missed a beat. He kept staring, wondering if it was a dream. The centre of his endless search that haunted him day and night, that which had grown roots in his dreams, in his heart – those shoes – there, in that showcase! Captivated, he stood still. Was it true? Was it false? Was this even possible?

He eventually recovered. The possibility of what had seemed impossible pierced his consciousness. He walked straight into the shop, but, unable to stand, he collapsed on a stool as if enchanted. He began to feel as if all the lights in the shop were focused on him, as if he was an extraordinary man. Fearing that someone else might get their hands on those shoes, he said, in a voice loud enough for the whole shop to hear, 'Give me those high-heeled shoes.'

Mehaboob Khan turned to look when he heard his brother's tone; Naseema was observing him too. Unmindful of all this, Nayaz Khan raised his voice even louder and called his wife. Having noticed Nayaz's strange behaviour in front of her brother-in-law, Arifa came and stood quietly behind her husband. Nayaz had become very emotional. He suddenly got up, turned to his wife and told her, 'Sit there, sit there.' Arifa was confused when she saw where he was pointing. The decorative throne-like chair was made of thick glass planks; she worried that it might break if she sat on it. Although she wondered why he was acting so strangely, she said nothing. Nayaz took her hand excitedly, urgently, and made her sit on that throne. Arifa shrank into herself. Her fear that it might break increased. Those high-heeled shoes in the salesman's hands, a husband who was not paying attention to anything, Mehaboob Khan gazing with empty eyes, and Naseema, trying very hard to control the amusement playing across her lips!

The salesman bent down, removed Arifa's blue-strapped Hawaii chappals and put those shoes on her feet. The yellow metal buckle on the shoes shone like gold under the lights. But it was impossible for her feet to fit. Made for dainty-footed women, the shoes would not encompass her wide feet. Nayaz Khan was not disappointed. He sat down and set about helping the salesman, and together they crammed his wife's toes, with great difficulty, into the shoes. He pulled the thin, delicate strap around her heel and somehow managed to put it through the buckle. The salesman imitated him and tightened the strap on her other foot as well. Her heels struck out of the shoes quite a lot. They had cracked here and there; their black lines stood out all the more now. It was evident that she was so occupied with household work that she never paid any attention to her feet. She was used to wearing her husband's Hawaii chappals without a care and walking about swiftly, comfortably. Now, when she saw the pointed heels on those shoes, she began to get scared.

The salesman looked at the pair of shoes that did not suit her in any way and hesitantly said, 'Walk a little and see, madam.' She got up very carefully. Somehow, she managed to stand upright. She was forced to take one slow step after another to move forward. By this time Nayaz Khan had already run to the counter, counted out notes and got a bill made. There was no limit to Naseema's amusement. She folded her arms to her chest, and encouragingly told Arifa,

'Hmm, walk now, my dear, take one step after the other, let's see.' She suppressed the waves of mockery that were rising within her, soon failed, and balloons of laughter began to burst forth not just from her lips, but also her entire face.

Stumbling, half out of fear and half out of shyness, Arifa realised that there was no way out; although she was fuming in her heart at her husband's extremely strange behaviour, she began to practise walking on the beautiful carpet. At that moment she did not have a choice. But she began to realise that walking was impossible. After a few steps, she came back and told the salesman, 'Look here, pack these shoes,' and glanced around for her Hawaii chappals. Where were they? Nayaz Khan had already had them packed and was waiting for her outside the shop. Arifa's eyes filled with tears.

She had to step outside the carpet and onto the shop floor now. The floor tiles were shining. Scared she would lose her footing, she began to walk very slowly. She took the support of pillars in the shop and the showcase and finally reached the front door. Seeing the smooth granite steps leading out of the shop, she stood still for a moment. Naseema understood her predicament. She was also angry at her brother-in-law's madness, and realised that he was doing all this to compete with her. But she took pity on Arifa and held her hand, telling her, 'Get down slowly,' until she was on the street.

Once they were on the road, how could she continue holding her hand saying, 'Pai, ma, pai,' as if encouraging a toddler to take one step after another? She slowly let go of Arifa's hand. Nayaz Khan was out of reach and running ahead. Although he thought it was strange of his younger brother to buy Arifa shoes that did not suit her, Mehaboob Khan did not notice anything else. Naseema added this to a collection in her brain, to use it to taunt her husband when the time was right, and soon became preoccupied with other things herself.

Arifa, the poor thing, still fearing she might slip and fall, limped and began to walk strangely. The new pair of shoes began to squeeze her toes. Her heels, spilling out the back, were hurting too. More than that, the thin, sharp three-inch high heels . . . It was OK even if she fell down, at the most she might break a few bones. But what about the baby inside her, she wondered?

She began to walk slower and slower. Nayaz, Mehaboob and Naseema disappeared into the distance. Every step she took felt like an impossible task. She had watched many young women wearing such heels with short skirts or bikinis, showing off their long, naked legs on TV. Remembering the way their legs danced, she tried to find the courage to take a firm step forward. But instead of feeling brave, she began to feel naked herself and started to stumble.

In the middle of all these worries came a terrible cough that occupied her body and heart for a long time. Arifa started shaking. Once the bout of coughing had subsided, she wiped the sweat off her reddened face and stood still for a few minutes. She realised for the first time how many problems feet could bring.

Arifa still did not understand her husband's demeanour. He had not shown any concern for her, forced onto her evil shoes which she didn't want and which could harm her unborn child, and swiftly walked away without a backward glance. She wondered if she should remove those unwanted shoes, and came to a conclusion that defied all her anxieties, fear and oppression in half a second. She stood straight, put all her strength on her toes and tried to wiggle them in the congested space. Since that hurt her, she began to stamp her heels, putting her entire weight on those pencil heels to try to bend them. Umm! Hoo! She realised those damned heels had not budged an inch. Arifa had become stronger after she made her decision. Her determination gave her a strange power. She stood upright again, put her weight on both her legs and, chanting, 'Left, right, left' in her heart, began to march.

It was evident from the way she was walking that she did not care who saw her. She soon became less careful, and twisted her left ankle. It was only because she managed to grab the shirt of a giant man walking in front of her that she did not fall. He felt his tucked-in shirt being pulled from the back with such force that the shirt buttons came up to his neck, and his collar fell all the way back. He turned around angrily. But his anger melted when he saw Arifa's condition. Though she had let go of his shirt, she was still struggling to stand up; he helped her up and gently asked her, 'The shoes you are wearing don't suit you, do they?' Moments in life are like this. Having never come face to face with a male stranger before, she stammered for a moment and then said, 'Yes, these shoes are not my size, they are not comfortable and are a torture.'

'Why don't you at least remove them and hold them in your hands?' She gave him a light smile, even in that unusual situation, saying, 'These are devil shoes. Even if I remove them, I'll have to wear them again and again.' She lifted her right foot and stamped it hard. Forget about the heel breaking, it didn't move even a little. She felt her eyes mist over. She extended her hand, hoping she would find something to hold on to.

There. When she was stumbling, whether she knew it or not, she felt it getting dark around her. Did the power go off? No. It would have turned dark all of a sudden. What kind of a darkness was this? Its touch was cool on the skin, it spread through her veins. It made her unconscious. With each second, her body became heavier, the darkness swallowing her every nerve. It strode through the door to her soul and froze her consciousness. It ate the last bit of resistance she put up, and finally the darkness entered her and sank in deep.

As she was experiencing each second of that strange sensation, she saw darkness putting down deep roots into her being. Those roots descended from her brain, down and all over her face, to her neck, her chest, till they burst through her lungs, further down, and then, by the time she noticed, the roots had come and stopped near her pregnant stomach. The sharp roots then became blunt. Their power to pierce reduced, the peak of darkness shrinking. That was when she realised that there were limits to the all-pervading darkness as well.

Suddenly she looked down at her belly. She began to feel that although she was buried in the mists of darkness there was still a ray of hope for her, when the life coiled under several layers began to knock on all sides of her womb. When all five of her senses were buried deep under darkness and she felt as if she was far away from feeling anything, then she made miraculous contact. The movement of life within her.

'Amma.'

'Tell me, my darling,' she immediately answered, but when she realised where that piteous cry was coming from, her entire body became slack. Her eyelids began to close involuntarily. She felt as if her senses were out of her control, and it seemed like she was communicating with this child from a consciousness that was not hers. A moment of silence. Then, curled up in some corner of her womb, it cried out again.

'Amma?'

'Tell me, tell me, talk to me, my darling.' She began to slowly rub the part of her stomach where it lay curled up like a ball.

It became a little lighter at this touch. It whispered, 'What has happened to you, Amma? There is a lot of weight on me.'

'How . . . how . . . what kind of weight, my child, my heart?'

'I don't know, Amma. Your stomach's weight is entirely on me, I cannot even move, Amma.'

'Aiyoo, my dear, what happened to you, I don't understand . . .'

'The weight of your whole body feels like it is on me, Amma, and now look, look, I . . . I don't have any space, Amma . . .'

Tears rolled down from Arifa's half-shut eyes.

'Oh my life, what is happening to you, what can I do?'

Her legs started shaking. She was determined not to fall down, but the more she tried to stand up straight, the more the strength in her knees reduced. By the time she began to think to herself that her child would get hurt if she fell down, it coiled into itself again and softly asked, 'What happened to your feet, Amma?', cutting her thoughts short.

Everything became clear to her in an instant. She was putting unnecessary pressure on her unborn child because of the high-heeled shoes. Her heart melted.

She struggled in the dark, pulling at the buckles and trying to remove the shoes. They did not budge. Not just that, but the more she tried to pull them, the more they seemed to tighten around her feet. They began to look like a layer of skin.

The more pressure there was on the womb, the less space the child had. She felt her child struggling between life and death.

I am not a mother, I am a mahamari, a demon. A thread of awareness began to arise in Arifa even amidst her distress.

There was still time. She had to try one last time to save her baby. She looked around for her husband, but he was nowhere to be seen. He had disappeared after putting those shoes on her feet.

She looked up at the sky in great distress. In that darkness, she saw nothing.

In the end, a weak voice floated up. 'Amma . . .'

The voice pierced through the well of her love, and filled Arifa with a strange emotion, with an incredible strength that she did not know she had.

She placed both her hands on her stomach, focused all her will on the child that was slowly stopping all movement, filled her heart with the innocent, sweet form of the baby who was going to be born soon, and with all her strength began to put pressure on those high-heeled shoes instead.

As she continued putting pressure on them, she was drenched in sweat. Just when it felt like her womb would become victim to their pressure, those high-heeled shoes, as if from some great power, exploded into thousands of pieces, lit up like a meteor, fell somewhere, somewhere were obliterated.

And then Arifa stood solid like the earth on the still, firm ground.

SOFT WHISPERS

It hadn't been long since I went to bed, but my sleep was already thick as the cream that sets over hot milk. My nightie was soaked with sweat and sticking to my back. It felt cold behind my ears. My neck and hair were wet too. Perhaps I wouldn't have woken up, but the sound of the phone ringing, relentlessly ... I had no choice.

'Hello?'

'Hello. Were you sleeping, my dear?'

'Mmm. Yes.' My voice was heavy.

'I wouldn't have called you at this hour; I knew you would be sleeping.' Ammi hesitated a moment. 'Abid has come from the village.'

'Abid? Which Abid?'

'Oh. Haven't you woken up fully yet? Mujawar Saheb's son. Now he is the mujawar of the Shahmir Ali Dargah and attends to the shrine.'

'What does he want?'

'You know the Urs festival is happening there at the end of this month. There must be someone from our family present during the sandalwood ritual. Iqbal is thousands of miles away. At least you have to be there, my daughter.'

'Me?'

'What is there to be shocked about?'

'No, Ammi, of all things, for the sandalwood ...'

'Leave it, leave it, I cannot talk much. Abid said he will come there. Talk to him and make arrangements, dear. Can we let go of family traditions?' Those were words of hurt. Unwilling to argue further, I said, 'Don't send him now. Let him come in an hour. Let's see.'

I put down the phone and drew the curtains apart; it was blazing hot outside. Inside, too, my life was soaked in the heat of difficulties. I went and fell on the bed again. Abid has come from the village. The village, Malenahalli, my grandparents' village. We went once a year for the Urs festival because Abbajaan forced us. Ammi used to go because he insisted. A village with about a hundred houses, of which more than sixty had Muslim families. It was not just Ajji's maternal home; everyone in the village was related to her as well.

Ajji was lean, fair and tall. She used to wear skirts made of Sussi silk, and white full-sleeved shirts with Nehru collars. On top of the shirt, which revealed not an inch of stomach, back or hands, she wore either a white Mul or Chikan-embroidered davani. In her shirt pocket, a box of snuff, small change, a piece of white ribbon for the hair, a few chalk pieces, some bits of pencils, grey nicker seeds, one or two pens.

In the evenings, Ajja would sit on the expansive jagali in front of the house, grinding the tobacco on stone and mixing the snuff gently with butter, while a little distance away, leaning against the door, sat Ajji. On her lap and around her we sat, that is, me and four of my father's eldest sister's children. Two of Asiya Athe's children, four of Noori Athe's . . . we used to jump up and down on Ajji's slender but strong thighs. We used to empty Ajji's pockets, take what we wanted and stuff the rest back. One or two of us hovered around Ajja too. Ajja's white beard was scraggy and looked very funny. He used to pound the snuff to a fine powder and send a pinch of it to Ajji. She would sniff it into her nose and comment either that the lime was not enough, or that it needed more butter or more powdering.

An evening like that. I had emptied Ajji's pocket, and, under the pretext of putting everything back, grabbed a ten-paise coin by sleight of hand, and was lying on her lap acting innocent. Ajji had a soft spot for me because I was her son's daughter and came to visit rarely. That day, Ammi could not stand still or sit in one place. She kept going in and coming out like a cat whose tail was on fire. 'Tomorrow is her birthday.' She pointed towards me and addressed Ajji.

'Is it? How old will my dear be?'

'She will turn eight tomorrow, and begin her ninth year.'

'Aha, my darling.' Ajji hugged me and it rained kisses. 'If this snuff smell was not there . . . '

Ammi said anxiously: 'She does not have new clothes for tomorrow. So far. He also has not come.' My mother must have felt like the sky had fallen on her.

'He will come, don't worry. Does he live close by? He has to travel by bus for five hours, then take some other vehicle or walk the rest of these ten miles.' Ajji had a lot of sympathy for the difficulties her son faced, working in a government job.

Dusk began to spread. My eldest Athe lit a brass lamp that had been polished till it shimmered, and brought it to the drawing room.

'It's OK if he can't come, but if he had sent her a frock, that would have been nice.'

Ajji smiled slightly. 'Is it OK if he doesn't come, as long as he sends a dress? The problem is about one frock? Leave it, we will get one stitched.' Ammi calmed down and hurried inside.

Looking at the way Ajji sniffed a pinch of tobacco and wiped her nose, I immediately got out of her lap. She laughed at my cleverness and, saying, 'Come here,' she held my hand and led me to the large bed standing in a corner of the drawing room. There was not enough light there. She bent down and pulled out an old trunk from under it. All the children came running into the room, even Asiya Athe, Ammi too. Noori Athe came holding the brass lamp.

The trunk was full of Sussi fabric and Mul davanis. Ajja's jubba. When she was bringing out these things one by one, a dry date caught the naughty Ghani's eye and he jumped for it. All the children screamed, 'Hoooo.' He quickly shoved it in his mouth and started dancing. I had had a better chance to grab it because I was sitting right next to Ajji. Ammi contorted her face, wrinkled her nose and tried to scold me for my laziness with her eyes. I turned my attention to the trunk again. A spinning top became Hamid's. Ajji was laughing softly when all the children screamed, each time one-one thing kept disappearing. This way, as ribbons, glittery decorations and mehendi packets got emptied, Ajji opened a small bundle wrapped in red cloth that lay at the bottom of the trunk. Seeing a small piece of white Achkan cloth, Ammi turned her face again. Ajji did not notice any of this; she put all the things back inside the trunk, carried me on her waist and came to the main door. My long legs dangled till Ajji's ankles, but still I wrapped myself tightly around her waist. All the children had come down to the street with us. I was feeling very happy. Our procession continued.

Once we crossed the street and went past the school, I saw Abbajaan. Holding a bag in his left hand, dusty black boots on his feet, he was walking towards us. Ajji saw him and stopped. I jumped down from Ajji's waist and ran into Abbajaan's arms. I told him before he asked: 'Abbajaan, Dadima is getting a frock stitched for me. We are going to Jaffar Baba,' I said happily.

'There is no need to get it stitched now. I have brought a nice frock, you can wear that.'

'No, I want the frock Dadima gets stitched,' I insisted. Ajji laughed and said, 'You have come walking just now. You go on home, I will come in a little while.' The herd behind Ajji had grown bigger. Children from the street had joined us.

An old machine was screeching pathetically on the jagali in front of Jaffar Baba's house. There was a frog figurine on top of the machine stand, and it looked strange under the lantern, as if the frog was about to leap down. We all gathered around the machine. Even when Ajji got up on the jagali platform, Jaffar Baba did not stop pedalling. He did not even ask what she wanted. Instead, he kept operating the machine, and began to make loud, scary sounds from his throat. By then, Ghani and a few others also stood on the pedal, attempting to move it, and, in the end, it became too heavy and the pedal stopped.

Jaffar Baba slowly lifted his neck, looked at Ajji and asked, 'Do you know, Jamaal Bi, why this whole world, the sun, the moon, the sky and stars have been created?'

Ajji took out the piece of cloth from her waist, but did not talk.

'For whom were all these created? For whom?' Jaffar Baba asked himself, mumbling. He pushed up his glasses which had slipped to the end of his nose and asked, 'Are you not ready to leave?'

Ajji laughed softly. 'Jaffar Baba, you are my sibling. The very guru who blessed you has also shown me the way. When the call comes, no one will remain. Philosophy is not your exclusive property,' she said.

'No, no. You have lost. You do not seek release. You have hidden the bird in the cage,' Jaffar Baba said.

Ajji's forehead crinkled. 'Has our guru given you some kind of authority or what? There are a few who are too weak to fly even if all the doors to the cage are open. There are also those who find a way through the darkness of ignorance. But the heart has to be pure. Haven't you listened to the guru's words?'

Jaffar Baba did not say anything for a couple of seconds. He sat still, staring into the void. Ajji went near the sewing machine. She placed the cloth on top and ordered, 'Stitch a nice dress for this darling of mine,' carried me on her waist, and walked out.

I looked back. Jaffar Baba sat unmoving. I leaned towards her and asked, 'Ajji, what did that mean?'

We were near Qasim Bi's house. She was sitting on a mat on the jagali and stuffing tobacco into a bidi roll. I sneezed because of the smell of the leaves. Ajji put me down and sat there. 'Qasim Bi, where is this tobacco from?'

'I don't know where it is from, but it is very nice,' she replied. She took out two bidis from the packet, examined them, folded their ends using a bamboo stick as thick as a pencil, gave one to Ajji, put the other in her mouth, lit it with the lamp kept nearby, blew out smoke and handed it over to Ajji. She lit her bidi with Qasim Bi's, gave his back and slowly blew out smoke. I was surprised – shocked: my beloved Ajji, who thinks deeply about spiritual matters, now bidi-smoking – Ajji! I clapped my hands and shouted, 'Ahaha! Women are smoking bidis! I will tell Abbajaan.' Qasim Bi immediately pressed the bidi to the floor and, when the light died, threw it out and grumbled, 'Bad children, bad children.' When Ajji nonchalantly took another two puffs and sat on calmly, I remembered the way she had made Jaffar Baba shut up. 'Dadima, what does it mean?' I asked.

'You will not understand it, my dear. But still, I will tell you. Our hearts should always be pure.' I did not understand. This grandmother! I began to feel bored. 'Dadima, let's go home.'

'Hmm. Let's go,' she said. I climbed onto her waist again.

When we got home, the fragrance of fish curry hit our senses. Ajja and Abbajaan were sitting in the drawing room. Ajja was asking, 'What do you say? Have Sheikh Abdullah and Nehru become friends now or not?'

Abbajaan used to spread the newspaper around and read every day, and he began to report in detail. I tugged at Ajji's seragu. Yawning widely, I said, 'I am going to sleep, I am sleepy.'

'No, my little one, wait a minute.' Ajji went inside and brought a plate of rice and fish curry.

'No! I don't want – no – I won't eat.' I closed my mouth with both hands.

'Look here, this is Malli fish. Just little bites. It is small, isn't it. If you don't eat this, you will grow up like your mother.'

'Like Ammi? Thoo! No.'

'Why are you saying no? She is so beautiful, she loves you so much.'

'Not at all. If I don't eat dinner, she threatens that Hitler will come and take me away, and then, and then, Dadima, I like bread a lot, isn't it? If I am eating bread, she says that it is made of mucus, isseee! I feel like puking. She cuts my nails very short. Ammi is bad,' I complained.

Abbajaan stopped talking to Ajja and paid attention to what I was saying. Ajji laughed wholeheartedly. 'Did you see? Your wife gives my darling a lot of trouble, it seems.'

Abbajaan looked troubled. 'Didn't I tell you before? To not get such a young girl married off? Did you all listen to me?' he scolded Ajji. 'No one asked about my pain. When Safiya got measles two years ago, her eyes had veiled over, she could not breathe and it seemed like she would not live. I made her lie down on my lap. Your daughter-in-law was relaxed about all this. I was very distressed looking at the child's condition. None of you lived close by, my tears overflowed from helplessness. Your daughter-in-law saw that and laughed so much. I don't know how I controlled myself. Once the child recovered, I asked her one day why she had laughed so much. She said she couldn't control her laughter seeing a grown man like me crying,' he complained. 'What do you say? When she got married to me, she must have been eleven years old. When Safiya was born, she had turned twelve, isn't it? But still. Now it is OK. She has matured a little bit,' he continued, softening, and added, 'But still, Amma, girls should not be married off at such a young age.'

Ajji took me into her lap with great love, remembered the measles attack I had had two years before and said, 'That is why the child is so weak. Yet how else can it be if she does not eat properly either? You are my dear one, open your mouth . . . no, no . . . don't clamp your teeth . . . just one mouthful . . . look here. Once I was cleaning a Malli fish when the Shanbhog's daughter-in-law came in. She was pregnant. She stood there and looked at me. 'What is this, Boobamma?' she asked. I replied, 'See, my dear, this is such and such fish.' 'What will you make with it?' 'I will make curry, dear,' I said. She stood there talking till I made the curry. When the curry came to a boil, its fragrance began to spread all around. She began to desire it too. She did not say anything. Here, here, open your mouth, don't bite your teeth down . . . another mouthful . . . and then, and then, she began to get labour pain.'

'Why did she get pain, Dadima? Does one get pain after eating fish curry?'

Ajji laughed again. 'Pain comes for some reason. You just say hmm, haa! Another mouthful now . . . She got pain, but she did not deliver. She ate pain for three days.'

'Can one eat pain, Dadima?'

Ajji stopped talking and stared at me for a minute. As if she was addressing someone else, she said, 'Correct, isn't it? One should eat pain and give happiness.'

'What happened then, Dadima?' I asked, pulling her back into the story.

'And then everyone gathered. In those days, there were no doctors or such others, after all. They asked her to tell what was in her heart. What did she want to eat, what did she want to wear, they asked. After a lot of persuasion, she finally opened her mouth. She said that she wanted to eat Malli fish curry from Boobamma's house. The people gathered there almost died in horror. After that, I got to know about this and went to her house. That is all? Why get worried about it? I came back home. A load of rice straw was lying there. I chopped them to finger-length size, took a handful of the sticks to their house and told them what all spices were needed for the fish curry masala. The Shanbhog's wife did exactly as I told her. The curry began to boil, the fragrance hit the senses, that girl drank a bit of curry, she sucked on a few rice straw sticks, she gave birth. A beautiful girl child like you was born.'

With some food still left in my mouth, I had slipped deep into a dream.

In the morning I was still asleep, and it was only when Ammi poked my ribs a couple of times that I woke up. Sunrays had seeped through the roof tiles into that small room. Delicate dust particles floated in rainbow colours inside the sphere of that light. I stretched my hand . . .

Ammijaan was shouting at me anxiously, 'Get up quickly! I will give you a bath. Look, what a beautiful frock this is!' The frock was covered with rose frills. I had never worn something like that before. Just as Ammijaan was happily smiling and holding it up to see, I don't know what I was feeling, but in one leap I was near the door. 'I will not wear this,' I said.

'Why?' Ammijaan was surprised, angry.

'Why, because I will wear what Ajji got stitched for me.'

'That white bit? Who knows if even a stitch or two has fallen on that piece. Go to the bathroom now, or else,' she scolded in a low voice so that Ajji would not hear. Just as Ammijaan was keeping one step in front of the other, carefully so as not to wake up Abbajaan, I jumped out. The pot of milk in Ajji's hands tilted, but did not fall. I disappeared into the folds of Ajji's Sussi skirt, and Ammijaan's angry looks could not touch me.

When Ajji and I reached Jaffar Baba's house, he was washing his face. He was seated on the jagali, three large shimmering brass pots of steaming hot water in front of him, charcoal powder in his left hand, a meswak stick in his right. Upon seeing us, he vigorously brushed his teeth, retched and spat out, brought up loud, strange sounds from his throat and exhibited all of his quirks. He splashed water on his face, scrubbed his face and then his legs with the towel on his shoulders, and sat down on a stool next to the sewing machine. His daughter placed a tall tumbler of dark black coffee in his hands. She brought me and Ajji the same coffee in small porcelain cups. Ajji had not yet had it. I had never had such coffee before. In fact, I was not supposed to drink coffee or tea. Ammijaan would chase after me with a glass of Ovaltine, I would make her run all around the house, and in the end would sometimes drink it and sometimes pour it out of the window. If Ammijaan saw me drink this coffee now! Even imagining it made me happy. I took a sip. My tongue singed. By the time I carefully finished drinking it, my body had warmed, it felt like I was going to sweat, my head felt strange.

Jaffar Baba took out a dozen or so pieces of the cloth Ajji had given him the previous day. Just like Ammijaan had said, not a single stitch had fallen on the cloth. I leaned on the machine and stepped on the pedal. The machine began to run, taking the weight of my leg with it. Every piece began to join together. When I wore Jaffar Baba's artwork, all my enthusiasm came crashing down. Stitched without any measurements, the frock stretched below my knees. The folds that were supposed to sit at the waist sagged pathetically. Shoulder, arms, neck, none of these were where they were supposed to be, and like footpaths in villages, went here and there haphazardly. But I liked the pocket Jaffar Baba had stitched on the right side. I knew that this would irritate Ammijaan very much. When I returned home wearing the frock, Abbajaan merely laughed. Asiya and Noori Athe giggled, as if I was a cartoon. I won't even go into Ammijaan's reaction; my desire was fulfilled.

After lunch, after making sure that Ammijaan was asleep, I sat on the jagali for a long time. After a while, I noticed that my companions were all screaming together and running around. I jumped down from my perch too. Everyone had gathered in the backyard of Rehman Chikkappa's house. Some had climbed on top of the hay pile, while others had climbed the guava tree. Although fifty-sixty children had gathered there, the yard fell silent. When I pushed the thorny partition aside and went in, everyone turned to look but no one said a word. It became clear that Abid, holding a thin, tall pole, was issuing orders. I hesitantly walked ahead. My eyes turned involuntarily towards Abid. As if he was expecting that, he gestured that I was to climb the guava tree. Seeing all this secrecy, my curiosity was stirred too. When I got to the tree, all my efforts to climb up were in vain. Even when I stood on tiptoe and stretched, I couldn't reach the dozen hands that dropped down from above. Abid put the pole aside carefully and came near. He was a tall, brown boy, about fifteen-sixteen years old. All of a sudden, he grabbed my waist, lifted me up and sat me on the nearest branch. Some giggled.

He approached the haystack slowly, taking careful steps. A few sparrows flew up. As I sat there watching, Abid held a winnow in his left hand and propped it up with the tall pole in his right. He took a fistful of finger millets from a bag inside his pocket and spread them below the winnow. He stood near the other end of the staff. Nothing happened for a few minutes. It was so still it felt like everyone had stopped breathing. After a while, a sparrow came to peck at the seeds, then soon another and yet another, until some five-six sparrows, with their small beaks, with their brown and grey feathers standing up, had bent their heads and were pecking at the seeds. The heartbeats of all the children must have stopped and perhaps mine too. Just then, in a blink, Abid pulled his end of the staff. The winnow fell face down. The children screamed ho ho ho and giddily fell out of the tree. They all surrounded the winnow and continued to shout, but no one dared touch it. They moved aside when Abid got close and sat around the winnow on their knees. Everyone was restless. He held the winnow tightly in his left hand, made a small opening to one side, put his fist in and searched around. He searched around again, and yet again. Something should have been there for him to find. He lifted the winnow up slowly. One sparrow, which must have hidden somewhere, flew out; some were disappointed, some confused, but still all of them hooted for more. Abid commanded, in a loud voice, 'All of you climb up.' We went back to our places without a word. He set his trap again. The sparrows had cleverly flown away the first time. He continued his task, the children feeling a mix of enthusiasm and disappointment. I started feeling sad at the cruelty of the game.

Abid continued to be deeply engrossed in designing the trap and running to a distance. His face began to redden under the sun.

Beads of sweat formed lines on his forehead. Ghani, sitting on a branch above me, deliberately swung his legs, trying to put them on my shoulders, but in the end dashed them against my cheeks, my ears. I was fed up. Just as I was about to get down from the tree, I realised I couldn't do it by myself, and just as I was about to call Abid, the winnow fell over once more. Abid ran ahead, searched inside the winnow and brought out a fat, cute sparrow. He held it tightly in his large hand, squeezing it and showing only its head. Everyone's excitement overflowed. It would be right to say that they all flew out of the tree and the haystack. As they were all hooting wildly, I tried to get down too, and fell. My knees hurt a lot. My elbows were bruised. A cut on my forehead started bleeding. Naturally, everyone surrounded me. Finding no other way to stop the bleeding, Abid took a fistful of mud, sieved it through his fingers to separate out the stones, and applied soft clay to the wound. The unexpected incident hurt and embarrassed me, and I started crying. Since I was not trying to control my tears, the crying soon turned into intense sobs.

'You only fell,' many of them said, trying to avoid taking responsibility. Abid, however, held my hand and led me to a rock. He wiped my tears and consoled me. 'Look here, don't cry, I will show you a funny thing. This is a female sparrow so there are eggs inside its stomach. I will give them to you; you can take them home and hatch them,' he said. His suggestion sounded very attractive to me. My sobbing reduced and gradually the tears stopped altogether. Abid held the sparrow in front of me, while Ghani held the sparrow's head and Abid took out a small knife from his pocket and cut its throat. Blood oozed out. Unable to watch, my eyes closed automatically.

Abid let the blood flow and placed the sparrow on a small piece of roof tile. Then, he slowly pierced open its chest and laid bare its insides.

What was inside? An oesophagus mixed with blood, the intestine wrapped spirally around it. A little heart that was still beating.

Although I did not like it, it was an incredible sight. I had never seen the world that was now opening before my eyes. Abid cut out the part of the intestine that looked swollen and told me, 'Here, put out your hand.' I stretched my right hand out, feeling a mix of fear, surprise, desire, curiosity and incredulity. Abid placed tiny eggs in my hand. They were warm. There were brown dots here and there on the white- and ash-coloured eggs. I felt as if I had the most precious wonder of the world. Just as my hand remained outstretched, several other hands came forward, saying let me see, let me see, and I quickly closed my fist. But they did not let me be. Several small hands began to pull my hand down. I closed my fist tighter and held it close to my chest. The eggs broke in this struggle. I did not notice at first. When my hands felt sticky, and I saw the runny eggs falling on my frock in strings, I screamed. Seeing me weep, Abid realised what had happened.

Just then, Rehman Chikkappa's wife Zubeida came to the yard, took in all the drama, and scolded Abid with whatever curses came to her mouth. When the children realised it was no longer wise to remain there, they began to slip away quietly. Abid whispered, 'Let's go to the pond.'

Everyone began to run in that direction. Only I limped slowly, wiping my hand on my frock.

By the time I reached the pond, most of the boys had already jumped in, and were splashing water on each other and swimming. The girls were sitting on the edge of the pond on rocks placed there for filling water, washing clothes and vessels, their legs. I inched into the water very hesitantly, and sat on a rock. The water came up to my waist. The water, warmed under the sun, looked pretty to me. I wondered what Ammijaan, who used to flare up in rage

145

if I stood one or two minutes longer than necessary by the public tap, would say if she saw me now; the thought made me laugh, even in the sorry state I was in. I washed my sticky hands. The moment I remembered Ammijaan, my heart began to shiver. I had to go home. With this injured knee, a cut-open forehead, dirty frock . . . abbaaa . . . there was nothing for it now.

I was thinking all this when I felt someone tug at my legs. Abid swam like a fish next to the rock and brushed against them again. By the time I thought to lift my feet up and squat on the rock, he brushed past once more, this time coming near and suddenly lifting me off the rock. I shouted, 'Let me go, let me go,' but he carried me to the shore and, with everyone looking on, kissed me on my cheek, deposited me on a rock, and disappeared into the water as suddenly as he had come.

The girls on the bank screamed thoo thoo thoo. Asiya Athe's daughter said, 'I will tell your Ammi.' I shrank in shyness, but a strong, protective voice was beating inside me, saying that I had not done anything wrong. Seeing no other way, I sat on a rock on the bank of the pond, covered my face with my hands and began to weep. I kept crying.

A strange fear gripped me. I did not realise the time and did not know how long I sat there; I lifted my head up when I felt the touch of a warm hand. Ajji!

All my pain, anxiety and fear disappeared with her touch. She hugged me to her chest and washed away my snot and the mud stuck to my forehead. She wiped my face gently with her seragu, and lifted me to her waist.

The girls playing around did not have the guts to say anything to Ajji. She carried me and started walking. My heart felt very heavy. My tears were eager to burst forth. 'Dadimaaaa,' I said, in a deadened voice.

'What is it, my love?' in a tone full of maternal affection.

'And then . . . and then . . . and then . . . ' I stuttered.

'Tell me, my dear.' Ajji's affection brought me some courage.

'And then . . . that bad Abid . . . he . . . he kissed me . . . here . . . ' I said, pointing to my cheek.

A very brief smile flitted across Ajji's face. I gave her more details. 'I did not do anything. Dadima, he only behaved like the Shaitan!' The moment I started to explain, a flood of tears, who knows where from, rushed in and engulfed me.

Ajji did not say anything. She hugged me tighter and with more affection to her chest and kissed my forehead. She soothed my back, cracked her knuckles and walked hurriedly towards the village, carrying me tightly.

I wonder what she felt looking at my dull face, for she lamented, 'My child has withered so much on her birthday.' She pushed open the gate to the backyard, went in and put me down. Attempting to cheer me up, she picked up a rusted sickle from the base of a distant tree.

She walked a little further away and began to dig the ground with the sickle. The ground was hard. She gathered her strength, dug harder, and soon the soil loosened and a hole began to form. I looked on. After some more digging, I was astonished to see a bunch of groundnuts suddenly hanging from Ajji's hand. My surprise was endless. Ajji began to look like a Gandharva who could magically detect things underground. I clapped my hands and danced and laughed joyfully. Does groundnut really grow underground? I hid some of them in my frock. 'Dadima, some more, I want some more!' I said. Wherever I pointed my finger, wherever I looked, wherever Ajji moved her hands, there were peanuts; my frock filled up.

I forgot all the shame I had felt because of Abid. Ajji engulfed me in her saree and protected me from Ammijaan's wrath. That night I got a high fever and the next day Abbajaan took me and Ammijaan and left the village. It took many days for my injured knees to heal, but that day remained special because of all the first experiences I had.

Abid. That naughty, uncivilised boy from Malenahalli was, today, the supervisor of the dargah under our family's management, a historically important place, famous among people as a spiritual centre! He was the guru there!

I was waiting for him. Would he be as rough as he was as a boy, would he have acquired a holy glow, or would he have a deceitful look on his face? I began to feel a new enthusiasm. I had a lot of faith in my ability to gauge the value of people just by looking at them. This was an opportunity to test my skill.

He arrived. A chequered panche, a full-sleeved white jubba reaching his knees, two-three silver rings with different coloured stones, a green rumaal on his head, sporting a beard and a moustache.

I did not know what to make of him at first. The scent from his attar was intense and overbearing, and spread throughout the room.

'Do you remember, Abid?' I don't know if the question in my heart reached him or not. He bent down and said, 'Assalamu alaikum, Apa.'

'Apa!' I wanted to laugh. So much propriety in just one word. But then I too was displaying so much cultured behaviour.

I replied and asked him to take a seat. He sat down. His eyes had been on the floor from the moment he entered the house. He continued to look down, and said, 'Apa, we have decided to hold the annual Syed Shah Mir Ali gandha mahotsava festival on the fifteenth of next month. You must come.'

He recited the lines like a good student who had learned a poem by heart and was now repeating it with his eyes closed. His eyes remained on the floor. I did not answer him for a long time. I thought he might look towards me at least in anticipation of my reply; I would have caught him then, immediately. Whether the naughtiness of his boyhood still remained housed in him or not. But no, he did not meet my eyes, and carefully escaped all evaluation.

Some people are like this. They turn everything upside down.

A TASTE OF HEAVEN

Shameem Banu's family found it very difficult to understand her. Saadat wondered what had made her change. An Urdu language teacher in a government secondary school, he spent all his free time analysing her behaviour; he sometimes thought that perhaps a jinn had stepped on her. Although he was not in the habit of reading, his eyes had by chance fallen on an article in a newspaper lying in the staffroom, and it seemed his attempts to solve his problem were bearing fruit at last. He decided, all by himself, that his wife was going through menopause, and that she needed his help during this time. His conclusion brought him a little relief. He learned to ignore her outbursts at home, the way she lost her temper for small-small things and screamed at the children. He had wanted a simple explanation for her behaviour; this was an easy road to walk.

The eldest of their children was Azeem. Perhaps it was because he was the oldest, or maybe it was because he was the son, but Shameem Banu had a special love for him. Saat khoon maaf, like they say — she would have forgiven him seven murders! It had become an everyday occurrence for Aseema and Sana, his two younger sisters, to complain, 'Ammi is doing partiality!' She was open about it as well. But when she got angry, and this happened often, she would weigh all three of them on the same scale, brand them all as Shaitan's group, thrash whoever she could catch hold of, and so cool her anger down.

Azeem, however, was rarely caught. Although Sana was the youngest, she was also the smartest and was able to gauge her mother's mood and vanish. Whether she was at fault or not, it was Aseema who was invariably thrashed, though she was for an odd reason willing to bear the brunt of her mother's anger. When that anger was spent, Shameem would be filled with remorse, and begin to feel immense love for the girl who suffered the worst of her bad temper. She would then buy Aseema a new dress, a new pair of chappals, maybe give her some extra pocket money or some sweet dish, in an attempt to fulfil any remaining wants her daughter had.

Their father's extraordinary patience with their mother surprised the children, and they decided that she controlled him fully. They took what Saadat and his sisters had to say about their mother and came to their own conclusions about why her behaviour had changed, and consoled and commiserated with each other.

Shameem had come into that house of three sons and three daughters as the eldest daughter-in-law, with the sky of limitless expectations in her eyes. When she dipped her hennaed palms in sandalwood paste and made an imprint on the western wall of the house, she was surprised to see small-small hands make imprints next to hers. She turned round to see her sisters-in-law, brothers-in-law, their expenses, food, clothing, a mother-in-law who was always sick and the prescribed diet she had to be cooked, her father-in-law's countless relatives and friends. Her own dreams withered away. She initially managed everything with a smile on her face, as they say. But as days passed by, her own pregnancies, and having to raise her little children in the middle of all the other weddings, pregnancies, deliveries and confinements of her husband's sisters, illnesses, and eventual deaths of her parents-in-law, brought her much irritation. Even then she had never lost her temper. A thread of hope spooled in

151

her mind that her responsibilities would reduce at least a little once her co-sisters came.

But what happened was the opposite; after the first brother-in-law's wife merrily left for Dubai with her husband within just a year of their wedding, Shameem's disappointment knew no bounds. When would she, her husband and their children ever be free from endless chores? Maybe after she died. So she began to hiss, unbashful, paying no heed to who heard her. Saadat's younger sisters and the rest of the family kept their distance.

She looked after her youngest brother-in-law Arif, orphaned after his parents' death, with much love. But after he got married, she became like a stepmother overnight. To Saadat's surprise, she told Arif and his new wife to live separately. Saadat was anguished. But would she let it go? When she raked up every issue, old and new, blamed Saadat wholeheartedly, cried and screamed and made a fuss and then banged the door to her room shut, Arif and his wife became very distressed. Poor Arif! He didn't ask why he had to leave, when it was his father's house and she could go if she wanted to. In the end we don't know what Arif and Saadat decided between themselves. Arif swallowed the embarrassment and insult he had endured in front of his wife, and within three days left the house, renting in the 2nd Cross of the same mohalla.

The Arif incident affected each member of that house differently. The three children discussed their mother's behaviour in whispers. They liked Arif Chikkappa a lot. Sana blurted out the mischievous thought in her head: 'Now after you get married, you will also have to pack your bags like this with your wife.' Azeem felt a mix of distress and fear, and did not react. He stared at her for a long time until Aseema came to his rescue.

'Say bidthu; may no one see such a terrible day,' she said, displaying wisdom far beyond her years. Azeem broke his silence and continued to whisper with them. Their paternal aunts used to explain away such things, saying, 'Poor Bhabhi! When she has high blood pressure, she behaves like this at times, but she is good at heart.' The children followed the same line of thought, saying, 'Poor Ammi! She is good . . . ' They completed the sentence, certified her heart, saw no other way but to forgive her and make up. Though they were ashamed to see Arif Chikkappa's face, they went to his house when he invited them to the milk-boiling-over ritual. Shameem Banu did not attend. Without offering a reason, she had stopped talking to Arif and his wife, and then, many days later, as casually as if nothing had happened, managed to build a good relationship once more.

Saadat, however, was deeply hurt by all this. He blamed himself a hundred and one times, accusing himself of uselessness. He rebuked himself for clinging to the excuse of her menopause and letting go of all relationships and kindness because of it. He called himself a coward for so justifying his helplessness. He suffered a great deal of shame, thinking his stature had shrunk before Arif and his wife, and saw himself unfit in his role as elder brother. In the face of his acute sorrow, he became stubborn about getting back his power and status, and decided that, as before, he would make his wife obey his every command. But then he deliberately gave up every chance he had to follow through on his decision, and felt even sorrier for himself.

By the time he understood the impossibility of tolerating her behaviour, he began to realise that some fear was stopping him from confronting her. He could not, however, identify what he was afraid of, and after his attempt at analysis failed, he built a wall of depression around himself. The day he broke those walls himself was the day he would be free of this torture. The sunshine in his life lost its warmth; he started to collapse internally.

One evening, he was about to leave for evening namaz and was looking for his cap. Usually it was kept where he could see it, but that day it must have fallen. He was getting impatient. The azaan from the masjid was about to end. He could just manage to offer namaz with the jama'at if he wore the cap and ran to the mosque. But the cap! 'Where is my cap?' he called out loudly, as if asking himself. Who was there to answer him? He still expected an answer; he would have been relieved if Shameem came out to scold him and throw his cap at him too. For all the other prayers, there was a half-hour after the call to prayer ended for people to gather and offer namaz. But there was no such time at evening prayers. People would gather quickly right after the azaan ended. If he couldn't even get a chance to pray during the holy evening hour, then . . . he was highly agitated. Shameem was sitting in front of him, her legs stretched out, immersed in something on TV.

'Will you switch that damn TV off? Can't you at least turn down the volume when the azaan is going on?' he said. 'Allah has created a special hell for you,' was the thought that came to the tip of his tongue, though he managed to stop himself from saying it. She neither turned to him nor cared. She had looked at him sympathetically during his hunt for the cap, and then turned her attention back to the TV. He wanted to lash out at her, slap her, but it was impossible. Why couldn't he do it? He was withering before some invisible fear; he was sweating profusely and about to collapse. Just as he was looking around, hoping there was at least a chair to catch him if he fainted, his invisible fear slowly came before his eyes, with a remarkable glow on her face despite her bent back, wrinkled skin, withered hands and legs and uncombed, matted hair. An elderly figure with the seragu of her white saree covering her head stepped slowly into the angry room on that dusky evening and stretched out her hand to give him his cap. He looked defeated.

Yes. For her, he tolerated all the torture Shameem Banu meted out. 'Oh Allah, what a test you are giving me!'

'Isn't this your cap? Take it and go offer namaz quickly. I have to go say my prayers too.' She held out the old cap in her right hand; on her left was a ja-namaz, as ancient as her.

'Aiyo, Ammaji, why did you take the trouble? I would have looked for it myself,' Saadat remarked, and came closer to take the old cap, faded from white to dull yellow, before putting it on. She lovingly kept a hand on his head, uttered some blessings and walked slowly back to her room.

Saadat ran to the mosque. He used to call her Ammaji a long time ago. But as his children began to grow older, they took to calling her Bi Dadi. Wonder who taught them to say that? And then everyone began to call her Bi Dadi, Saadat included. She was his aunty, his father's younger sister, who had been married off as a child. Her husband died just a month after their wedding. Someone said he had died of a snake bite, but she never found out for sure. A year after his death, she got her first period, and while there were no official restrictions in her maternal home, the family did not have a tradition of remarriage. Her body shed its layers every month and became one with the earth. Her body, her mind, her dreams, none were fulfilled. She remained an eternal virgin.

She lived like a shadow and gave shade to her elder brother's family. She managed the illness of her sister-in-law, that is, Saadat's mother, cleaning her urine and faeces, without complaint. There were times Saadat wondered whether Bi Dadi had been born to manage his mother's illness, or whether his mother saw her and then fell sick. She finished everything his mother asked her to do, and then continued to work, constantly looking for another chore. She never once looked at the pile of used dishes with disdain; she merely bent down her head and washed them. He couldn't remember a single day when that house had been empty and locked; she herself became the lock. She opened the door for him, no matter what time he knocked. When she was given a set of new clothes for Ramzan, she folded them neatly and put them away in her iron trunk. She kept the ja-namaz and the namaz chador she was given at her wedding folded on top of that trunk. Every now and then, a few jasmine flowers would blossom within the chador's folds.

She was also a skilled hand at killing insects and little creatures without mercy, and for this reason was a saviour among women and children and beloved by many. If someone shouted 'Bi Dadi' loudly, that was enough, and within an instant she would present herself, broom in hand. This way, while killing little worms and insects . . .

One day she left her broom to one side, picked up a split log of wood and killed a snake. Several men were afraid, looking at the dead snake with blood splattered all around it. Even as people were identifying the dead snake, some calling it a cobra, others saying it was a viper, she thrashed it some more, angrily shouting, 'Why do these snakes have to bite?! What is this job of killing men?' Some bystanders insisted that her eyes were full of tears as she spoke.

Shameem Banu had learned her domestic skills under the super-vision of Bi Dadi and had paid her immense respect at first. But as time passed, Shameem began to speak to her with disregard. Saadat's fear had started from there. Would Shameem chase away Bi Dadi, who had given her life to them, like she did cruelly with Arif? If she did throw her out, where would she chase her to? It was at least OK for Arif; he had a job, a wife. Who did Bi Dadi have except Saadat? If Shameem behaved like that . . . even thinking about it made him shiver. Although he consoled himself, saying, 'It is all Allah's mercy,' peace of mind had fled far away.

One day, Azeem shouted to his sister from outside. 'Hey, Sana. Sanaaaa! Where are you?'

'Coming, coming. What do you want?'

'It's OK, I don't really need you – just bring me a piece of old cloth, I want to clean my bike.'

'One minute,' she said, dashed inside for an old cloth, and gave it to him before vanishing. Azeem was unsure about the cloth he was holding. But since he was in a hurry, and too lazy to tire out his mind by thinking, he quickly wiped his bike and left, throwing the cloth near the door. When he returned in the afternoon, it did not take him long to realise that he was directly responsible for the great disaster that had transpired.

Bi Dadi and his mother were standing in the front yard. Bi Dadi, who never cried, was crying so much that her eyes were about to fall out. The old cloth he had thrown down was in her hands, and she was trying her best, with her feeble hands, to wipe away the grease stains. A distressed Shameem Banu stood near her, holding a new silk mat and trying to console her.

'Here. This is a new ja-namaz. Please take this, Bi Dadi.' Bi Dadi wiped her eyes some more and burst into tears again. 'No. I don't want this. Why does a dying woman need this?'

'Say bidthu! May it be your enemies who die. This is not just any ja-namaz. When my elder sister went to Hajj, she brought this for me. There she sprinkled the holy Zamzam water on it too. I beg you, please take it . . . please offer namaz on this.'

Azeem realised his mistake. He felt like he had been caught red-handed with stolen goods. The oil marks on the ja-namaz were telling all the stories.

He came between them, saying, 'Ammi,' and tried to speak. He got flustered under her sharp stare and became quiet. When he looked for Sana, he felt that, like always, she had anticipated disaster and vanished. Aseema was staring at him, indicating that she was willing to be the sacrificial lamb, and this confused Azeem even further.

'I don't want . . . didn't I say I don't want this? If your sister got this for you, then keep it yourself. Why are you giving it to me? My ja-namaz is enough for me.'

Shameem Banu seemed to have acquired extraordinary and surprising patience all of a sudden. 'What does it matter if you offer the namaz or I do? I don't know who did this. Maybe the children did this unknowingly. It is very old, after all.'

'Is it? Is it too old? I am also very old, isn't it?' Bi Dadi stubbornly began to pick a fight. She had never before fought with anyone. In that full house, when relatives visited, she would butcher three chickens, faithfully clean them herself and cook the meat into a fragrant saaru, and even when she didn't get a single piece of meat, she never fought about it; when she made a big vessel of payasa and didn't get a teaspoon of it to taste, she did not feel sad. During weddings, when there were countless zaratari silk sarees on display, she never desired one. Seeing her shed copious tears over a threadbare ja-namaz shocked Shameem Banu.

'No, Bi Dadi, please don't cry. Azeem did not realise that it was your ja-namaz. He is not a bad boy; please forgive him. Take this ja-namaz.' The more she begged, the more Bi Dadi's grief increased.

Shameem Banu's patience snapped. 'Che! What a headache this is. Damned ja-namaz! For the sake of an old ja-namaz you are being as stubborn as a child. Are you out of your mind?'

Just as she was shouting at Bi Dadi, Saadat came in through the front door and at the sight of the scene before him his hands and feet went cold. He thought he was witnessing what he had feared for so long. Before he could fully understand what was happening, Bi Dadi went pale and collapsed on the floor. The frail ja-namaz fell from her hands. Saadat immediately hugged her to his chest, not knowing what words to use to console her. Azeem brought a glass of water. After taking a sip or two, she stared up at Saadat intensely and asked, as if to prove a point, 'You know which ja-namaz it is, don't you?'

To be honest, he did not know. His parents got married ten years after Bi Dadi returned to her maternal home; he was his parents' sixth son. How was he to know these wedding things? But he merely nodded his head. 'My father had it brought from Gujarat for my wedding. When I went to my mother-in-law's place, the first namaz I prayed was on this ja-namaz, and then, and then—' She paused a little and continued. 'I had spread out my ja-namaz next to the window in my room for the evening prayers, when someone threw a handful of jasmine blossoms on my mat from outside. I got scared. Back then we had only chimney oil lamps. When I looked out in bewilderment, he was standing there, laughing.' She was floating away to some other world, as if she did not have any connection with the present. Her marital secrets. Oh god! Saadat had a lump in his throat. He did not say anything. Although warning bells were ringing in a corner of his heart, saying, no, no, he ignored them and looked accusingly at his wife. She remained still, as if she hadn't noticed or seen any of this from the corner of her eye.

The whole family stood still like idols, each lost in their own thoughts, feeling accused in the court of conscience. Nobody had thought that an unexpected incident could upset the whole family to this extent. Everyone was in the middle of justifying their actions to themselves. Who could say that it was wrong for Bi Dadi to have delicately washed her old ja-namaz and hung it on a wire to dry carefully so that the smell of jasmine did not fade? Responding to Azeem's urgent call, Sana's decision – that the hanging cloth was an old one and could be handed over to clean the bike – was not wrong either. That was how the piece of cloth looked. Azeem, poor fellow, was not at fault. Fearful of what curse the old woman might heap on her innocent children for desecrating the ja-namaz she had been praying on for decades, the protective mother in Shameem Banu had lost her temper. So, unable to assign blame, everyone remained upset about what happened.

Saadat, however, did not bother with any of these details and imagined what he wanted about his wife. His worry that his fear was coming true was followed by anxiety over Bi Dadi's future life. He had managed to console her a little and walked her slowly to her room. He held on to her hand for a long time, even after she had lain down on her bed. Not knowing what to do with the ja-namaz, Shameem Banu washed the mat some more to try to remove all its stains, hung it on a wire to dry, and walked inside.

There was no indication that the ja-namaz incident would be solved easily any time soon. Instead it began to take a strange turn. Bi Dadi's entire daily routine changed. She did not again touch the ja-namaz that was drying on the wire outside. It remained there, letting itself catch the sun. For a few days Bi Dadi did not offer namaz, though she had never before missed a prayer. When it was close to prayer time, Shameem left spare prayer mats where Bi Dadi could see them, but Bi Dadi didn't even glance in their direction.

The always-cheerful Bi Dadi began to cry constantly. There were no times, rhymes or reasons, rules or regulations for her grief. Her spontaneous crying did not have any impact on the children. But it affected Shameem Banu and Saadat immensely. He had decided that his wife was the sole reason for Bi Dadi's sadness and suffered all the more thinking there was nothing he could do to make it better. He became a slave to dangerous levels of silence, and began to pay more attention to Bi Dadi, determined to repair all mistakes.

Shameem Banu got very irritated with Bi Dadi's tears. There were bound to be some highs and lows in a family; what was the need to make it a big deal, she wondered. Although she had given her a new ja-namaz, Bi Dadi hadn't accepted it and was being stubborn. Shameem decided that her husband was furthering Bi Dadi's stubbornness and stopped talking to him. What did it matter which ja-namaz it was? Offering namaz was the main thing. Shameem was boiling in frustration that the old woman had stopped doing that, and she felt sad and anxious about any curse she might have put on her son. She began to offer namaz at all the proper times, praying for her son's protection. Once the morning namaz was over, she recited the Surah Yasin, blew over half a cup of pure water and began to make her son drink it. She looked for the poorest among their relatives and distributed rice, wheat, lentils, eggs and new clothes. She had a black chicken brought in, circled it over Azeem's head without his knowledge, and had it fly off the roof of their house to ward off the evil eye. Still unsatisfied, she fasted for three days and prayed for her son's welfare.

Bi Dadi behaved as if none of this concerned her and kept up her programme of crying continuously. Who knows what all pains she was crying away; denial built up over many years must have been frozen in her. Every now and then she let out a deep sigh, and was even beginning to address Allah directly: 'Allah, Allah, you must look after me,' she would utter. Shameem Banu lost the last thread of her patience at this.

No matter how hard the children tried, they couldn't extinguish Bi Dadi's sadness. Azeem plotted with his sisters and took that ja-namaz to the dry cleaners. All the stains were removed, but it became even more threadbare. He got scared and hung it back on the wire, not wanting anything more to do with it.

This way, for about fifteen or twenty days, Saadat's family was caught in a ja-namaz whirlpool. Then one day, Aseema placed a plate of food and a glass of water in front of Bi Dadi and stood there, urging her to eat. Bi Dadi remained lost in her own world. When Aseema broke off a piece of dosè and put it in the old woman's mouth, she not only spat it out, thoo thoo, but also cried again: 'Allah, Allah, you must look after me.' Shameem Banu, who was busy in the kitchen, got irritated. She rushed in with Bi Dadi's trunk in one hand and dragged her to the door. Aseema got between them and begged, 'Ammi, Ammi, no, let her be!' Shameem ignored her and called to an auto plying on the road, made Bi Dadi climb in with her trunk, placed some money in the auto driver's hand and told him to drop her off at Arif's house before storming back in.

The auto driver was familiar with the family; he took one look at Shameem's angry face and drove to Arif's. Even though she had passed off Bi Dadi to her brother-in-law, peace eluded Shameem. She began to snap at her children without reason. Aseema willingly bore the brunt of her anger as always but she did not get repentance gifts like she used to. Although the children were being punished more than ever before, they were also determined to do something about the situation. Whenever they had time they went to Arif's house and tried to talk to Bi Dadi. They all decided that Bi Dadi was doing a little better there. They noticed that she was eating with Arif and offering namaz at all the designated times like before.

After about fifteen days Azeem sat Bi Dadi in an autorickshaw and brought her home. Shameem Banu glared but did not say a word. Azeem spotted a brief look of peace on his mother's face and heaved a sigh of relief, thinking he was saved from her anger. He shifted Bi Dadi and her trunk into one of the inner rooms, but unfortunately her habits began to change again. After sitting for the morning namaz, she would remain sitting there till noon. She could no longer remember which namaz she was reading, which of the five prayers it was, or which surah she was reciting. Right after having food, she began to complain directly to Allah, saying, 'Allah, Allah, they have not given me food! You have to look after me now . . . ' The problems started again.

Azeem decided that he had to find a solution, that doing nothing was no longer an option. Shameem Banu had gone out. Saadat, as usual, was out of the house too. Azeem called his two sisters for a meeting. Sana, as usual, began to create mischief. What was a meeting without food? She blackmailed him, claiming she would attend the meeting only if he brought her pani puri from the vendor at the corner of the street, and if not she would report this meeting in detail to their mother. Azeem had to pause the meeting before it had even begun, go out and come back with chicken kebabs and a bottle of Pepsi. Sana was happy. By the time Aseema passed the plate of kebabs to her siblings and was about to eat a piece, Bi Dadi came into the room. Azeem jokingly said, 'Oho! How can we have a meeting without the president?' and shifted a little to make her sit next to him. Wondering whether to give Bi Dadi a piece of chicken, he looked up at Aseema. Sana, noticing their wordless communication, gave a glass of the bubbly drink to Bi Dadi without any forewarning and encouraged her to drink it. Everyone looked on as Bi Dadi placed the glass to her lips and took a sip. She drank the whole glass in one long gulp.

Running her tongue over her lips, she glanced at Azeem's glass and asked, 'What is that?' Before he could answer, Sana, smiling mischievously said 'It has gone to her head already! That is aab-e-kausar,' and burst out laughing. The other two did not like her joke one bit. Bi Dadi's face beamed and she asked, 'Aab-e-kausar? Really? Isn't that only in heaven?'

'Yes, yes, this is the drink of heaven. Only the fortunate get to drink it. You are now in heaven. We are the houris, ready to serve you,' Sana answered, theatrically. Bi Dadi began to worry.

'If I am in heaven, then where is he?' she asked. Sana did not stop her naughtiness. Instead she tore off the string of jasmine flowers from her hair, went behind Bi Dadi and threw it into her lap, replying, 'See, see, he is right behind you, he is throwing jasmine flowers at you. But you must not turn back and look.' Bi Dadi was ecstatic. She did not turn back and hesitantly touched the jasmine flowers in her lap. After a while she said, 'I want aab-e-kausar.' Watching the two of them, Azeem neither stopped Sana nor got angry with her. He could not decide whether the situation that seemed to be bringing so much joy to Bi Dadi was really making her happy, or whether she was, like Sana, acting; he gave his glass to her. She happily put the glass to her lips.

The moment the doorbell rang, Aseema took the plates and glasses and ran into the kitchen. They wiped their hands and mouths and sat still. Even Azeem glanced at the door cautiously. Shameem Banu came inside the house, and their drama ended.

After drinking the aab-e-kausar, many of Bi Dadi's problems vanished. What issues can the residents of heaven have? She saw her husband around her, felt him, and found peace in her heaven at home. Once she drank that liquid, she never returned from her heavenly world. Even though there was no alcohol in it, Sana helplessly wondered how it had managed to intoxicate Bi Dadi. Every now and then, when Bi Dadi asked, 'Where is my houri?' and looked around, Shameem Banu did not know who she was searching for. But when she stepped out on some work, Sana would pretend to be a houri. It was mandatory to wear a sequined saree when she played the angel because that was how Bi Dadi imagined angels to look. If she didn't dress the part, Bi Dadi would feel sick and get agitated.

Between the experience of her special drink in heaven and her own personal houri, Bi Dadi lost all connection to this world and lived peacefully in her husband's company. Even though Shameem Banu felt agonised when she saw Bi Dadi talk and laugh to herself, she was relieved there were no other problems. Never again did she try to send her to Arif's house. Saadat was also peaceful, knowing that his wife would never again throw Bi Dadi out.

It was Azeem who had problems now. He must continue the heaven drama, which had started without forewarning. Anger, tears and stubbornness had left Bi Dadi. But still she did not touch food. Except for aab-e-kausar, she seemed to need no other sustenance. Azeem felt defeated trying to supply her with aab-e-kausar. She began to demand the nectar of heaven whenever she felt like it. If he gave her coconut water, juice or any other drink, she threw it away without hesitation. Azeem's pocket money was spent entirely on the drink her tongue had got used to and which made her happy. She talked about aab-e-kausar relentlessly, even in front of Saadat and Shameem Banu. Both of them decided that she had lost her mind.

Stuck in that mess, Azeem borrowed money from his friends. He got fake accounts added to the family's tab at the provision store. In the end, unable to manage Bi Dadi's demands, he went and confessed to Arif. His uncle burst out laughing, and even though he slapped Azeem's back a couple of times in mock anger, he arranged for him to get a bottle of the bubbly drink every day. Because of the heavenly drink, there seemed to be some peace and quiet in the house.

Azeem was sick with worry, wondering what to do if Bi Dadi died from only drinking Pepsi without eating any food. But Bi Dadi has been living for the last six months, as if to ease his fear. Shameem Banu is endlessly surprised. She wonders how this old woman is living on no food and just water. Trying to forget the ja-namaz incident, Saadat thinks about his wife and tells himself, 'Poor Shameem is a good woman. She behaves like this at times when the menopause jinn steps on her,' thus drawing the conclusion convenient for him. Only Azeem and Arif sometimes wish for Bi Dadi's death, though they pray it shouldn't be from malnutrition. Only if it is a natural death will they be spared the guilt of becoming her murderers. Meanwhile, Bi Dadi continues to live in the heaven she achieved so effortlessly, free from all worry, in the company of her long-lost husband.

THE SHROUD

On days when it was impossible for Shaziya to wake up in time for the dawn namaz, she would blame it on her high blood pressure, and had a habit of saying she had no peace because of those damn tablets.

Her mother used to say, 'All this is Shaitan's game. Shaitan comes early in the morning, presses your legs, drapes a blanket around you, pats you back to sleep and stops you from offering namaz. You must kick him away and practise waking up at the right time to pray.' The idea of Shaitan being her personal servant and pressing her legs seemed romantic to Shaziya, and so she'd pretend to kick him a few times, enjoying the thought. It became a habit for her to wake up late and blame Shaitan for it.

She was deep asleep that day too, and it was well past dawn. She woke up with a start and looked down at herself, unsure of where she was, though she touched her husband when she stretched her hand to the side. It was only when she noticed that her head was on her own pillow, that her imported blanket was draped around her body, that she realised she was in her own room in her own house. This made her both happy and content, to wake up in a familiar environment.

But contentment did not last long. She heard someone crying outside and by the time she slowly got up and went to the door, she heard her son Farman speaking. She hurriedly came out to the veranda and saw Altaf standing there, looking distraught. Farman was consoling him. 'What has happened has happened,' he said. 'All this is in nobody's hands. Don't worry, go home. I will get everything to your house once Ammi wakes up. She is asleep now, let me not wake her up, she is not very well. The doctor has told her to get lots of rest.'

'But Bhaiyya, the jama'at has decided that the burial will be tonight at five. There is no one else we are waiting for. That's why the ghusal and other rituals must be done quickly,' Altaf repeated. Farman lost his temper and said, 'Look, you did not give me any kafan for safekeeping. It is already six-seven years since Ammi returned from Hajj. Why didn't Yaseen Bua take her shroud from Ammi all these years ago? Or maybe she took it and kept it somewhere. Search the house once again and see.'

Shaziya felt shocked as she came and stood behind her son. 'What is happening here?' she called. 'Farman, who are you speaking with, beta?' Farman turned towards his mother; impatience had pressed itself on his face. He thought to himself, 'These women cannot be quiet, eat, dress up and mind their own business. If they don't get involved in one thing or the other, it is as if their food won't be digested.' But he did not express his disapproval, and instead said, 'Go sleep, Ammi. Why did you get up and come? Altaf is here. He says he is Yaseen Bua's son; he is asking about some kafan.'

She felt as if she had been struck by a thousand bolts of lightning. She anxiously rushed forward, looking at the young man questioningly, and asked in an angered tone: 'What is all this ruckus you are creating first thing in the morning? Where will the kafan run away to? Don't you have the sense to know whose house you should go to and when?' It became clear to her that Farman did not like all this. Altaf lowered his voice and stared back, distressed, and said, 'Chikkamma, Ammi died this morning, around the time of the dawn namaz. That is why I came to ask for the kafan.' The moment she heard the news, Shaziya collapsed inwardly. Unable to control herself, she sat down with a thud on a chair nearby. The unimaginable, the impossible had happened. How to face it now? How to fix it? These thoughts did not remain within her control. She was devastated. 'Oh God, what has ended up happening,' she lamented.

Even though she didn't want it to, her mind raced back. There was a function in her house that day. Her family and friends had gathered in large numbers. Shaziya and her husband Subhan were going on Hajj. They had already visited most of their closest relatives and friends. They had hugged everyone and requested that any kaha-suna, any hurt they might have caused, any complaints their loved ones might have, any rumours the couple might have unwittingly spread be forgiven. These relatives had also laid out feasts for the couple, given them both whatever clothes and gifts they could afford, assured them of their forgiveness and requested that Shaziya and Subhan forgive any transgressions too. Content that their mistakes were mutually forgiven and the protocol followed, their closest family and friends had sent them off with light hearts.

Even so, with a week left before their pilgrimage, there were still many relatives to meet. The husband and wife called up their family living in distant places and asked them for forgiveness for any mistakes they might have committed. Subhan, the owner of an extended business enterprise, and Shaziya, the mistress of a spacious bungalow, did not have the time to meet all their family and friends individually before leaving. That was why they had organised a feast to bring everyone together. The ritual of asking for mutual forgiveness continued there too.

The one who came, uninvited yet without any arrogance or ill will in her heart, was Yaseen Bua. Her husband had given her two children within three years of marriage and then walked away without a backward glance. He used to work as a loader at the APMC yard, and one day, while carrying a load, he died of a heart attack. After his death she had not observed iddat. A very young woman back then, she wore a scarf around her head and started washing vessels in the front yards of several houses, sweeping and cleaning, a loner amidst weddings, festivals, ceremonies, birthdays, and bearing the chaos and happiness of such events in these houses to fill the empty stomachs of her little children. During the iddat, she did not sit with her head covered in a room, praying for her departed husband and observing the mandatory period of mourning. Many tongues wagged. Despite the mud-slinging, however, the welfare and the hungry stomachs of her children were more important to her. Thanks to her hard work, her children built their lives. Having studied a little, her daughter taught the Qur'an to girls and earned a few rupees. Yaseen Bua added this money to what she had managed to save herself, got her daughter married off and lived with her son, an auto driver. When her bones started making creaky lata-lata sounds, when the veins in her hands began to swell as age advanced, she cut back on working for others.

She had a great wish to get her son married. But more than that, another desire had overtaken her, her heart and her body and her soul. All day long she became a kite around the flames of desire. Her habit of saving every single paise indicated not a miserly nature, but the anxiety of an unsecure future. When she took a little money out from the bundle that she had saved for her son's wedding to buy herself a shroud, she began to feel as if she had stolen it from someone else. She could not shake off her immense guilt, she became restless, and for three days tied the money to her seragu and protected it. But even her maternal instincts could not defeat the intensity of her private dream. A strange stubbornness to get her way doubled Yaseen Bua's enthusiasm. She held on tightly to the bundle at the end of her saree and walked swiftly towards Shaziya's house. There were a lot of people, celebrations, festivities under way there . . .

She had no invitation. There was no one to welcome her, saying, 'Oh, you have come!' Neither was there anyone to say, 'Come, eat,' or to show her any hospitality. She had never in her life known what it meant to be honoured and held in esteem. She did not recognise disrespect either. She worked as much as she could. Her hands nearly fell off washing the porcelain dinner plates. The grease of biriyani doesn't wash off so easily now, does it? After everyone had eaten, she sat down on the cement in the front yard and had a few mouthfuls. All her attention was on Shaziya. 'A lucky woman, a fortunate woman,' she repeated to herself. She wondered when Shaziya would be free, and how she could express her desire, all the while patiently observing everything Shaziya was doing.

When would Shaziya find some free time? She was exhausted from receiving wishes and gifts from her innumerable relatives and friends. Some people ended up talking about their own life problems when they hugged and wished her well, and asked her to say duas for them during Hajj. 'Shaziya Apa, I cannot find a suitable groom for my youngest daughter. Please say a dua for her,' one requested. Another asked, 'My sister-in-law is suffering from cancer. Please pray that she recovers soon.' 'My son is not able to find a job. He is suffering a lot. Please say a dua for him.' The list of demands grew longer. Shaziya kept replying with a smile, 'Inshallah, I will pray for them,' and although she was getting tired, she did not show it and happily sent everyone off. Although they had organised the feast for lunch, people kept coming by well into the evening. Yaseen Bua kept on washing vessels, cleaning the plates, sweeping, waiting her turn.

At around eleven o'clock at night, when a tired Shaziya finally sat on the sofa and stretched her legs out on the soft carpet, she saw Yaseen Bua's shadow near the living room door. Bua was fretting, 'Aiyoo poor thing. How tired this soul is,' and felt bad for Shaziya. She wiped both her hands on her seragu and tiptoed towards her, ensuring she did not set her dirty and cracked heels down on the precious carpet. 'When did you come, Bua?' Shaziya asked, reluctantly.

Immensely happy to have finally met with Shaziya, she replied, 'I came a long time ago, my dear.' 'Oh, is it? I've barely seen you all evening,' Shaziya said, and in a softer tone enquired, 'Did you eat?' 'Yes, taayi. My life is still holding on to itself only because of the rice from your house. May everything you touch turn into gold. May your house prosper.' Shaziya felt gratified. 'It is already so late, Bua. How will you get home?' To this very feminine of concerns, she replied, 'Altaf said he will take me home in his auto. I will leave the moment he comes.' Shaziya had noticed Yaseen Bua occupied with some work or other the whole day. So she dragged her feet heavily to her room and brought out some money. 'Take this, Bua, some money for your expenses. We are leaving for Hajj in three days, and will come back after forty-five days. May Allah accept our Hajj. Please say a dua for us.'

She clasped both Bua's hands in hers and placed the money in them. Yaseen Bua was overwhelmed. Her eyes welled up to see Shaziya being so kind and friendly with even a hakir-fakir like her. She did not take the money from Shaziya. Instead, she removed the two-three knots at the end of her saree and pulled out some crumpled notes. Extending her hands towards Shaziya, she pleaded: 'My avva, there is six thousand rupees here. You are anyway going to Hajj. Please bring me a kafan from there after dipping it in the holy Zamzam water. At least I might go to heaven because of that holy shroud.'

For a moment Shaziya did not know what to say. It didn't seem like a difficult task at the time. 'Aiyoo, it is one kafan after all. I can bring it for her even if it costs a little more money,' she thought to herself, finding herself taken in by the spontaneity of that situation. She did not think twice and agreed.

It was when the notes passed from Bua's hands into her own that Shaziya understood. Money from the pockets of poor people was, just like them, broken, shattered, crumpled, wrinkly, diminished in essence and form. She had at times felt that even if the poor were given crisp notes, the money would turn into something strange and ugly; now she became sure of it. 'OK, Bua, you go and come,' she said, and sent her off. Shaziya immediately went to the en-suite bathroom, placed the money on top of the sink, and washed her hands thoroughly with a disinfecting soap before lying down on her bed.

Shaziya did not remember if she picked up the money Yaseen Bua had given her from the sink or not. Everyone boarded a morning flight arranged by the Hajj Committee and reached Madina. With the new environment, visits to religious places, and the compulsory forty namaz over their eight-day stay, she did not notice the time passing. Subhan had forbidden her from shopping. Yet what did she care about restrictions? She believed that rules were meant to be broken, and she did what she wanted without hesitation. This situation was no different.

Subhan brought up the topic of niyyat. Before they left for Hajj, they had set intentions for the pilgrimage and for prayers. He told her that she could do her shopping after Hajj, and made her believe that any shopping done during would spoil the niyyat they had set. When they left Madina for Mecca, it was again a new experience for Shaziya. She had forgotten her village and her house in the middle of all this. Her stay at Mecca was unforgettable. India's Hajj Committee had rented out several buildings. Pilgrims were allotted rooms depending on the rent money they had paid in instalments. For two rooms there was one shared bathroom, along with one small shared kitchen, a gas cylinder and a stove, a fridge, a washing machine and other facilities for the residents. Since four members of Shaziya's maternal family had travelled together, they had been allocated a large room. As usual, the women in the group looked after the cooking. Most of their time was spent in namaz, in circling the Ka'aba, in prayers and other religious activities. Visiting the cave of Hira, where the Prophet received his first revelations, and other historically significant mosques and offering namaz at the determined times kept them all occupied. The Saudi government, along with owners of large businesses and other donors, distributed food packets, juice and water bottles from huge trucks to pilgrims after namaz. Since Hajj pilgrims were the guests of Allah, they believed that treating the pilgrims well would make Allah happy. Thus, everyone behaved as if hospitality was the main aim in life.

Shaziya and her group were making arrangements to finish the rest of the Hajj rituals. One afternoon, she came back from the Ka'aba after offering namaz. Her eyes shut involuntarily, perhaps because of the hot sun, or maybe it was post-meal lethargy. When she woke up from her short nap, she felt a little refreshed. Soon the group had to go to Masjid al-Haram for the Asr namaz. When she went to the bathroom to perform wudu, she saw something that gave her pause: Zainab from the room next door was pouring water from their drinking water dispenser into a ten-litre bucket. Shaziya was surprised, and asked, 'Zainab, what are you doing?'

Zainab looked around her and said, 'I have to wash the kafan.'

'What did you say?' Shaziya asked, her anger rising. 'You are stealing drinking water. Is this fair? You have not let go of your cheap behaviour even during Hajj.' She started shouting and Zainab quickly ran into her room with the bucket, slamming the door shut. Shaziya realised what was going on. The Saudi government was responsible for supplying drinking water to the pilgrims. The water companies did not bring it in huge plastic tubs. Instead, they would load tankers with Zamzam water from the well inside the Kaaba complex, and use that to fill up the dispenser shared by the two rooms. It held ten to fifteen litres, and was refilled at around three o'clock every afternoon. Shaziya rarely got drinking water from it. Most nights Subhan would buy a five-litre bottle for their use on his way back from namaz.

Shaziya was furious. Zainab's feeble answer only made her feel like her body was on fire. Disillusioned by her audacity, she wondered how many shrouds Zainab had soaked in the stolen drinking water. Ya Allah! Was she going to make her entire family lie in Zamzam-soaked kafans? Shaziya imagined all this, and Subhan, who upon hearing his wife's loud voice had come running out of the room, arrived to see her hooting with laughter. Unsure whether he had imagined her shouting just a moment ago, he asked his wife, 'What is it, Shaziya? What is making you laugh so much?' Continuing to laugh, she told him what had happened, and said, 'Look at this, rii, these people cannot understand the importance of Hajj. They come here and cheat even for little things like this.' He smiled slightly and replied, 'Did you get to know this only today? I noticed it the day we got here. But I didn't get angry and pick a fight like you. This is why I started buying water for our use. Let it go. It is not something to fight over.'

Shaziya suddenly remembered Bua's kafan. 'And then, rii, look here, we have to buy a kafan for Yaseen Bua. Let's do that when we return from the evening namaz,' she said, remembering her promise, and deciding to honour it right away. He nodded, and got ready hurriedly, for it was getting late. As they had anticipated, al-Haram was busy by the time they reached it, the women and men gathered separately according to practice. They were all standing between the pillars of the mosque, hands folded reverentially, heads bent. Since they were late, Shaziya and Subhan stood next to each other in the mosque's extensive yard, which filled up very quickly with other latecomers. It was sunny, and the huge umbrellas programmed to open automatically when the sun was out had spread their wings wide to provide shade. As the sun went down, the wings folded in to look like pillars – Shaziya always found them a fascinating sight.

After the Isha namaz, they walked back from the Ka'aba complex. With lakhs and lakhs of people walking on the main road and the side streets, Subhan could not figure out where they might find a kafan shop for Shaziya to buy one for Yaseen Bua. He walked on, holding his wife's hand tightly, worried about having to look for her amidst all the people should she get lost. He had made a habit of holding hands with her, or wrapping his arm around her waist, without any shyness or hesitation. He had to walk a little slower and match his stride to his wife's saunter. Before pulling her in, he stood before each shop to first confirm that they sold kafans. Yet, while looking for kafans, a carpet shop stole all of Shaziya's attention. She was so taken in by the wares, it looked like she would never leave. She found the beauty, the designs, the colours, the weaving at the centre very attractive. Without asking her husband she began to bargain over the price of one, and Subhan's plan to stop her from shopping crumbled. The fact that her niyyat would be ruined, that her intentions would now be in doubt, were emotional matters that flew out with the wind. Nor was she moved by his promise that she could shop as much as she wanted once the Hajj rituals were complete. He tried his best to get her out of that shop, but all his efforts were in vain.

Unmindful of everything and everyone, she was lost in the Turkish carpet she had chosen. Defeated, Subhan whispered to the shop assistant, 'Can we get kafans here?' The assistant instantly brought out a shroud, wrapped in plastic and heavy as a corpse. Subhan tried his best to catch Shaziya's attention. She held on to the carpet firmly, and tried to lift the kafan with her left hand. 'Aiyyappaa, how heavy this is! How can we take this and go back?' she said, dismissing the matter in an instant, and returning her attention to the carpet.

Finally, her shopping was over. Subhan counted out notes from his pocket and walked out, placing the carpet the shopkeeper had packed on his shoulder. They could not expect to find an autorickshaw or a coolie there, so he lugged the carpet himself, and although he hoped no one would see him he kept coming across people he knew. Midway, Shaziya also felt bad and tenderly asked, 'It is not too heavy, is it, rii?' He did not utter a word. He was furious enough to beat her senseless, but he very patiently dumped the devil-carpet in a corner of their room and let out a sigh. Under any other circumstance, he would have at least glared in anger, maybe scolded her too. But since this was Hajj, and since the others in the room were all her relatives, he calmed himself.

Their Hajj pilgrimage ended. Although they worried over mistakes made here and there, they were both satisfied. Once they returned from Mina, Shaziya took to her bed, which was cause for some anxiety. Her blood pressure had shot up, and she had to be admitted to the hospital for two days. It was only after her discharge and a day of rest that her blood pressure came under control. More than anything, however, she was annoyed about wasting her shopping time. She insisted her health was fine, fine, in front of Subhan, and soon began to feel better. He thought of various strategies to put off the shopping. He was not worried about money, but having seen the problems that excess luggage can lead to in flights, he did not want to fall into that trap. But neither did he want to disappoint her, or make her blood pressure shoot up again uncontrollably, so all his plans to curtail her shopping foundered. There was no one to stop Shaziya.

While rushing about on her shopping spree, thoughts of Yaseen Bua and her kafan passed regularly through Shaziya's mind in flashes, coming and going, until eventually they began to hide and she soon forgot about the matter completely. In this magical place, to think of a depressing, heavy object like a kafan taking up so much space . . . oh God . . . can't one get it in India also? Won't we get it in our village also? I can say that I couldn't find it in Mecca. Ahm! Can I tell such lies the moment I return from Hajj? She said, 'Tauba, tauba,' lightly hitting her cheeks. She said goodbye to lies. She had not expected Yaseen Bua's desire to end up being such a bother.

Now, hearing of Yaseen Bua's death, Shaziya was distraught, thinking about the consequences of that unfulfilled wish. Aiyoo, if she had known, she would have kept her word, even if she had had to face some difficulties as a result, she agonised.

When they had returned, she had bought so much stuff that her excess had to be distributed among the baggage of others in their group. By the time he managed it, Subhan was exhausted. Then there were the five-litre cans of Zamzam water to distribute to everyone, several kilos of dates, and weren't all these things heavy too? All she had done, wearing her burkha, was hold on to her handbag and run to her husband for every little thing, which only made him more irritated. Finally, after a great deal of trouble, they'd managed to load all their bags, and themselves, on the flight.

Even a month after their return, Shaziya had not finished distributing everything to everyone. For the first three days, she couldn't get out of bed because of ill health and jet lag. After that there was the unpacking. Then she made arrangements to send the gold and other expensive gifts she had bought for her nearest and dearest ones. She unrolled the precious carpet and felt happy. She did not even notice Subhan's lack of reaction; he had just walked away, irritated. Then she distributed clothes, toys, etc. to everyone she had bought them for. A few of her closest friends and some close relatives had told her that they wanted burkhas with this particular design and kasuti work, in these particular colours, cut in such style with such and such embroidery. Some had given her money. For others, she sent the burkhas as gifts, out of a sense of obligation. For everyone else, she dispatched one ja-namaz, prayer beads, a fistful of dates and a bottle of Zamzam water. Although she didn't do everything herself, she had to supervise it, and the whole task tired her. Over a month had passed by the time she finished.

There is a belief that those who return from Hajj embody immense positive and spiritual energies. In order to ensure that these energies are not wasted and instead are used to offer prayers to Allah, Muslims stay at home for a period of about forty days, observing this practice strictly, like a vow. Shaziya observed this too. As was her habit, Yaseen Bua came to the house a few times, and returned without announcing her presence. Each time Shaziya was either asleep, or was resting, or doing namaz, else was occupied with some important work: these were the messages given to Yaseen Bua, who was in tears. On one hand, she was very impatient to see her kafan. On the other hand, she was eager to stand close to the Hajj-returned Shaziya, to take her hands in her own rough ones, to clasp them. She waited and waited, in the hope that Shaziya might have brought some gift for her.

Finally, Shaziya made an appearance, having borne witness to Bua's excruciating period of waiting. She had just had a bath, and her hair was still half wet. When she came out wearing a grand sky-blue churidhar set, fashionably draping a matching kasuti-embroidered dupatta on her head, Yaseen Bua could have burst with happiness. Her joy knew no bounds when she ran and pressed Shaziya's hands to her eyes. Touching the hands of a Hajjin made her feel as if she too had become spiritually pure, and she got goosebumps on her arms. Shaziya freed her hands and made small talk. 'How are you, Bua?' She swiftly went into her room to get a ja-namaz and prayer beads and gave it to her: 'Take it, this is for you.' What Yaseen Bua wanted to see was not there. That was the moment her desire to journey towards Allah wrapped in a Zamzam water-soaked kafan was going to be fulfilled. She did not stretch out her hands to take her gifts, but only looked at Shaziya in disbelief, blinded for a moment by disappointment. Drawing on some internal courage, she addressed Shaziya, speaking very clearly in a firm tone: 'I don't want these. Give me my kafan.' Not expecting this, Shaziya got very angry. Without bothering to hide it, she scolded Bua in a loud voice, 'Che! Does anyone say no to a prayer mat?' But Bua did not budge an inch. She stood her ground. 'I still have the ja-namaz that your mother-in-law gave me after she returned from Hajj. I offer namaz on it when I get time. Where will I keep such a new and beautiful ja-namaz? How much longer do I have to live? How many more namaz will I offer? Society is telling me to go, and the forest is calling me to come and retire. All I want is the kafan.'

Shaziya had never seen Yaseen Bua like this before. Bending at the waist in reverence while walking, Bua would praise Shaziya to the skies every other minute, cracking her knuckles to remove any evil eye on her beauty, always wishing her well, *May Allah give you a long life, give you wealth. May your family be well, may your marital status be safe. May Allah give you a coral house in heaven.* Where was the Bua who always showered her with blessings, always saying duas for her? Who was this Bua who was standing so stiffly?

Shaziya's anger bubbled and flowed over. She forgot that she had only recently returned from Hajj. 'What kafan, which kafan after falling down dead? Someone or other will put you in a kafan. Why make such a fuss? What has happened to you, Bua? Have you lost your mind? How much money did you give me? I will throw ten times that at your face. Wait, and hereafter don't show your face to me again,' she screamed, and angrily rushed to her room. When she came out holding two five-hundred-rupee notes, she could not see Yaseen Bua anywhere. Given her temper, she was unlikely to let Bua go so easily. She hurried into the kitchen. She went to the backyard. She peeped into the gully nearby, but no matter where she looked, she couldn't see Bua anywhere. Thinking 'Let her go to hell,' she dumped the notes on the teapoy and lay down on the sofa. As Shaziya had wanted, Yaseen Bua did not come into her sight again. Thinking it was good riddance, she relaxed into a sense of peace and contentment. But how could Bua do this? The question rose up in her mind now and then and raked up the anger hidden in her memory. But what could she do when Bua would not show her face? Let her go? Maybe she would come by for Ramzan or Bakrid to beg. She hoped that Bua, who would bend her back and become small enough to fit inside a fist, would come by during Ramzan. But Bua's self-respect was not to be underestimated. She had been so eager for one look at her kafan, for one touch, like a bride awaiting her nikah gift. The way Shaziya, decked up in jewellery and grand clothes, had treated her like a lowly destitute had left a permanent scar in her heart.

Even in her wildest dreams, she had not thought that Bua would haunt her after death. She collapsed under the weight of sudden anguish. What must she do? What must she not do? Even if Bua asked for a kafan costing one lakh rupees, Shaziya was ready to give it to her, but a kafan from Mecca that had been soaked in holy Zamzam water, ya Allah, what to do? She agonised over how to rectify her mistake, what shall I do, what shall I do, holding her mobile phone anxiously and hurrying upstairs to take refuge in a corner of an empty room. Whether it was her body temperature rising, or whether she was shivering, or why she was sweating, she didn't know. How unfortunate. If this poor woman were to hold out her seragu and beg Allah for justice on Judgement Day, even if I poured out all my good deeds, I will still be at fault, Shaziya thought, alarmed. It became clear to her that she was poorer than Bua, more unfortunate too.

That kafan had been the dead woman's last wish. Otherwise why would her son come looking for it? Why would he beg for it on his dead mother's behalf? He spoke softly, but it was evident that he was determined to fulfil her last desire. How could she get out of this? A shiver ran down her spine. If he did not agree to use any other kafan, her burial would not take place that day. The jama'at would call her husband and son to the masjid and question them. The thought of them standing with their hands folded and heads bent frightened her. Farman would certainly not let her off. He was as capable of cruelly belittling her as he was of loving her. Her thoughts flew back and forth and fluttered around like a kite. She sat and cried till it felt like her heart would burst with sorrow, her cries coming out in gasps. Did she feel light after crying so much? No. Intense sorrow stuck in her throat; even to her enemies, she did not wish God to give such agony. She began to struggle to take breath.

A ray of hope arose, after she had spent one-two hours sitting and crying alone. She could hear Subhan's voice from downstairs. He was calling for her loudly. 'Shaziya, Shaziya, where are my clothes? Where is my pen? Is my breakfast ready?' Although she heard him, her voice refused to come out. But Saba answered him straight away. Coming out of her room, she said, 'Abbaji, Ammi is not at home. News came early in the morning that someone had died. She must have gone there.'

'What? Who died? Who told you?' he asked.

'Farman told me, and went out without having breakfast or drinking tea. Ammi must have gone with him too,' she suggested. Shaziya let out a deep sigh of relief. No matter how terrible Saba was – being the daughter-in-law, she had all the cunningness that came with the role – Shaziya felt a little softness for her after that. She was arranging chapattis and palya for Subhan in porcelain vessels on the dining table, serving him food made by the cook. After a while, she heard Subhan's car drive to the gate and then beyond the compound wall. There was no use crying any more. Now she felt she had to try and do something.

Shaziya had not shed this many tears when other people had died, not even her own father. Then again, on those occasions there were innumerable people around to make her drink water, to wipe her tears away with cotton dipped in rose water, to soothe her back, to hug her to their chests and console her, friends and relatives falling over each other to help. Surrounded by all that, her sorrow was manageable. Having to hide in a corner of the house, however, alone like an orphan – this was something she had brought upon herself. She must get out of it now. Having made a decision, she swiftly began calling her relatives and friends.

'I'm looking for a kafan that has been soaked in Zamzam water—' Her query would not even be complete when they would reply, 'Haam . . . is it Shaziya? No, we don't have a kafan at home. Our mother brought one when she went on Hajj, but we gave it to whoever had asked for it and finished the job.' Another reacted, 'What, you want a kafan?' Laughter. 'We don't keep kafans in our house. We don't make promises to anyone about bringing a kafan. That is a bothersome task.' Yet another responded, 'What is the need for a kafan from there? So what if the kafan is from here? It is only according to our deeds that we reap benefits in the afterlife, isn't it?'

After hearing no from everyone, Shaziya called Saba's mother, though she did not want to, though her heart was not OK with it. Once the formalities of hello . . . hello . . . were over, she put her dignity and self-respect aside and came to the point. 'Might you have a kafan brought from Mecca with you?' Saba's mother did not like Shaziya very much. According to Saba's regular dispatches, Shaziya was a muttering demon, a cruel woman who kept a sharp eye on her daughter-in-law, a witch who gave her too much grief, a python in the way of her peace. Given all this, Saba's mother was willing to arrange for a kafan at any cost – provided it was meant for Shaziya herself. She asked, 'Do you want the kafan?' and paused for a few seconds to let the emphasis sink in. 'But why do you want it?' she asked. Her sarcasm was clear and Shaziya cut the call wordlessly. Starting from her own maternal home, this request for a kafan expanded and spread to all her relatives and friends. She had never imagined she could be this helpless, and shed a flood of tears again.

Realising it was no use crying, she decided to come out of her room, have something to eat and take her medicines. But none of these made her any better. Feeling defeated, she wondered if she should get a kafan locally, soak it in the Zamzam water stored at home and send it there. But that would not be a kafan from Mecca. Disgusted with the abyss into which she was falling, she helplessly cursed herself: 'Thoo, Shaziya, may your life be damned.' The pain, the agony, the loss of dignity, the helplessness and suffering of that moment could not be explained in words.

Farman came home around three o'clock in the afternoon. Walking up to the dining table he asked Saba, 'Where is Ammi?' She had guessed that her mother-in-law was in a very bad mood and said nothing, instead gesturing towards Shaziya's room with her eyes. Farman rushed in, and despite his mother's wordlessness he understood everything when he saw her face. He sat next to her and said, 'Ammi,' holding her hand. Shaziya found a shoulder to cry on. No matter how hard he tried to console her, she kept crying in gasps. Was my mother-in-law so sensitive that she is grieving the death of a servant this much, wondered Saba, surprised. She was standing by the door; Farman gestured to his wife and sent her away.

He had been upset with Shaziya in the morning. 'She should not have agreed to this . . . but after agreeing, shouldn't she have kept her promise? What is the big deal in bringing one kafan? That too for that poor woman.' He had felt very bad. 'Couldn't Ammi have told us to bring it when Saba and I went to Umrah last year at least? I would have brought it.' Wondering why bringing the kafan had become such a problem, he'd come close to blaming her, but stopped just short and managed to calm down. Feeling sorry for how much she had suffered, he said, 'Ammi, leave it, sometimes these things happen. Whether because of forgetfulness or just bad luck, these things end up happening. Don't take it to heart. Also, Ammi, I went with Altaf to his house in the morning, finished all the burial rituals for Bua and just got back. I bought a kafan, incense sticks, perfume and other things needed for the rituals, then had the grave dug at the spot he had chosen in the graveyard, and arranged for the bathing of the corpse. I thought I would have lunch and then take you with me. I know you will not be at peace otherwise. Come have lunch with me. Then we will go and see Yaseen Bua one last time.'

Shaziya's sorrow rose again. Farman pushed a plate of food before her. After a little rice went into her stomach, he told Saba, 'You don't have to come, it is enough if only Ammi comes,' and took his mother to Yaseen Bua's house. He pictured all that was going to happen there. After seeing Yaseen Bua's face, she was going to burst into tears again. Perhaps Shaziya had shed as many tears as Yaseen Bua's daughter and son had. But still she was not going to forgive herself. He realised that she was going to continue grieving.

When they reached Yaseen Bua's house, everything happened just like he had known it would. There was no end to Shaziya's sorrow, no drought for her tears. Those who saw her face, her reddened eyes, her swollen lips were surprised. Many people sympathised, thinking that they had never seen a woman from a prominent, rich family feel so much grief over the death of a servant. Who knows what kind of relationship they had, they thought, before shifting the burden onto God. Only God knows. Shaziya alone knew the truth: it was not Yaseen Bua's last rites being conducted, but her own.

THE ARABIC TEACHER
AND GOBI MANCHURI

No matter how simple some things might seem, they're not, or at least not always. People behave in strange and illogical ways when they're afraid they may have to take responsibility. I have reason to think about such things. The revelation that I can no longer justify my own erratic behaviour on these terms is a recent one, however; it came to me many years after the event itself. No doubt this awareness gradually became stronger over time, but, even so, various aspects of that incident jump up from the depths of my memory every now and then, with a thud and without any warning.

Back then, along with the pressures of my career in law, I had the responsibility of raising two daughters, educating them, monitoring their behaviour, managing religious festivals and such other things. More than anything else, the children had to be given a proper religious education. Predictably, though their father had plenty of time, his entire family had issued a fatwa exempting my husband from this responsibility, saying that the proper bringing-up of children was the mother's, that is, my duty alone. This decision was in keeping, you could say, with society back then. I've never been surprised by the expression *a saree like its thread, a daughter like her mother.* The only difference was that while my husband's relatives dumped these responsibilities on me and kept quiet, my side of the family at least tried to help me deal with it all.

In keeping with this spirit of helpfulness, my younger brother Imaad called me a week after I was given this task. 'Didi, I have found an Arabic teacher for the kids. Tell me when you are at home. I will bring him,' he said.

'How have you managed to appoint him already? Shouldn't we interview him first?' I asked.

'Interview him, oh ho! As if you are giving him a government job and thousands of rupees as salary!' he replied, irritated and angry that I was dismissing his efforts to help.

'It is not like that. You misunderstand me. I won't be at home. Only the girls will be here, that is why I asked if it is alright, that's all. Is that teacher married?'

He got angrier. 'I don't know all that, I didn't ask. If you want, ask him yourself, else leave it. What do I care if your children study or not? I went looking for a teacher because Ammi would not let me sit in peace at home and kept bugging me to do this,' he said, ready to pick a fight. The very next instant he added, 'Tell your dear husband he can look for a messenger of God and bring him to you instead,' blaming his indifference.

'Look, don't add words to words and start an argument. There are great gentlemen out there; many people spend lots of money on madrasas so that their children can learn Arabic and get a good religious education. What kind of a Shakuni-like uncle are you? Aren't they your children also? Isn't their education your responsibility too?' I emotionally blackmailed my brother a little.

He immediately protested. 'When learning the Qur'an is the big story here, don't bring in the Ramayana and Mahabharata to distract me. Then someone else will enter the conversation and it will become a different thing altogether,' he cried, trying to get away.

'Uff, all that only happens when mad people like you get into a muddle. It's not that they both have never learned Arabic at all.

They have read the Qur'an three times already. Now they just have to learn the Qira'at, to recite the verses properly. Then they have to learn grammar and the meaning of the words, like learning a language. I want someone who can teach all that properly, do you understand? Come in the evening at five o'clock and bring the teacher along,' I said, and ended the conversation.

Imaad's words kept bothering me all day. When I was about to leave for home in the evening, Gowri called to say, 'Madam, please come to the appellate court right away.'

'Why, what is there?'

'There is that Muniswamy case.'

'Oh! But this morning Vivek said it was adjourned.'

'Aiyo, you know how Vivek is, madam. Even if they call our case in front of him, he will be floating in another world,' she replied sourly, but without losing her cool.

'Take one week's time, let us see.'

'It might be difficult to get more time. Can I make the argument, madam?'

I, however, did lose my cool. 'No, no, I will come myself. The different points of law must be discussed in detail,' I replied and rushed to the court.

I called my husband on the way, told him what Imaad had said and asked him to see if that teacher could be appointed. He coolly replied, 'Oh, they both came here over fifteen minutes ago. We are drinking tea. I don't know about those other things. I don't want any trouble from you if I end up appointing him. You come and decide.'

I had prepared my arguments already by familiarising myself with precedent in a similar Supreme Court case. I was initially irritated that the case – which kept getting adjourned because the court didn't have time for it – had now suddenly come up for argument. The moment I began to present before the judge, however, I forgot about everything else. By the time I finished my work and returned home, it had struck six.

It was time for the evening prayers, the teacher was getting restless, and he was taken a little aback when he saw my black coat. He was still young. He was from Uttar Pradesh and had learned the entire Qur'an by heart in a madrasa there and received the title of Hafiz-e-Qur'an at a young age. I would have preferred a teacher for my daughters who was a little older and a local. By the time I removed my coat and entered the living room, Asiya and Aamina were sitting on either side of their father. Asiya must have been thirteen or fourteen years old then, Aamina must have been twelve. I was embarrassed by my own ignorance of these details as their mother. The teacher remained very restless, as if he was sitting on thorns.

Before I could say a word, Imaad asked, 'So from when will you come to teach?' as if he had already decided everything. The teacher agreed to start the very next day. He found it difficult to say what time he could come because, whenever children are not in school, that is, between six and eight o'clock in the morning and after five o'clock in the evening, his time was torn into pieces and distributed all around. I suggested that it was best if he could come between five and six o'clock in the evenings. Imaad seconded my suggestion. The teacher looked strained. 'I go to teach the fruit seller Ghaffar Saheb's children at that time. Forgive me, I don't want to speak badly of anyone, but those children are not interested in learning anything. That is why I will stop going to their house and come to teach your children instead,' he said, addressing Imaad and my husband in the chaste Urdu of the Uttar Pradesh region. He did not glance at me even once by mistake. Teachers like him are taught not to meet women's eyes or talk to them directly; that is the purdah to be observed by men. Thus, he looked at the wall, or at the floor, or at times at the ceiling, or at the two other men present there while talking. In the end, it was decided that he would come to our house to teach Arabic to our children at five o'clock every evening and would be paid five hundred rupees a month for it.

The children began their lessons. I had told our cook to give the teacher a cup of tea along with some snacks or biscuits when he arrived. The cook would do that and go home. Once in a while, in the middle of a work day, I would get anxious wondering if the teacher was behaving himself with my daughters. I was just being overly protective as a mother, of course. Nothing untoward could happen; I trusted in the good sense Asiya and Aamina had. Even so, I had asked my husband to be at home in the evenings and pay attention to their classes. But he had looked at me with such pity and disdain that I did not have the guts to bring it up with him again.

Although I had decided on a salary of five hundred rupees, I did not stick to it. I was well aware of how necessary religious education was for the children's future. Thus, I began to pay the teacher a little more money to encourage him to give their lessons extra attention. Perhaps this is the working mothers' solution: trying to make up for the guilt of not being able to spend time with their children by giving them money and gifts. But it is impossible to avoid guilt in impossible situations, and in the strange relationships and problems that ensue. Only God can save us working mothers!

Despite these confusions and anxieties, I felt that the Arabic teacher was doing a good job with the lessons. Some six months had passed since he had started. One day, the Fathima Women's Organisation was celebrating the Prophet's birthday. When I went to the event, Aamina was there, and gave me a slight smile. By the

191

time I wondered why the girls had come to the event without telling me, both of them went onstage and began to sing a song on the struggles of the Prophet in his life. Their pronunciation was clear, their stance confident. Several women came up to congratulate me later, and, naturally, I was happy. When even my sister-in-law expressed her envy-laced appreciation, I truly felt that the girls had made a lot of progress.

Singing the song again in front of their father, they looked like houris. 'Ammi, we wanted to give you a surprise, so we planned this with Hazrat. We didn't know till the last minute whether you were going to attend or not,' Aamina said. That month, I added an extra five hundred rupees to Hazrat's salary. But I did not imagine that this teacher would soon give me a bigger surprise.

Another three months must have passed. That day too, I was to argue one of my cases, but was feeling a bit unwell. I had prepared a written argument on behalf of my client, and gave the file to Gowri, who was always standing on her toes for any such opportunity. 'Read this argument a couple of times and present it in the court effectively. In the end, submit the written argument to the court,' I instructed her and left.

'Are the children back from school?' I asked, the moment my cook opened the door. I went into my bedroom and immediately slipped into a deep sleep. By the time I woke and was about to get out of bed, several voices, all talking at once, drifted from the kitchen. In an instant, all the suspicions I had about the Arabic teacher grew like a giant, and I hurried down, taking two steps at a time to reach the kitchen, where I saw oil heating in a pan. A heap of cauliflower florets sitting in a bowl. Asiya and Aamina's hands were decorated with oil, dough and such other things. The Arabic teacher was sitting on a chair in a corner. Their faces fell when they saw me. The teacher became so pale that he seemed about to faint.

I did not understand what was happening, and, seeing me furious, the teacher got up and ran out into the street.

The kitchen was telling a different story altogether. Both Asiya and Aamina explained in detail, between copious amounts of crying. From what I understood, the Arabic teacher was crazy about gobi manchuri. Thanks to his passion for the cauliflower snack, he was spending a lot of money every day to buy a plate of it and satisfy his desire, though the desire to eat it to his heart's content remained unfulfilled. He had decided that only in our kitchen was there to be found an unending supply of the dish, which was why he had hatched a plan with the girls. They had asked the cook and got the recipe from her. The cook did not know how to make such junk food, but, unable to refuse when the children asked, she gave them a made-up recipe. It was when the three of them were in the process of executing their plan that I had barged in on them.

I breathed a sigh of relief after listening to all this, happy that nothing untoward had taken place. If relatives had seen them instead of me, it would have been a disaster. The incident would have grown wings and spread, taking on strange forms depending on the fertility of the gossiper's imagination. Thankfully, we were spared that, and I breathed another sigh of relief. My guess turned out to be right: that teacher wouldn't even look in the direction of our house again.

I kept hearing news about him though. He had looked for a bride in a few of my clients' houses, but for strange reasons none of the proposals had worked out. Abdul Subhan, an old client, would often come to discuss his case just as the office was closing, and would talk about personal matters as well. One evening he stood near the door and said: 'See, madam, there is a proposal which has come for my youngest daughter. The boy is a maulvi in our Azeem Masjid. But he is not from our state, he is from somewhere in the north. I could get her married off to a thief from here even, but one cannot trust outsiders.'

'That is true. What happened then?'

'He gave your name, which is why initially I thought I could get a house on rent, pay the advance myself, buy whatever was needed for the house and have them live close to me. But then, where will I search for him if he disappears after fathering one or two children? Who will look after my daughter and her children? I decided I did not want that trouble and dropped it, madam,' he said.

I thought he had done the right thing. Another two-three months passed. Saleema Jaan, a cook who used to work in our house and had then quit because of ill health, came looking for me one Sunday evening. She knew when I would be under pressure and when I would be free. She started chatting about this and that.

'Akka, a proposal has come for my sister's daughter. I don't do anything without asking you, that is why I have come. The girl has passed her Bachelor of Arts exam and is a teacher in a corment school.' Saleema, like others in the area, mixed the words for convent and government schools together. She continued, 'This girl is the only child of her parents, nor does he have a family to boast of. They thought they could have him live with them.'

For some reason, the moment I heard this introduction, I knew our hero had a part to play. I reined in my curiosity and casually asked, 'Who is the boy?'

'That maulvi Hazrat. The teacher who used to come to teach your children, that same boy.' I began to suspect that something was amiss here, given how my name was being dragged into all this.

'Hmm. Did the proposal work out? When is the wedding?' I asked.

'How could it work out? Even when she goes to the corment, our girl wears the burkha. He didn't ask to meet her even once. He

194

didn't ask about what we would give or take during the wedding. He waited for the girl to leave the house, stopped her in the middle of the road and asked whether she knows how to make gube manchari, whatever that is! What sort of a man is he?!' she asked herself, and became quiet for a minute.

She then scanned the whole room with her eyes and ears to see if there was any indication of the man of the house or the children. She was relieved that there didn't seem to be anyone around. Even so, she came close to me, pulled the veil of her burkha down to ensure no one could see even the movement of her lips and said, 'See, Akka, this fellow doesn't even behave like a man. There are no elders with him to talk about marriage. But still, the boy is educated, and spends his time at the masjid all day and night. He always has God's name on his lips. He is someone who advises people and solves problems for them. Later, even if he leaves her and goes off to his home town, she can still fend for herself. We thought she could somehow look after herself if needed, but the truth is he doesn't care about marriage or the girl at all. He wants us to prepare some kind of gube curry and something else for the wedding feast. This is why I thought to come and ask you about him. You meet such crack people a lot, so, tell me, what should we do?'

I realised she meant he had asked for his favourite gobi snack to be served at the wedding, and became a little worried about this Arabic teacher's antics. I also felt a little sympathy. Wondering who could rid him of his obsession with gobi manchuri, I replied, 'I don't know much about him; he seems like a good man. He came to teach Arabic to our children for some time. You can get the couple married if you want; enquire with a few others and then take a decision.' It was a noncommittal answer, and she was not willing to let me go so easily.

She leaned even closer and whispered, 'How can we find out if he is fully male or not?' I began to feel fed up. She seemed to realise I was getting angry. 'Not like that, Akka, don't misunderstand me. I asked because you are a lawyer, that's all. How will I know if he is crazy? On the face of it, he has learned Arabic and Urdu. But what can we do if he stops the girl in the middle of the road to ask if she can make some gube curry? To think he is a teacher in the masjid,' she said, combining praise and censure for the things he had done.

I began to think that this was really some madness on his part. Perhaps if he had demanded biriyani, kurma sukha, pulao or other similar dishes, the girl's family would have accepted happily. But this vegetarian whatever-it's-called, this gube manchali, this weird gobi manchuri . . . I wondered if I should call Imaad and ask him to talk some sense into the Arabic teacher. But then I realised it was not appropriate for me to even show this kind of interest in him. Thoughts of the teacher flew away like sparrows in the face of my never-ending responsibilities, and I once again became immersed in my professional world.

Another six months must have passed. One fine day, Imaad himself came to tell me the news just as I was getting ready to leave the house and go to court. He came bearing two boxes filled with dates, almonds and rock sugar. Calling Asiya and Aamina, he said, 'Your teacher's nikah is over. I've come straight from the mosque. Your teacher remembered you both even in the middle of all the chaos of a wedding and sent you these dry fruits,' handing them each a box. They vanished when the treats landed in their hands. I remembered that scene in the kitchen with the three of them that day and laughed to myself. I felt a little lighter in the heart after hearing that the Arabic teacher had finally got married. Hoping that he would live peacefully, I let the tiny smile forming on my face float about and went on with my work.

However, just when I thought the devil had left the building, there he came again through the back door, and with him came the Arabic teacher back into my life. As if to prove that the world was indeed small and round, I began to hear news of him again and again. While I was glad that he seemed settled, I remained curious about who had given him their daughter in marriage. I told myself that if it had been some acquaintance of mine, I would have either received an invitation to the wedding or at least heard about it.

Whatever sense of relief I'd felt did not last long. As if to confirm the truth that I would have little peace, a young man and a burkha-clad woman came to my office one day. I did not know them. The girl had moved the veil only a little from her face. There seemed to be a scratch mark on her nose, and marks on both her hands from where glass bangles had broken and pierced her skin. Her eyes welled up when she showed me these wounds.

The young man got agitated and said, 'Madam, this is my younger sister. It's been six months since she got married. The boy is a maulvi. No matter what she tolerated, so as to maintain a maulvi's dignity, his torture has not stopped. He has been beating her from the day they got married. We also are fed up; we have held three panchayats at the mosque already. The mutawalli there and other committee members have tried a lot to talk some sense into him. But he is not in a position to listen to anyone. In the end they fired him from his job at the mosque. Even then he did not stop torturing my sister. Please write a police complaint about this for us.'

I felt very sad about the tragedy taking place because of that Arabic teacher's obsession with gobi manchuri. I did not ask for details from that young man, but he, furious, began to give me more details himself. 'He tells her to cook some dish, madam. She does not understand what he wants, and he does not find what she makes tasty. He starts thrashing her like a madman. We cannot tolerate this; please send him to jail,' he said.

Without doubt, it was a crime which deserved jail. But also without doubt he would disappear the moment a criminal case was filed against him. What about her after that? I decided I had to try and save him from this mess somehow. More than that, I thought, I must try and save this woman's life, and possibly her marriage. On one phone I searched for a recipe for gobi manchuri, while on the other I called my brother Imaad.

BE A WOMAN ONCE,
OH LORD!

After creating crores and crores of tiny organisms like me over lakhs and lakhs of years, after establishing heaven for our good deeds and hell for our sins, oh Lord who sits waiting for us: Prabhu, you must be on your way now to enjoy the sweet fragrance of the garden in heaven. Or perhaps you are issuing orders to the angels, who stand there with hands folded, radiant faces aglow. I may be a mere tiny fragment of your soul, but I do have the right to make a request, don't I? Because . . .

This is about a period when I was particularly fragile and vulnerable, though I didn't really have many problems then. There were four walls around me at all times, and freedom, in the form of a breeze, that marvellous product of your pure imagination, touched my face only when I opened the window. The only time I stroked the jasmine plant that infused the air with a heady fragrance was at night. The white cottony clouds, embroidered at their edges by flame-like rays of the setting sun, and, glimpsed through the branches of the lone curry leaf tree in the backyard, the view of roaring black-black clouds that looked like elephants in heat – these I saw from the window in the middle room of the house. It was only in my heart that I saw the ferociousness of the rain like strung pearls. My feet never touched the front yard, and stepped only on the floor inside the threshold of the house. My seragu never once slipped from my head. My eyelids were filled to the brim with shyness. Laughter did not cross my lips, and neither did my eyes wander round like bees. This was why Amma did not keep a strict eye on me. Don't do this, don't do that, don't stand like this, don't look like that . . . she did not need to tell me such things. I did not have the habit of thinking of many things either.

But still, I have one small question! All of these – that is, these sparkling green-coloured crickets, these colours everywhere, shining stones, the fragrant mud, the breeze, this sweet smell, these plants and trees and fields and forests, the roaring ocean, this rain, a paper boat in the rain – these are not things I can touch or immerse myself in, cannot smell, cannot see, up to which I cannot raise my face. You have given all these for him, for your supreme creation, isn't it? This is the only truth I know. That is why I did not cause much trouble, because this is your order, it seems. Poor Amma! What could she do, after all?

So I never talked back and I listened to everything Amma said. Let me say it: You should be obedient, she said, he is God to you, you should do whatever he tells you to, you should serve him loyally. These things were carved very deeply into my heart.

As for Appa? Let it be. When I had to leave Amma and go, it felt like my heart had been ripped out, placed on a palm and squeezed hard. Amma was also suffering. Even so, she said nothing. A saw was running wildly over her innards. But still her eyes gleamed; only the edges were wet. Perhaps you will understand. They say you carry the love of hundreds of mothers for us; the burning in one mother's heart must have touched the hundreds of other hearts within you. But I did not see you anywhere. I was very scared. Amma hugged me to her chest, her cold hands stroking my burning cheeks. But then he pulled me away from my mother's embrace and carried me away. I was a precious jewel wrapped in gold- and silver-embroidered cloth.

I knew Amma was sobbing. No matter how far we went, I could still hear her sobs. Here too, one small question: what would have happened if he came and set down roots with us? When you so leisurely created the animal kingdom, the delicate threadlike parts inside flowers with gold coating, these marvellous ponds and lakes, rivers and streams, did you not have the time to peep into my heart and see my fears, my wishes, dreams and disappointments?

I had nothing left that was just my own. I had to set down roots in another's front yard, grow new shoots there, bloom there. He was getting attached, while my identity was melting away. Even my name got lost. Do you know what my new name was? His wife. My body, my mind were not my own. To my surprise, he desired my body, whose power to bounce back even I was unaware of. He devoured me. Except in those moments, the sceptre of power you had bestowed on him shone in his hands.

From where all his cunningness sprang and in what ways, I don't know. In an instant he could break my heart into pieces, and would scatter each piece to different corners. My body was his playground; my heart, a toy in his hand. This way, like this, I used to apply balm, to attempt to repair my heart, but he continued to break it at whim. Prabhu, why did I have to become a toy? I do not hate him, nor do I wish for him to be my plaything either. If only I had been his backbone and he the hands that would wipe my tears away . . .

He had been using me for less than a week when he screamed like a madman. *What am I? What is my status, there are people who will give me lakhs of rupees, but I ended up bringing home a beggar like you!* How was I supposed to answer? As per Amma's advice, I remained silent. He ordered, 'You must bring fifty thousand rupees from your parents' house immediately. If not, you can never set foot there ever again.' I went back to Amma, like costume jewellery wrapped in a dirty cloth.

Amma's face lit up. Hundreds of suns and moons shone in her eyes in an instant. They immediately dimmed when she saw that he had not come with me. She gently took me in. The demand for fifty thousand rupees had disturbed the happiness on my face. That night when I slept next to Amma, I felt at peace, but soon he came to mind. A hole opened up in the fortress of Amma's loving heart. He had crept in. By the time three days had passed, even I waited eagerly on my tiptoes. When he enquired if I'd got the money and saw my withered face, he said: 'This is the last time we will come here. You cannot return from now on; nor should your parents come to our house.'

Amma fed me to my stomach's content. She blessed me with all her heart. She combed all the knots out, and braided my hair as if threading all her loving kisses together. The string of jasmine she tied in my hair was, like her, fragrant. Kanakambara flowers played hide-and-seek with the jasmine. Looking back at Amma every other second, I peeled my reluctant footsteps off the ground and walked behind him.

He was not one to go back on his word. Shouldn't there be a limit to his arrogance? I did not open my braid out for three days after I went back to his house. I was scared of Amma's loving kisses slipping away. My heart was attached to her; his was attached to having the last word. I did not meet Amma after that. There is no need for me to bring this to your attention either. You know all this; your own bookkeepers bring you crores and crores of such reports every day, but they are all written with a pen, whereas this report was written from the heart, a woman's heart, a string of letters written with the heart's sharp nib and the red ink inside. Perhaps no such requests have reached you till now because you have no bookkeepers who have a heart like mine.

As always, I am a prisoner of a soul whose doors and windows are shut. I did not see Amma, or Appa, or my younger brother ever again. There was a distant hope that Amma would not remain quiet. I know that she tried to see me many times. But he had built such a strong fort that all her efforts were in vain. His greed for money swallowed all our attachments, love and affection. He was blind but strong about his stand.

Several neighbours used to advise me to be the way he thinks is right. Even you have preached the same thing, that he is my God, that it is my duty to obey him, that in this world he can meet anyone anywhere any time he wants. But me? It was you who said that mother too is equal to God, it was you who said that there was heaven under her feet, and yet I cannot meet her even once. Whether you have time for these small problems striking my limited thoughts, whether you feel my entire life is a three-hour play, whether I seem like an actor to you, keep one thing in mind: my happiness and sadness are not borrowed. They are not to be performed. They are to be experienced. You are just a detached director. When one of your own characters assaults my mind, have you no duties as a director? Grant me one solace at least. What is my fault in all this, tell me?

He never asked me if I had eaten or had something to drink. But he ploughed, he sowed; despite its shattered heart and fatigue-filled soul, the body was ripe, the womb ready, and his hunger was great too. I was on the road to becoming a mother myself but I stood in a corner constantly looking back down the road to my maternal home. I could not see any form or shape no matter how far into the horizon I looked. All I could see were a few green memory trees, as they shed their leaves and grew bare.

I later learned that Amma had somehow convinced Appa to sell everything they called their own, make a bundle of twenty thousand rupees, and come to our house. That day the crow had cawed, the right eye had fluttered, the fireplace had hummed. Perhaps Amma would come. Amma had started but did not arrive. There was an accident somewhere it seems. Everything is anthe-kanthe, hearsay. He didn't let me go see Amma's body. Instead, he took care to ensure I didn't hear about what had happened.

Here, in the big hospital in our town, it seems they cut into her dead body. Perhaps they didn't cut into her heart. They wouldn't have found clotted blood if they had; instead they would find a clotted soul, several uncrossable Lakshmana Rekha, several dozen signs of tests by fire. But one thing is true: even if her body was shattered into pieces when she was alive, when she was dead no one touched her heart. Or her soul. An eternal virgin, her eyes remained open. I wonder who she was expecting to see. Her unfortunate eyes had remained open in anticipation, awaiting someone's arrival.

From here and from there. From the window. Although I had heard bits of news through the ventilator, he who had gone to see everything remained stubborn. It seems that Appa, sitting beside Amma's dead body, removed the bundle of twenty thousand rupees tied around Amma's waist and placed it in his hands. It seems he begged, 'At least now bring her here.' He did not tell me about any of this. Neither did he take me there.

A daughter was born, her face just like Amma's, her eyes deep ponds. Just like Amma, I held her up, cuddled her and played with her. Now my tears did not flow or make ponds and rivers. Instead, they would gleam at the edges of my eyes like mist. Thank you for your marvellous gift; you gave me the power and determination to forget. The cool breeze of old memories was peaceful over the desert of life. I became pregnant again even though I was still breastfeeding, and as I carried her in my arms, the soft kicks of another pair of legs and the beat of a little heart had taken root in me.

I was greatly agitated. He twirled his moustache and said, 'I am the one raising them, what is your problem in bearing them?' Poor thing. What he is saying is right. If only you had told him, just once, about the difficulties of giving birth, he might not have uttered these words. As easily as clearing one's throat, as easily as pissing to relieve pressure, you have created a simple being that is arrogant and happy, and now you are indifferent. Should he be made uncomfortable with blood and flesh? Should the salt of his bones be ground and fed to the womb? Should he live in between not just the flesh and blood but also a pain so intense it breaks the ribs? If only he had had these experiences. No, I don't have the opportunity to ask these things, because you are the creator, and he is your beloved creation. Does that make me the creation unloved?

There was no limit to his happiness when, just as he wished, a boy was born. Although I was not happy, one thing gave me satisfaction. At least we had not created another helpless prisoner of life like me. Instead of someone who had to live pathetically, without stability, a son was born who could step ahead proudly, in full arrogance of being male!

I poured more love on my daughter.

Both the children were growing up. His status, superiority complex and arrogance all kept laying eggs and procreating. I had morphed into the most dutiful servant; it was the only available path. Giving nothing to the world, getting nothing from the world, with no awareness of social relationships, nameless, less than a person, I was only his wife, that is, free labour. At night if I imagined what would happen to me without his protection, I started shivering. I was nothing without him and that stark reality was constantly before my eyes. I was a mere shadow. I hadn't been ready to accept this at first. There was a lot of conflict within me. At the slightest hint of a future without him, I would get frightened. I was scared to even imagine the situation. I was a slave; even so, the owner who gave me food, water and shelter in return for my labour seemed like a mahatma to me.

Perhaps this could have continued, and I would have eventually married off the children and then died, just like Amma. But one day he admitted me to hospital. Apparently there was a tumour growing in my stomach. The doctors conducted many tests and said that I needed surgery. His face screwed up like he was angry with me. He didn't say anything in front of the doctors. Once my surgery was over, he returned and just stood there. 'Give me the neck chain you are wearing,' he ordered. It is better to say a few things about this chain. Amma had this two-strand chain made when I got married. She had melted the gold her mother had given her for her own wedding in order to make it. I wore it always, in memory of Amma. This was why my heart was reluctant to hand it over. I asked, stammering, 'Why do you want it now?' I think that was the first time I had ever questioned him in my life. Without an ounce of hesitation or mercy, he very casually replied, 'I am getting married again. I want to give it to the new girl.' Darkness surrounded me. Do I rip off these glucose bottles and run away? Where do I run to? Do I give him a slap? Che! That is impossible. What will happen to the children? The possibility that even the four walls of my house could be closed to me became a truth that solidified before my eyes, and I was crushed.

I held on to the chain in my left hand as if it was my life and said, 'I will not give it to you.' He was taken aback, perhaps because he had not expected it. He looked at me with hatred. My refusal insulted him more than not getting the chain. He burned, wanting revenge. 'Oho! You think my wedding won't happen if you don't give me your chain?!' he shouted. In a timid voice I asked, 'Why do you want to get married again now?'

'Should I give you an explanation also? OK, listen then. I do not wish to waste my life with a beggar like you. What is the use of a sick person? I am marrying a good girl from a good family.'

You gave me the strength to bear a lot of pain. But you should not have given him the cruelty to cause so much of it. What is the limit of patience? Even though patience was my life's mantra, I collapsed, helpless. Before I could speak he said, 'Do you want to hear more? What pleasure have I got from you? Every time I touched you, you lay there like a corpse. That is why I am getting married again.'

I'd lost the ability to think straight. My words had become silence. My eyes had misted behind a veil of tears. I was being thrown on the street like trash and I was filled with anger. I wanted to get up from the bed but I couldn't. Slowly I started to think. Was it possible for me to stop him? In my time as his loyal servant I had asked only three or four simple questions, to which I received thousands of answers in reply.

'Look, you are not well. Let him get married again.' If one voice said, 'Arey, this is all very well, he is a man, not just one, he can marry four, what can you ask?', others advised with fake sympathy, smiling under their moustaches: 'Look here, my dear, let him get married if he wants to. File a case demanding that he give you some money every month. It will take about four or five years for the judgement. Until then do some daily wage work or something.' That means society has accepted what he's doing. They even say that you help with these things! It is in your name that he does this, because I am your incomplete creation, hey Prabhu? Can you hear my grievances? Are my cries reaching you? What will I do . . . what will I do . . .

He has not come to the hospital in three days. My children and I have been sharing the free food given by the hospital people. That too has ended, now the doctors have discharged me. Taking the children along I walked towards my house with great difficulty. There is a fat lock on the front door. A green canopy of coconut fronds is in front of the house. There is no one at home. Neighbours peeped out and disappeared from view. The children sit huddled against me. The day was spent and night stepped in, even as I continued to sit in front of the house.

The door to hearts and houses had shut. The darkness was deepening. Seeing my helplessness, the children didn't mention their hunger. Since my feet were stiff, I spread out my legs. The children stuck to me and laid down. I was half asleep, I didn't know what time it was. When a scream loud enough to burn my heart opened my eyes, I saw that my son, who was sleeping next to me, had fallen into the ditch. In one leap I jumped down and hugged his slush-covered body. That was when I heard a tempo stopping under the canopy, the noise of people, excitement, the bustle of celebration. He got down. From the back door of the tempo with his too-strong hands he lifted a woman wearing red clothes, like a precious jewel wrapped in gold embroidered cloth. He walked ahead, taking purposeful steps. The front door of the house opened. Everyone was with him. My son shivered and hugged me. I looked at it all with wide eyes.

The nib of my red ink-filled heart has broken. My mouth can speak no more. No more letters to write. I do not know the meaning of patience. If you were to build the world again, to create males and females again, do not be like an inexperienced potter. Come to earth as a woman, Prabhu!

Be a woman once, oh Lord!

AGAINST ITALICS

Translator's Note

Banu Mushtaq's entire career, be it as a writer or as a journalist, lawyer and activist, can be summed up in one Kannada word – bandaya. Bandaya means dissent, rebellion, protest, resistance to authority, revolution and its adjacent ideas; combine it with sahitya, meaning literature, and we get the name of a short-lived but highly influential literary movement in the Kannada language in the 1970s and '80s. Bandaya Sahitya started as an act of protest against the hegemony of upper caste and mostly male-led writing that was then being published and celebrated. The movement urged women, Dalits and other social and religious minorities to tell stories from within their own lived experiences and in the Kannada they spoke. Of the many Kannadas that exist, theirs was dismissed as folksy, in contrast to the 'prestige dialect' from the Mysuru region that remains most used in popular culture.

Banu grew up in a progressive family and was educated in Kannada and not, as was common for Muslims then, in Urdu. She came of age during the decades when the personal-is-political emerged as a major theme in intellectual thought. Writing during and in the aftermath of the Bandaya movement, her works consciously moved away from what she calls the boy-meets-girl tropes of romantic fiction, and instead sought out narratives that critiqued patriarchy and its hypocritical traditions and practices. While there were several women who were inspired by the literary and political landscape of the '80s, Banu remains one of the few who have continued to write regularly in the ensuing decades.

Hassan, the southwestern town in the plains in Karnataka state where she has lived most of her life, and Madikeri, the town in the Western Ghat mountain range where I was born and now live in again, are barely a hundred kilometres apart. Both are compact in size, and are replete with the distinct socio-linguistic features and rightward political leanings that characterise small-town India. At home Banu speaks Dakhni, often wrongly identified as a dialect of Urdu, but which in fact is a mix of Persian, Dehlavi, Marathi, Kannada, and Telugu. Kannada is Banu's language at work and what she encounters on the street. Her Kannada, however, and the Kannada I grew up speaking, one heavily influenced by coastal inflections and Havyaka, a dialect of the caste I was born into, are both very different. Between us, we also speak over half a dozen other languages, many of which invariably slip in and out when we converse or write. In Banu's stories, this code switching between the three-four languages we engage with daily results in a delightful mix of Kannada, Urdu, Arabic, Dakhni and a Kannada as spoken by specific communities in specific localities of the Hassan region.

Such multilingualism is not rare or unusual for many Indians, and is not necessarily a function of caste, class, education or community, identifiers that otherwise determine every aspect of private privilege and public life in the country. When I began to work with Banu's stories, I grappled with what this project would be: a lapsed Hindu and an upper-caste person translating a minority voice into our shared alien language. It would be a disservice to reduce Banu's work to her religious identity, for her stories transcend the confines of a faith and its cultural traditions. Nonetheless, in today's India, where a decade of far-right politics has descended dangerously into Hindutva-led majoritarianism, hatred and severe persecution of minorities – iterations of such violence are found in many other countries of the world too, lest we forget – it is essential to note the milieu that she lives in and works out of. While of course a translator need not be from the same background as the writer, it still felt important to me to acknowledge our differences, our respective positions and privileges, and use this awareness to be more responsible and sensitive in my translation.

That said, I choose to attribute my gustakhi, my imprudence, to translate Banu to something she once said to me. She said that she does not see herself writing only about a certain kind of woman belonging to a certain community, that women everywhere face similar, if not the exact same problems, and those are the issues that she writes about. This sisterhood to which those of us who identify as women belong is the cushion I place my translation on. The coping mechanisms we devise, the solutions we find and the adjustments we make around men are survival strategies nurtured across generations. The particulars may be different, but at the core is a resistance to being controlled, 'tamed', or disallowed the exploration of our full potential. These experiences, both Banu and I believe, can be found anywhere in the world. Some of us step on the cindering balls of coal and carve a space for ourselves. Some of us learn to exist too close to the fire. None of us are left unscarred.

The Kannada language, as is the case with many languages that have been in use for over a thousand years, has a rich and vibrant tradition of oral storytelling. This lineage is visible in Banu's stories as well, where she regularly mixes her tenses, trails off, interjects an observation or a soliloquy in the middle of a dialogue and so on, as if she is sitting across from you. Kannada, like several other Indian languages, is a language filled with expressions, sayings and phrases that not only sound poetic but also give a wonderful sense of theatre to everyday speech. Here, speech is as much a physical, almost musical performance, where a word's meaning depends on haava-bhaava – gestures and expressions – on tone, etc., as much as it does on the information it expresses.

I have tried my best to retain that sense wherever possible, without making the sentences and the jerks and stops in them visually jarring on the page. For instance, hyperbole ('let him get married a thousand times') and repetitions of words ('shining-shining' or 'dip-dipping') are common in everyday speech. I believe they add a delightful amount of drama to a conversation, and have chosen to retain such quirks in English too.

It bears reminding that translation of a text is never merely an act of replacing words in one language with equivalent words in another: every language, with its idioms and speech conventions, brings with it a lot of cultural knowledge that often needs translating too. For instance, in 'Stone Slabs for Shaista Mahal', Shaista is speaking to her new friend Zeenat about her husband Iftikhar. Instead of saying 'my husband' or using his name, however, Shaista refers to him as 'your Bhai Saheb' ['your elder brother']. Zeenat is not a biological relative of Iftikhar's – in fact they've only just met – but the gesture immediately welcomes Zeenat into the family, and she is indeed warmly received. The phrase encodes a wealth of other information too: how women in conservative households do not, for example, typically call their husbands by name, instead referring to their husband's relationship with the addressee (here, 'bhai') or using words like 'rii' if addressing them directly. Nor do people typically address their elders by name without adding a suffix to denote the equivalent of aunty, uncle, elder brother or elder sister, and so on (here 'saheb'). These conventions show respect, yes, but also fulfil a cultural practice of making space for a new person in one's family, bringing them into a circle of closeness by building these relationships. It implies that kinship is not determined by blood or marriage relationships alone and strengthens the idea, in a family-oriented society like India, that everyone belongs to a group, thus taking the edge off foreign ideas like individualism and personal identity. Having to think through socio-cultural traditions like this made translating stories with complicated tiers of relationships both a challenge, and a welcome chance to stop and notice practices so internalised that one takes them for granted. In the spirit of transmitting the flavour of each relationship, whether Banu used the Kannada or Urdu equivalents, I have retained each term as is instead of flattening the nuances with a generic 'aunty' or 'uncle.'

While Kannada is a major language spoken by an estimated 65 million people, its presence online is something of a wilderness when compared to Urdu and Arabic. There are very few words which are google-able in transliteration. Hence, while spelling them in English I have sometimes gone with what is closest to how they are pronounced, and sometimes with how they are more likely to have been spelled in the scant resources available online. For instance, I've transliterated flatbreads as 'rottis' and not as the more familiar 'rotis', since the latter is a northern-centric pronunciation. Same with 'lungi' and 'panche' instead of 'dhoti.'

When transliterating words from Urdu or Arabic, there were plenty of options to choose from, and I again followed the same rationale. Words like Qur'an and jama'at retain the hamza (') to honour the clipped glottal stop used by native speakers. Speakers of Dakhni, including Banu, transliterate 'q' as 'kh' owing to a slight difference in pronunciation. Thus, the word for a Muslim cemetery is transliterated as 'khabaristan' and not as 'qabaristan' as is more often used.

Setting aside the futile debate of what is lost and found in translation, I am delighted that here, in this collection, the Kannada language has found new readers. I was very deliberate in my choice to not use italics for the Kannada, Urdu and Arabic words that remain untranslated in English. Italics serve to not only distract visually, but more importantly, they announce words as imported from another language, exoticising them and keeping them alien to English. By not italicising them, I hope the reader can come to these words without interference, and in the process of reading with the flow, perhaps even learn a new word or two in another language. Same goes for footnotes – there are none.

TRANSLATOR'S ACKNOWLEDGEMENTS

It takes a village to make a book. Among the many inhabiting mine, all my gratitude and love to –

First and foremost, Banu Mushtaq, for trusting me with her work, and for her friendship;

Basav Biradar, for introducing me and Banu;

Hammad Rind, my friend, fellow writer and multilingual translator, for so patiently helping with the Arabic and Urdu words in this book;

Kanishka Gupta, my agent, for the cheering on;

Tara Tobler, editor extraordinaire, for making this translation shine, for always having my back as we navigated through the quirks of many cultures;

Stefan Tobler and everyone else at And Other Stories, I could not have wished for a better team to help shape this book;

Will Forrester and others at English PEN, for the support and encouragement.

Two stories in this collection, 'Red Lungi' and 'Be a Woman Once, Oh Lord' appeared in differently edited translations in, respectively, *The Paris Review*'s Summer 2024 issue and as part of *The Greatest Kannada Stories Ever Told* anthology published by Aleph Book Company, India. Many thank yous to the editor Emily Stokes at the *Review*, and to Chandan Gowda, who selected and edited the anthology, for including my translations.

Last, certainly not the least, all my love to N, my main cheerleader.

AUTHOR'S ACKNOWLEDGEMENTS

Banu Mushtaq wishes to thank her husband Mushtaq Mohiyudin for all his support and encouragement over the years.

THIS BOOK WAS MADE POSSIBLE
THANKS TO THE SUPPORT OF

Aaron McEnery
Aaron Schneider
Abigail Walton
Ada Gokay
Adam Lenson
Adam Murphy
Adris Lorenzato
Aija Kanbergs
Ajay Sharma
Al Ullman
Alan Hunter
Alan McMonagle
Alasdair Cross
Alastair Maude
Albert Puente
Alena Callaghan
Alex Johnstone
Alex (Anna) Turner
Alexander Bunin
Alexandra Buchler
Alexandra German
Alexandra Stewart
Alexandria Levitt
Ali Boston
Ali Riley
Ali Smith
Ali Usman
Alice Carrick-Smith
Alice Wilkinson
Aliki Giakou
Allan & Mo Tennant
Alyssa Rinaldi
Amado Floresca
Amaia Gabantxo
Amanda
Amanda Milanetti
Amber Casiot

Amber Da
Amelia Dowe
Amitav Hajra
Amos Hintermann
Amy and Jamie
Amy Hatch
Amy Lloyd
Amy Raphael
Amy Schoffelen
Amy Sousa
Amy Tabb
Ana Novak
Andrea Barlien
Andrea Larsen
Andrea Lucard
Andrea Oyarzabal Koppes
Andreas Zbinden
Andrew Burns
Andrew Kerr-Jarrett
Andrew Marston
Andrew Martino
Andrew McCallum
Andrew Milam
Andrew Place
Andrew Wright
Andy Marshall
Anna-Maria Aurich
Anna Finneran
Anna French
Anna Gibson
Anna Hawthorne
Anna Holmes
Anna Kornilova
Anna Milsom
Anne Edyvean
Anne Frost
Anne Germanacos

Anne-Marie Renshaw
Anne Willborn
Anonymous
Ant Cotton
Anthea Parker
Anthony Fortenberry
Anthony Quinn
Archie Davies
Aron Trauring
Asako Serizawa
Audrey Holmes
Audrey Small
Avi Blinder
Barbara Mellor
Barbara Spicer
Barry John Fletcher
Barry Norton
Becky Matthewson
Ben Buchwald
Ben Peterson
Ben Schofield
Ben Thornton
Ben Walter
Ben Wasson
Benjamin Heanue
Benjamin Judge
Benjamin Oliver
Benjamin Pester
Benjamin Winfield
Beth Heim de Bera
Bianca Winter
Bill Fletcher
Billy-Ray Belcourt
Birgitta Karlén
Björn Dade
Blazej Jedras
Brandon Clar

Brett Parker
Briallen Hopper
Brian Anderson
Brian Byrne
Brian Callaghan
Brian Isabelle
Brian Smith
Bridget Ingle
Brittany Redgate
Brooke Williams
Brooks Williams
Buck Johnston & Camp
  Bosworth
Burkhard Fehsenfeld
Buzz Poole
Caitlin Halpern
Caleb Bedford
Callie Steven
Cam Scott
Cameron Adams
Cameron Johnson
Camilla Imperiali
Carl Emery
Carmen Smith
Carole Burns
Carole Parkhouse
Carolina Pineiro
Caroline Montanari
Caroline Musgrove
Caroline West
Carrie Brogoitti
Caryn Cochran
Catharine Braithwaite
Catherine Connell
Catherine Fisher
Catherine Jacobs
Catherine McBeth
Catherine Tandy
Catherine Williamson
Cathryn Siegal-Bergman
Cathy Leow
Cecilia Rossi

Cecilia Uribe
Ceri Lumley-Sim
Cerileigh Guichelaar
Chandler Sanchez
Charles Fernyhough
Charles Heiner
Charles Dee Mitchell
Charles Rowe
Charlie Hope D'Anieri
Charlie Small
Charlotte Holtam
Charlotte Middleton
Charlotte Ryland
Charlotte Whittle
Chelsey Blankenship
Chenxin Jiang
China Miéville
Chris Clamp
Chris Johnstone
Chris Lintott
Chris McCann
Chris Potts
Chris Senior
Chris Stevenson
Christina Sarver
Christine Bartels
Christopher Chambers
Christopher Fox
Christopher Lin
Christopher Scott
Christopher Stout
Cian McAulay
Ciara Callaghan
Ciara Windsor
Claire Mackintosh
Claire Riley
Clare Buckeridge
Clare Wilkins
Claudia Mazzoncini
Cliona Quigley
Colin Denyer
Colin Matthews

Collin Brooke
Courtney Lilly
Craig Kennedy
Cynthia De La Torre
Cyrus Massoudi
Daina Chiu
Daisy Savage
Dale Wisely
Dalia Cavazos
Daniel Cossai
Daniel Hahn
Daniel Sanford
Daniel Scarah
Daniel Syrovy
Daniela Steierberg
Danielle Moylan
Darren Boyling
Darren Gillen
Darryll Rogers
Darya Lisouskaya
Dave Appleby
Dave Lander
David Alderson
David Anderson
David Ball
David Eales
David Gray
David Greenlaw
David Gunnarsson
David Hebblethwaite
David Higgins
David Johnson-Davies
David F Long
David Miller
David Morris
David Shriver
David Smith
David Toft
David Wacks
Davis MacMillan
Dean Taucher
Debbie Pinfold

Deborah Gardner
Debra Manskey
Denis Larose
Denis Stillewagt &
  Anca Fronescu
Derek Meins
Diane Hamilton
Dinesh Prasad
Dominic Bailey
Dominic Nolan
Dominick Santa Cattarina
Dominique Brocard
Dominique Hudson
Doris Duhennois
Dugald Mackie
Duncan Chambers
Duncan Clubb
Duncan Macgregor
Dyanne Prinsen
Ed Smith
Ekaterina Beliakova
Eleanor Anstruther
Eleanor Maier
Elif Kolcuoglu
Elina Zicmane
Elizabeth Atkinson
Elizabeth Balmain
Elizabeth Braswell
Elizabeth Cochrane
Elizabeth Draper
Elizabeth Eva Leach
Elizabeth Seals
Elizabeth Sieminski
Ella Sabiduria
Ellen Agnew
Ellen Beardsworth
Emily Drabinski
Emily Tran
Emily Walker
Emma Barraclough
Emma Coulson
Emma Louise Grove

Emma-Jane Lacey
Emma Teale
Emma Wakefield
Eric Anderson
Erin Cameron Allen
Erin Wroe
Ethan White
Ethan Wood
Eunice Rodríguez
  Ferguson
Evelyn Reis
Ewan Tant
Fay Barrett
Faye Williams
Felicity Le Quesne
Felix Valdivieso
Finbarr Farragher
Fiona Wilson
Fran Sanderson
Frances Gillon
Frances Harvey
Francesca Rhydderch
Frank Rodrigues
Frank van Orsouw
Gabriel Garcia
Gabriella Roncone
Garland Gardner
Gavin Aitchison
Gawain Espley
Gemma Alexander
Gemma Bird
Gemma Hopkins
Geoff Stewart
Geoff Thrower
Geoffrey Urland
George McCaig
George Stanbury
George Wilkinson
Georgia Panteli
Georgina Norton
Gerhard Maier
Gerry Craddock

Gillian Grant
Giorgia Tolfo
Glen Bornais
Glenn Russell
Gloria Gunn
Gordon Cameron
Graham Blenkinsop
Graham R Foster
Grainne Otoole
Grant Ray-Howett
Hadil Balzan
Halina Schiffman-Shilo
Hannah Levinson
Hannah Jane Lownsbrough
Hannah Madonia
Hans Lazda
Harriet Stiles
Haydon Spenceley
Hayley Maynard
Heidi Gilhooly
Helen Alexander
Helen Berry
Helen Mort
Henrike Laehnemann
Howard Norman
Howard Robinson
HumDrumPress Amy
  Gowen
Hyoung-Won Park
Ian Betteridge
Ian McMillan
Ian Mond
Ian Whiteley
Ilya Markov
Inbar Haramati
Ines Alfano
Inga Gaile
Irene Mansfield
Irina Tzanova
Isabella Livorni
J Drew Hancock-Teed
J Shmotkina

Jack Brown
Jaclyn Schultz
Jacqueline Lademann
Jacqueline Vint
James Attlee
James Avery
James Beck
James Cubbon
James Kinsley
James Lehmann
James Leonard
James Portlock
James Richards
James Saunders
James Scudamore
James Thomson
James Ward
Jan Hicks
Jane Dolman
Jane Leuchter
Jane Roberts
Jane Rogers
Jane Woollard
Janis Carpenter
Jason Montano
Jason Timermanis
Jeff Collins
Jeffrey Davies
Jen Hardwicke
Jennifer Fain
Jennifer Harvey
Jennifer Mills
Jennifer Rothschild
Jennifer Sarha
Jennifer Yanoschak
Jenny Huth
Jeremy Koenig
Jeremy Morton
Jeremy Sabol
Jerry Simcock
Jess Decamps
Jess Hannar

Jess Wood
Jessica Harkins
Jessica Kibler
Jessica Queree
Jessica Weetch
Jethro Soutar
Jill Harrison
Jo Clarke
Jo Lateu
Joanna Luloff
Joanna Bibby-Scullion
Joanna Trachtenberg
Joao Pedro Bragatti
   Winckler
Jodie Adams
Joe Edwardes-Evans
Johannah May Black
Johannes Holmqvist
Johannes Menzel
John Berube
John Bogg
John Carnahan
John Conway
John Gent
John Hodgson
John Kelly
John Miller
John Purser
John Reid
John Shaw
John Steigerwald
John Walsh
John Whiteside
John Winkelman
Jon McGregor
Jon Riches
Jonah Benton
Jonathan Blaney
Jonathan Busser
Jonathan Leaver
Jonny Kiehlmann
Jorge Cino

José Echeverría Vega
Joseph Darlington
Josh Glitz
Josh Ramos
Joshua Briggs
Joshua Davis
Joy Paul
Judith Gruet-Kaye
Júlia Révay
Julia Von Dem
   Knesebeck
Julie Atherton
Julie Greenwalt
Juliet Swann
Juliet Willsher
Juliette Loesch
Junius Hoffman
Jupiter Jones
Juraj Janik
Kaarina Hollo
Kalina Rose
Karen Gilbert
Karen Mahinski
Kari Rodgers
Karina Cicero
Kat Brealey
Katarzyna Bartoszynska
Kate Beswick
Kate Wille
Katharine Robbins
Katherine Spalding
Kathryn Drabinski
Kathryn Edwards
Kathryn Williams
Kati Hallikainen
Katie Freeman
Katie Zegar
Keith Walker
Kelly Hydrick
Kenneth Blythe
Keno Jüchems
Kent McKernan

Kerri Marusiak
Kerry Broderick
Kevin Winter
Kieran Cutting
Kieran Rollin
Kieron James
Kirsten Benites
Kitty Golden
KL Ee
Kris Fernandez-Everett
Kris Ann Trimis
Kristen Tracey
Kristin Djuve
Kristin Glenn
Krystine Phelps
Kurt Navratil
Kyle Pienaar
Lana Selby
Laura Ling
Laura Rangeley
Lauren Pout
Lauren Trestler
Laurence Laluyaux
Leah Binns
Leda Brittenham
Lee Harbour
Leelynn Brady
Leona Iosifidou
Liam Buell
Liliana Lobato
Lilie Weaver
Linda Jones
Linden Franz
Lindsay Attree
Lindsay Brammer
Lisa Adler
Lisa Hess
Liviu Tanase
Liz Clifford
Liz Ketch
Liz Ladd
Liz Rice & Max Spitz

Lorna Bleach
Lorraine Cushnie
Louis Lewarne
Louise Evans
Louise Jolliffe
Lucinda Smith
Lucy Moffatt
Luiz Cesar Peres
Luke Gaillet
Luke Murphy
Lydia Syson
Lyndia Thomas
Lynn Fung
Lynn Grant
Lynn Martin
Mack McKenna
Madalyn Marcus
Maeve Lambe
Mairead Beeson
Maja Luna
Mandy Wight
Margaret Jull Costa
Mari-Liis Calloway
Marian Zelman
Mariann Wang
Marie Cloutier
Marijana Rimac
Marina Jones
Mario Sifuentez
Mark Reynolds
Mark Sargent
Mark Sheets
Mark Sztyber
Mark Troop
Mark Waters
Marlene Gray
Marten van der Meulen
Martha Wakenshaw
Martin Ewing
Martin Haller
Martin Nathan
Martin Rathgeber

Mary Clarke
Mary Tinebinal
Mary Ann Dulcich
Matt Davies
Matthew Cooke
Matthew Crawford
Matthew Crossan
Matthew Eatough
Matthew Lowe
Matthew Woodman
Matthias Rosenberg
Maxwell Mankoff
McKenzie MacDonald
Meaghan Delahunt
Meg Lovelock
Mel Pryor
Michael Bichko
Michael Boog
Michael James Eastwood
Michael Gavin
Michael Parsons
Michael Schneiderman
Michaela Anchan
Michele Whitfeld
Michelle Mirabella
Mike Abram
Mike Barrie
Mike James
Mike Schneider
Miles Smith-Morris
Mim Lucy
Miranda Gold
Mohamed Tonsy
Molly Foster
Molly Schneider
Mona Arshi
Morgan Lyons
Moriah Haefner
Myza Gouthro
Nancy Chen
Nancy Cohen
Nancy Jacobson

Nancy Oakes
Naomi Morauf
Natalie Jones
Natalie Middleton
Natalie Shpringman
Nathalia Robbins-Cherry
Nathan Weida
Nichola Smalley
Nick Cain
Nick James
Nick Judd
Nick Marshall
Nick Nelson &
  Rachel Eley
Nick Rushworth
Nick Sidwell
Nick Twemlow
Nico Parfitt
Nicola Mira
Nicolas Sampson
Nicole Matteini
Niharika Jain
Niki Sammut
Nikola Ristovski
Nina Aron
Nina Laddon
Nina Todorova
Niven Kumar
Norman Batchelor
Odilia Corneth
Olga Zilberbourg
Owen Burke
Pamela Ritchie
Pankaj Mishra
Pankhuri Sahare
Pat Winslow
Patricia Schirmer
Patrick Hawley
Patrick Hoare
Patrick Liptak
Patrick McGee
Patrick Pagni

Paul Bangert
Paul Cray
Paul Ewing
Paul Jones
Paul Jordan
Paul Milhofer
Paul Munday
Paul Myatt
Paul Nightingale
Paul Scott
Paul Stuart
Paul Tran-Hoang
Paula Melendez
Pavlos Stavropoulos
Pawel Szeliga
Pedro Ponce
Perlita Payne
Perry
Pete Clough
Pete Keeley
Peter Wells
Petra Hendrickson
Philip Herbert
Philip Leichauer
Philip Warren
Phillipa Clements
Phoebe Millerwhite
Piet Van Bockstal
Prakash Nayak
Rachael de Moravia
Rachael Williams
Rachel Beddow
Rachel Belt
Rachel Coburn
Rachel Rothe
Rachel Van Riel
Rahul Kanakia
Rajni Aldridge
Ralph Jacobowitz
Rebecca Caldwell
Rebecca Carter
Rebecca Maddox

Rebecca Marriott
Rebecca Milne
Rebecca Moss
Rebecca Rushforth
Rebecca Shaak
Rebekah Lattin-
  Rawstrone
Renee Thomas
Rhea Pokorny
Rhiannon Armstrong
Rich Sutherland
Richard Clesham
Richard Corley
Richard Dew
Richard Ellis
Richard Hughes
Richard Ley-Hamilton
Richard Mansell
Richard Smith
Richard Soundy
Richard Village
Ricka Kohnstamm
Risheeta Joshi
Rita Kaar
Rita Marrinson
Rita O'Brien
Robbie Matlock
Robert Gillett
Robert Hamilton
Robert Selcov
Robert Sliman
Robin McLean
Robin Taylor
Robina Frank
Roger Ramsden
Ronan O'Shea
Rory Williamson
Rosabella Reeves
Rosalind Ramsay
Rosanna Foster
Rosemary Horsewood
Royston Tester

Roz Simpson
Ruth Curry
Ryan Bestford
Ryan Day
Ryan Pierce
S E Guine
Sabine Little
Saidy Bober
Sally Ayhan
Sally Baker
Sally Warner
Sam Ramsay
Sara Kittleson
Sarah Arboleda
Sarah Arkle
Sarah Jones
Sarah Lucas
Sarah Manvel
Sarah Stevns
Scott Adams
Scott Baxter
Scott Chiddister
Sean Johnston
Sean McGivern
Sean Myers
Selina Guinness
Severijn Hagemeijer
Shamala Gallagher
Shannon Knapp
Sharon Levy
Sharon McCammon
Sharon White Gilson
Shaun Whiteside
Sian Hannah
Sienna Kang
Silje Bergum Kinsten
Simak Ali
Simon Pitney
Simon Robertson
SK Grout
Sophie Rees
Stacy Rodgers

Stefano Mula
Stella Rieck
Stephan Eggum
Stephanie Miller
Stephanie Wasek
Stephen Eisenhammer
Stephen Fuller
Stephen Wilson
Stephen Yates
Steve Chapman
Steve Clough
Steve Dearden
Steven Diggin
Steven Hess
Steven Norton
Stewart Eastham
Stuart Allen
Stuart Wilkinson
Summer Migliori Soto
Susan Ferguson
Susan Jaken
Susan Morgan
Susan Wachowski
Susan Winter
Suzanne Kirkham
Suzanne Wiggins
Sylvie Zannier-Betts
Tamar Drukker
Tania Hershman
Tania Marlowe
Tara Roman
Tatjana Soli
Tatyana Reshetnik
Taylor Ball
Taylor Ffitch
Terry Bone
Tess Lewis
Tessa Lang
The Mighty Douche
   Softball Team
Theresa Kelsay
Therese Oulton

Thomas Alt
Thomas Campbell
Thomas Fritz
Thomas Noone
Thomas O'Rourke
Thomas van den Bout
Thuy Dinh
Tiffany Lehr
Tim Hosgood
Timothy Baker
Toby Ryan
Tom Darby
Tom Doyle
Tom Franklin
Tom Gray
Tom Stafford
Tom Whatmore
Tracy Bauld
Tracy Lee-Newman
Tracy Northup
Trevor Brent Marta Berto
Trevor Latimer
Trevor Wald
Tulta Behm
Tyler Giesen
Val Challen
Valerie Carroll
Vanessa Dodd
Vanessa Heggie
Vanessa Nolan
Vanessa Rush
Victor Meadowcroft
Victoria Goodbody
Victoria Huggins
Vijay Pattisapu
Vilma Nikolaidou
Wendy Langridge
William Brockenborough
William Schwartz
William Wilson
Zachary Maricondia
Zoe Thomas